RESCUED BY HALFLING HOUSE

VICTORIA VASSALLO

Rescued by Halfling House.

ISBN eBook – 978 1 7635391 4 3.

ISBN Paperback – 978 1 7635391 5 0.

Edited by Clever Editors, Christine Driver.

Cover Designed by Miblart.

I would like to acknowledge the traditional Owners and Custodians of the land on which this story was written, specifically the Dharug and Dharawal peoples, and pay my respects to their Elders past and present.

DEDICATION

To the warmth in your heart,
The magic in your soul,
And the love in these pages.

Welcome home again, my friend, we missed you.

CONTENTS

CONTENT WARNING

I believe that Content Warnings exist as a special relationship between myself, the author, and you, the reader.

I want you to enjoy the story but most of all, I care about you taking care of yourself, first and foremost.

If any of the following themes bring up emotions for you that you would rather avoid, please consider stopping here.

- Car accident/injuries, illness and hospitalisation.
- Bushfires and the loss of native wildlife.
- Loss of a parent/orphaning of a child.
- Violence.
- Fantasy creatures in animal-like forms being injured/dying.

Always remember, your mental health matters.

A QUICK NOTE

THIS BOOK IS WRITTEN in British English, with mostly Australian phrases, just to spice things up!

It means that there will likely be an 's' where you might expect a 'z' or a 'kilometre' where you would expect a 'mile'. I'm sure there's more, but you get the idea.

If you think that you've found a typo or would like some clarification, please email:

victoria@victoriavassalloauthor.com

I'm always happy to hear from you!

NEWSLETTER

WOULD YOU LIKE A FREE EBOOK?

Join Victoria's newsletter and you will receive your very own copy of **Halfling House Origins** for **FREE!**

Plus, you'll be the first to get updates on Victoria's newest books, her writing process, sneak peeks, and book reviews.

http://www.victoriavassalloauthor.com

Don't want to miss a thing? You can also follow Victoria on socials:

Facebook | Instagram | Goodreads | TikTok | Amazon| Bookbub

CHAPTER ONE

Autumn was creeping in. I saw it in the way the trees around Halfling House were starting to shed their golden leaves. Soon, they would stand tall and bare in the face of the powerful southern winds that spun through them. Mist surrounded the base of the mountains as though cradling the valleys below them. It was a transformation I'd seen a million times, in a million places, but here, on the southern coast of Australia, it had a magick to it that didn't compare to anywhere else.

That morning, clear blue skies surrounded Halfling House. The scent of the ocean and the fresh grass of the nearby paddocks was intoxicating. It was still as refreshing as it had been that first morning we'd woken in our home after the battle we'd waged with the Animus to protect Storm, and all of us, within Halfling House and Briarmoor.

I leaned forward, resting my forearms on the verandah railing, my hands wrapping around the warmth of my mug, filled to the brim with a fragrant French Earl Grey tea. I breathed in the floral scent and closed my eyes, feeling grateful for the moment happening at all.

When we returned to the house the day after the battle, it looked like we were on the losing side.

Mason's truck had been reversed out—very, very carefully—once it'd been determined that it wasn't holding anything structural up, but it had still sent half the upstairs hallway falling down. Bits and pieces of our everyday life lay interspersed with broken floorboards, shattered plasterboard, and jagged timber wall frames. The electrical wiring had always been a little so-so, although after the battle, when it flickered, I swore I smelled something burning, like singed toast.

The good news was that Gabe and the Faoladh had a few sets of trade skills between them and contacts for the skills they didn't have in-house. It took almost three months, but the front of the house had been rebuilt, better than before. The termite-ridden decking was gone, replaced with new pest-protected timbers and posts, along with reinforced cladding and extra insulation at the front of the house.

We had faced so much in such little time, and our world had changed.

My world had changed.

Even at that moment, I felt my power coursing throughout my body, filling all the empty spaces where it had ceased to be. Thankfully, it hadn't all returned at once. Just the thought of that was terrifying. No, it was returning slowly, as though it was steadily reclaiming its place within me, a moment at a time. At some point, I would be at full power, but I wasn't yet, and, in a way, I was grateful. While being able to flash anywhere in an instant would be useful, I wasn't ready to return to my duties as a goddess, and without my powers at full capacity, I couldn't. It was a reprieve, however slight.

My body had adjusted to the restoration of my powers better than my mind, welcoming the warmth of the magick back like an old friend while my mind struggled with the reality that the distance between me and the Pantheon had disappeared in an instant. I hadn't heard another word from any of the other gods or goddesses, so I assumed Zeus hadn't divulged the bargain we'd struck. He was a prideful God. Sharing that Nyx or I had bested him in any way was not something he would reveal easily. Not that it stopped me from looking over my shoulder, waiting for him to exploit the sanctuary he'd granted.

As for my mother, she remained quiet, as distant from me as before.

Only Thanatos checked in occasionally, although it was mostly to try to guilt me into reaching out to her. I took a gulp of my tea.

I do not want to think about that this morning.

Seeking a distraction from my thoughts, I reached out for my power, my mind easily grasping a tendril. It slowly pooled in my chest and started trailing down my arms until a warm glow emanated from my hands, even as they remained wrapped around my mug.

I'd forgotten how beautiful it felt to pull on those feelings of compassion and wrap myself in them, as though I could forget all the other emotions that usually came along with them, just for that moment.

"Mama E!" Zane's voice broke through my thoughts. "Alora's gone!"

Oh, Gods, not again. I took one more look at the morning view. Alora had been going through a rough patch since we'd moved back into the house. She missed Storm and all the other Faoladh kids more than any of us had expected. Usually, she was so caught up in her world of flowers and trees that anything else was more of an inconvenience, so her connections with the others surprised me.

"I'm coming, Z."

My patience was running out. I'd had to collect her from Denny's three times in the last week. Whenever she felt hard done by, she would flash as far as she could go before flashing again. And then again, and again, until she reached Denny's.

Clara and I were hoping it would be a couple of years before she worked that trick out, but we'd clearly underestimated how clever she was.

I let out a sigh, turned away from the view, and headed back through the front door. "Clara?"

"Kitchen," she responded. I followed her voice and found her setting Zane up with some cereal and milk.

"She's gone again?"

"Yep, as soon as I said we weren't planning on a visit today."

"Alright," I sighed. "Do you want me to go get her? You look like you have things covered here." I gestured to Zane, who was happily munching away, his ombre blue wing tips fluttering with each mouthful.

"Yeah," Clara replied. "I'll keep everything under control. I don't think Shade will show his face for a few hours yet, and this little guy and I will keep ourselves occupied while you grab Alora." She ruffled the top of Zane's head, mussing the blonde hair that trailed to a peak between his pointed scaly ears, momentarily distracting him from his food as he looked up to her with his deep, golden eyes.

"Okay." I put my mug down next to the sink and collected the car keys from the bench top. "Can I get away with this?" I gestured to my pyjamas.

"El, your pyjamas are just sweats and fandom shirts. They're normal clothes for other people. Besides, there's no outfit for 'my Fae kid keeps flashing to your house'. You'll be fine," Clara chuckled.

"Good point," I agreed. "I'll call Denny on the way, just in case they haven't noticed an extra kiddo running around yet."

"Good idea," she replied. "Hopefully, it'll only be one trip today."

"Fingers crossed." I headed back outside to the car, got inside, and turned the engine over, the car growling to life as I guided it out of the driveway and onto the road to the Faoladh house.

I made a quick call to Denny and gave her the heads up, but as usual, she'd already scouted Alora in the backyard, playing with a few of the younger pups. Thankfully, she didn't mind the extra kiddo, but these trips were getting tiresome, and I couldn't shake the worry that Alora would start venturing further out—to somewhere where people didn't know or understand her.

Fifteen minutes later, I pulled up to the front of Denny's house and parked next to one of the bigger SUVs. I'd discovered during our stay that there were more Faoladh in town than I'd expected. Quite a few of their families had litters of young ones because they often had twins or triplets with each pregnancy. It had made for a fair few noisy gatherings, especially by our standards, but it was comforting to know that we weren't the only ones in the thick of trying to raise good halflings—Faoladh, mortals, or whatever the little ones were.

I flicked the mirror down and checked that I had nothing on my face before jumping out and heading to the front door. I'd just raised my hand to ring the doorbell when it swung open, Denny's shock of white hair and a generous smile greeting me.

"Come in, come in." She gestured. "I have a pot of tea boiling already," she told me, walking toward the kitchen.

I shut the door behind me and followed. "You really don't have to, Denny. It's bad enough that Alora keeps popping up here unannounced. You don't need to host me too."

"Pst." Denny shooed me away and into a seat at a small table in the kitchen. "There'll be none of that, darl. The little one is just lonely, and she feels a pull to our kind. Most Fae do. It's in their nature. Kin is kin, after all."

"What do you mean?" I asked, furrowing my brow in confusion. I knew the Faoladh were from the Celtic Pantheon, as were the Fae, but that was the extent of my knowledge. I only knew the intricacies of my messed-up family and our Pantheon.

"Well, there's an old story that tells of the beginning of the Faoladh," Denny started as she finished making up the tea and brought it over, sitting down next to me. "A long time ago, our people were blessed by the Morrigan, one of the most powerful Fae in all of existence, to have the power to change between human and wolf form as a reward for our service to her. All that she asked was that we never tasted the meat of another being unless at her orders. As with all the old ways, they slowly disappeared into the past, and we could integrate into society and create lives for ourselves. But it all harkens back to the magick of the Morrigan. It is her magick which runs through our veins, as alive now as it was the day she created us."

"I had no idea," I murmured, holding the warm mug close to my chest and absorbing its comforting heat. "I guess that could explain some of the connection Alora has with the young Faoladh."

"It could," Denny agreed. "It could also just be that she's lonely."

"That was my first thought," I admitted. "Until everything happened with the Animus, we thought we were the only magickal beings in Briarmoor. Alora and Zane never got to leave the house, so it was just us and the kids."

"It makes sense." Denny gave me a small smile. "The good news is that you're not alone anymore, love."

"I know." I returned the smile, "And that means more than you know, but I just feel so clueless about how to manage all of this running away stuff with Alora. I mean, do I come down hard and fast, ground her from leaving Halfling House? We both know she'll just flash again. Or do I go with my instincts and talk to her, go softly and gently? I've tried that, and I'm back here again a few days later." I placed the mug on the table, the sound louder than I intended.

"Oh, Ellie. If it were easy, everyone would do it, love." She patted my hand comfortingly. "There doesn't have to be such a wide gap between approaches. You can be kind and loving, and firm and strong, all at once. You just have to find the right solution to your problem first."

"Well, I can't say I know what that is just yet, but your advice is more helpful than anything else I've come across. And it's not like I can just dial up my mother and ask for her advice."

"Have you thought about it?" Denny asked. "Talking to your mum?"

I sighed and picked up the mug again. *It'd be a waste of tea to let it go cold.* "I have thought about it, but her way of dealing with things is more suited to gods and goddesses, not halflings. And I'm pretty sure she's not their biggest fan anyway."

"Why not think about giving her a chance rather than writing her off straight away?" Denny suggested. "She did step up and save your bacon last time, love. That's got to count for something."

Does it? I debated internally. I'd had a lifetime of either being too unimportant to register on my mother's radar or only popping up when I was disappointing her on a much larger scale. It made my stomach churn with a mix of anxiety and trepidation.

"I'll think about it," I told her. Denny gave me a look like she didn't quite believe me. "I mean it. I will," I reassured her.

"Alright, darl. I suppose I can settle for that." Denny got up and put her cup in the sink. "How about we go collect that troublemaker of yours?"

"Sounds like a plan," I agreed, my thoughts immediately returning to Alora and the challenge I'd have of keeping her at home after her latest trip. "I might as well face it head-on."

"Well, that was an early morning adventure I wasn't expecting." I kept my voice even as I glanced in the rearview mirror at Alora, who was fastened safely into her seat at the back of the car. We were nearly halfway home, and she hadn't said a thing since we'd gotten in the car.

"Go back, I want to," she replied, the golden etchings on her brow furrowing as though she were close to tears.

"I know, honey, I do," I reassured her, "But we don't live there anymore, so you can't just keep showing up there when you want to."

"Please, I want to." Alora's bottom lip started trembling.

"Oh, Alora," I sighed, my chest contracting as I felt the wave of sadness washing over her.

The urge to take away her pain was overwhelming, but I'd been alive long enough to know that she needed to learn how to process these feelings, not have them taken away. When I was powerless, the hardest part had been not being able to take away others' pain, but now that my powers were back, the choice not to use them was just as challenging.

I'd cheated emotions for others before, and it had never ended well. *It had always ended though.* The thought escaped my mind before I could stop it.

The sound of small sobs tightened the grip on my heart. Fortunately, we pulled into the driveway of Halfling House, so I parked and got out quickly, unbuckling Alora and picking her up in a big hug.

Slowly, her tears stopped, and the vice-like sadness that had her in its grasp loosened. I held her close until she started wriggling a little more. Although she was nearly ten, as a Fae, she was still quite small and lithe, more like the size of an average six-year-old. Nothing out of the ordinary enough to attract attention, or at least not as much as the golden threaded design that adorned her forehead could, tracing along her hairline until it disappeared under her curls. The wriggling continued as she buried her face into the crook of my neck, and one of her hands started twisting itself in my own unruly hair. I closed my eyes for a second and took a deep breath, my relief pulling the grip of Alora's sadness away from my heart.

"Feeling a little better, honey?" I pulled back a few inches so I could see her face more clearly.

She looked up at me, those piercing violet eyes connecting with mine. "I am, I think."

"That's good. It can be hard when you have big feelings, can't it?"

Alora nodded. The tears from earlier dried on her cheeks. "Miss them, I really do. Boring, Zane is."

The corners of my mouth curled up as I tried not to smile at her assessment of her little foster brother. "It's hard, I know. I can talk to Denny and the other kids' parents, and we can organise something more often." Fortnightly playdates clearly weren't enough.

Alora's eyes lit up, brighter than usual—if that was even possible.

"Ah!" I cautioned. "I'm only going to do it if you promise me you will stop flashing there without me or Clara, okay?"

I could see her weighing it up in her mind, those same beautiful eyes becoming a little more shrewd and calculating. Her youth provided a thin veil of distraction from what was already a far too intelligent mind.

The moment she accepted my deal was as clear in her eyes as it was in her voice. "Mama E, okay. Promise?"

"I promise," I swore. With a quick squeeze, I popped her down on the floor and shut the car door. "Now, how about we go inside and see if Clara has any breakfast left?"

Alora looked up at me and smiled, grabbing my hand and keeping pace with me as we headed inside Halfling House.

Home at last.

CHAPTER TWO

"We're home," I called out loudly as I shut the door behind us, instinctively locking it. The Animus attacks had left behind some emotional scars. My hand fluttered toward my neck, rubbing at the spot where I'd been wounded. Mortally.

Even if the physical marks had disappeared from Asclepius's work, the emotional ones ran far deeper than traditional healing could manage. Immortality had taught me that some scars would never heal.

The house was unusually quiet, and there had still been no response to my greeting. A trickle of anxiety ran through me, and I widened my senses—my power—so that I could seek out any traces of fear or pain nearby, but I came up empty. Whatever Clara and Zane were caught up with, it wasn't something nasty. I could sense Shade in the basement, alone with his ever-simmering frustration. Still, I found it hard to trust my growing magick. Even though I couldn't sense any fear or distress coming from them, marrying that with the fear the attacks had left me with sometimes felt impossible. I wouldn't feel satisfied until I could see them with my own eyes to be sure they were safe, but I couldn't let Alora know that. For her sake, I needed to keep my anxiety to myself.

Alora ran ahead of me into the kitchen as I kicked off my shoes and slid on my slippers instead. It was still before noon, so it was acceptable. Ish. I followed her into the kitchen and found it was also empty.

"It looks like it's just us," I told her. "Cereal it is!" I opened the cupboard door and started listing off the most boring ones I could see. "Granola, Fiber One, Special K, porridge ..."

"Yuck, they are." Alora wrinkled her pert little nose in disgust and bounced on the balls of her feet.

"You don't want those?" My brows knitted together in faux confusion. "But you don't like the others. I mean, Cheerios, Froot Loops, Cap'n Crunch ..." I grimaced exaggeratedly.

"Yummy, yummy, yummy, they are!" Alora shouted excitedly. "Please, can I?" She pointed at the Froot Loops. "Please, please!"

"Ugh, I suppose you could have these yucky ones," I said with a loud sigh and a quick glance around to see if Shade was in earshot. It was an unspoken rule that he got first dibs on the Froot Loops. Always. But he wasn't in sight—or hearing.

"Mama E, thank you." Alora smiled ear to ear and raced over to the table where she launched herself into her chair and waited for her breakfast delivery.

I quickly poured the colourful mini-donut-like cereal into one of the plastic kid's bowls, soaked it in milk, plopped a spoon in, and placed it on the table in front of her. Alora gave another wide grin before delving into the bowl of sugary goodness.

The kitchen was clean, the timber counters clear, and the floor empty of any evidence of Zane's typically messy eating, so I figured that perhaps Clara and Zane had headed outside for some early morning fire-pit practice or maybe upstairs to play in his room.

Now that Alora was settled, I decided to do a quick search. A quick skim at the backyard confirmed it was empty, so while Alora was still distracted by her breakfast, I hurried up the stairs. As soon as I hit the upstairs landing, I heard them in the bathroom, and my anxiety disappeared almost as fast as it had appeared.

They're okay. I headed back downstairs, my mind at peace, and decided to rustle up a cup of Earl Grey tea. There'd be enough of our ordinary chaos shortly. I'd just settled down at the table when I heard Clara scream.

Hot tea flew from my mouth and landed on my sweatpants. "Fudge nuggets!" I cursed loudly. Alora's pointed ears perked up straight while her violet eyes flickered with panic. I grabbed the nearest tea towel and patted myself down while reassuring her. "It's okay, it's okay. I'll go see what all this is about. I'm sure it's nothing."

It's not Zeus, it's not. I tried to reassure myself, to clamp down on the reactive anxiety that hit me in the gut every time something unexpected happened. But I couldn't let the others—especially the kids—see it.

Alora nodded, but the look in her eyes remained cautious.

Clara let out another scream, although that one sounded far less, 'My life is in danger,' and much more, 'There's a bug in the room.'

"See, that's not as bad. Can you stay here and watch my tea while I go and sort it out?"

Alora nodded again, this time with a little more colour in her face and calm in her eyes.

"Okay, I'll be right back." I gave her shoulder a gentle squeeze and headed toward the stairs. Another scream, more of a shriek really, reverberated as I climbed the first couple of stairs.

"Zane! Stop it! Get down now!" Clara shouted, panic—not fear—filling her voice. "Zane. No!"

Not Zeus then. Thank the Gods.

My fear receded, and curiosity—most likely the kind that killed the cat—had a hold on me. There was not much that could spike the panic I was hearing in Clara's voice. Except for bugs, of course. She had a remarkably powerful fear of daddy-long-leg spiders. Something about the bulbous body and spindly legs really set her off.

I followed the sounds to the kids' room, where the sight of Zane's antics took my breath away. Laughter chased out any breath I had left in me before I could even make a single sound.

Clara sat on the floor in the middle of the room with wipes and nappies nearby, her legs splayed out in front of her as though she'd been in the midst of a nappy change. Her hair flickered with shades of bright green while she hid her face in her hands.

Meanwhile, Zane was zipping about the room, his ombre blue wings flapping loudly as he laughed at Clara's reactions and dropped pellets of poop all around, each punctuated with a particularly loud chortle. The grin on his face was only matched by the disgust on Clara's.

"Z-Zane," I managed to squeak out between a bout of laughter. "You need to come down now."

Zane pulled up midair, his wings flapping hard to keep him in place almost a foot above Clara. A single pellet dropped as he remained there, falling onto Clara's head and then rolling down onto the floor, only stopping at my feet where I stood in the doorway.

"Mama E!" he shouted, delight in his voice as he pointed at the pellet. "Poop! I pooped!"

"Yes, yes, you did," I acknowledged as I tried to pull the corners of my mouth downward so Clara's stink-eye would lessen somewhat. She had definitely not appreciated my reaction. I could tell that much for sure. "It's time for you to come down so we can count them."

Clara winced at my words.

"Mama E and Zane are going to pick up all the poop, aren't we?"

The wince on her face dropped and was replaced by relief. She quickly got up from the ground, carefully avoiding the poop pellets littering the floor, and looked up at me in the doorway.

"Thank you," she mouthed and then pointed to the bathroom. Her next word was no surprise. "Shower."

I'd managed to compose myself enough to nod and move out of the way so she could get past and clean herself up. "I've got it covered. I'll just shout down and let Alora know it's okay. She's in the kitchen eating breakfast, and she was quite worried."

Clara disappeared into the bathroom while I took a few steps out of the room and into the hallway where it met the stairwell.

"Alora, honey?"

"Mama E! Okay, is it all?"

"It's all okay. Zane just needs help to get changed. Can you come upstairs once you finish your breakfast, please?

"Yes, Mama E," Alora yelled back.

"Good girl!"

With that taken care of, I returned to the bedroom where Zane had found his feet on the floor and was diligently filling a toy tip truck tray with his pellets of poop.

"So, Mister Zane," I started as I knelt down next to him. "I think you're ready to start using the toilet like a big dragon. What do you think?"

"Yes, Mama E." Zane stopped and looked up at me, a big smile on his face and a couple of pellets in his hands. "I wanna be a big-boy dragon!"

"Oh, you'll be a big boy dragon." I smiled back. "There's no doubt about that. But first, let's see how much poop we can find. First one to fill a nappy bag wins!"

The mundane flow of our day was delightfully interrupted when Mason popped in a couple of hours after we'd survived the toilet-training fiasco with Zane. Clara had taken longer to calm down. Her hair remained green for most of the morning, a sure sign that she was still grossed out. I wasn't sure what colour would come next, but hopefully, something a little less disgusted and more positive.

We still had to get through the rest of the day. Mason's arrival was a welcome distraction for my head and my heart.

"Now, this is coffee." Mason closed his eyes and savoured the taste of the fresh brew made with the new fiddly coffee machine I'd bought for Shade in a bout of maternal guilt. It turns out buying his forgiveness was more expensive than I'd thought.

"You're welcome." Shade nodded at Mason, lingering at the machine, finishing making his own. "I can smell the coffee all the way in the basement if I make it strong enough." Shade shot a piercing glare at me.

Despite his initial agreement, Shade still held a grudge against me for sticking him with babysitting duty during the Animus attack, and then for a while more when we were living with the Faoladh.

Like most teenagers, he had phases, and coffee was the newest one. Entirely unnecessary, but most things were for Shade.

"I'm sorry, Shade. I don't know how many times I can tell you that before you know I mean it." *Who knew? Today might be the day.*

Shade responded with the same stony stare he'd been perfecting over the last few months. "So that means you're ready to let me out of the basement, out of the house, and into the real world then?"

Mason's eyes flickered between Shade and me cautiously. He'd tried mediating a few times before with very little success. Sometimes, the words not said were the best choice.

I looked down at my hands, flexing my fingers between each other anxiously. "You know it's not safe. Not yet. You need more control over your powers."

"Thought so," he chuckled sarcastically. "And you're the one who can teach me *all* about it, I guess. Your way, as usual. Thanks, but no thanks."

"Enjoy your coffee. It's not like anyone else here appreciates it." Shade turned to Mason. "Be careful. She might find a way to trap you here too. She's a *real* goddess now, don't forget."

"I think I can hold my own, but thanks anyway, mate."

Shade smirked and shot another frustrated look at me. "Whatever. I'll be in the basement. Where I apparently *belong*." And with that, he left as quickly as he'd appeared.

The kettle flicked off, steam creating condensation on the clear windowpanes. My mug sat there, two sugars crowded inside with a black tea bag, waiting for me to fill it, but, for once, I didn't want to. *Tea wasn't going to fix this.*

I sighed loudly and sat down beside Mason, who scooted his chair closer and wrapped one of his arms around me, the other still holding his cup of coffee tight.

"You're doing your best," he reassured me. "He'll come around."

"Yeah, maybe in a million years." I sighed again and rolled my eyes as I relaxed into his hug, relishing the familiar tug of the compassion within him that had attracted me to him in the first place.

"Luckily, I'm dating an immortal goddess with a million years to wait." He grinned shyly, the curve of his lips obscured slightly by his beard.

"Ugh, don't remind me." I closed my eyes. "I just wish he could see that trusting him with the kids is a bigger honour than being able to fight. It's taken a long time for me to trust anyone with the kids. It means something, you know?"

"I know," Mason agreed. "But he's a teenager. I know it's been a while since you were, but you must remember, they're always the first to rush in and want to save the day."

"With not a single care as to what the cost would be. I do. I saw it far too many times on the battlefield. And they were always the first ones who died." My breath caught in my throat as I tried my best not to see the faces of the young men I'd ministered to throughout my time with the Pantheon.

"So maybe some of it is that you don't trust him enough then?" Mason raised his brow as his big brown eyes looked right into my soul. "You don't think he'll make the right decisions yet. The ones that will let him come home safe, do you?"

I pulled away from Mason and shot him a look that I imagined was not too dissimilar to the one Shade had given me a few minutes ago.

"I don't. He reminds me too much of all the young ones I lost," I explained. "These past few months with you, the Faoladh—it's helped me feel safe again. I don't want to lose that. I don't want to lose him."

Mason held me close, comforting me.

"But he doesn't deserve to be bound to this house forever. He doesn't want my protection, and I don't know what to do," I admitted.

"It seems like family drama is everywhere these days." Mason breathed out a sigh. "Denny and the Faoladh have all been on high alert as well. Something's not going the way they wanted. Gabe wouldn't give me any answers, but I'm starting to think that I'm surrounded by control freaks."

"That's not fair," I protested, tangling one of my fingers in his hair.

"It's not?" he replied, adjusting to look me in the eye directly. "This isn't because you think that as long as you can keep Shade here, with you—control him, a braver man would say—you can keep him safe?"

I felt my heart pound in my chest harder than usual. It was as though he'd read my mind, the part I barely even let myself admit. "Why do I feel like you just pulled a quick one on me, handsome?"

"If it's a quick one you want ..." Mason grinned cheekily and put down his coffee so he could use both hands to pull me onto his lap.

A bubble of laughter escaped me, and my stern look disappeared. "You're supposed to be here for a coffee date, not to discover my unhealed trauma and make me reckon with my faults."

"Mmm," he murmured, nuzzling his scratchy, bearded chin into the crook of my neck, "Do you think you could forgive me?"

"You ..." I looked down into his dark brown eyes, forgetting myself for a moment. "You, I could forgive, over and over again, if I had to," I whispered softly.

The air in the kitchen somehow felt heavier and hotter as the world shrunk to just the two of us. I'm not sure who reached for whom first, but none of it mattered the moment our lips met, the bitterness of the coffee creating a sharp edge to the taste of him. I luxuriated in the feeling of him close to me, his arms cradling me to him as we took our time with one another. Eventually, I nipped at his bottom lip and eased away, resting my forehead against his as we caught our breath.

"Well, that makes us two to one now, I guess." He smiled coyly. "A whole kiss without a single kid walking in and making gross sounds."

"I believe that you're right," I laughed. "Care to make it three to one before I head off to see Storm?"

"Now that's an offer I can't refuse." Mason grinned and tilted my lips to meet his.

CHAPTER THREE

"STORM," I CAUTIONED FROM my seat on the deck at the back of Denny's house, a hot cup of honey and chamomile tea in my hand. "Storm, do not even think about it."

I tried to sound authoritarian, but this was pretty par for the course as far as these playdates with the Faoladh went. It had become part of our routine once we'd moved back to Halfling House. Zane and Alora practically counted the minutes until it was time to go and see Storm and the rest of the clan.

Wren sat in the opposite seat, helping keep an eye on some of the young Faoladh as they played alongside Storm, Alora, and Zane. The pups' movements were lithe and quick, where even an unplanned fumble would turn into a graceful landing. Of course, they were all a few years ahead of Storm, who, despite her determination to keep up, was still establishing the basics of her balance in both wolf and human form.

Right now, she was testing the waters of the balance beam that the others had just crossed, putting one paw in front of another while her cheeky gaze held mine, almost daring me to caution her again. Alora, fortunately, was much more cautious and aware that she didn't have the same natural coordination as the pups. Zane, on the other hand, remained childishly optimistic that his wings would make up for any other skill he lacked in comparison.

Before Storm could test me again, another Faoladh, Conrad, barked loudly, catching her attention. Excitedly, she turned tail and chased the path back along the wooden playground to where the others had gathered.

"How's she doing? Have you had any luck tracking down her mother?" I asked as I settled back into my seat, warming my hands on my mug. Storm had kept living at Denny's, which I'd discovered was something of a commune for all the Faoladh in Briarmoor. A few lived in their own places, but many of them chose to live together, similar to the typical wolf packs I'd encountered over the centuries. Conrad's parents, Sean and Maree, had the youngest pup, and when they'd heard of Storm, they'd offered to take her in and raise her amongst the Faoladh.

It still made my heart ache, the deep kind that you're not sure will ever quite heal over, but I knew it was the right choice for Storm. I found myself on the phone or popping in everyday or so, checking in, making sure that Storm knew I was always there for her if she needed it.

"She's good," Wren replied. "She seems to have fit right in with Conrad. They're practically besties now. Sean and Maree are enjoying having another pup around. After Conrad's birth, Maree was devastated. She couldn't have any more. I think Storm eases that a bit. She knows it's not guaranteed to be forever, but we're still drawing a blank on her mum. There are a few possibilities, some cousins, but they're mostly off-grid at the moment, so it's like drawing blood from a stone. Gabe and Farron keep taking off chasing leads, but ..." She shrugged.

I took a sip of my tea. That explained why I'd had such a hard time getting a hold of Gabe lately. Farron still wasn't my biggest fan, but we'd found some common footing.

"At least she's happy while it all gets worked out. I'm not going to say I don't miss the nighttime cuddles, but it makes me happy that she's helping them as much as they're helping her."

"She'll always have a home here now, no matter what," Wren said. "It's the way it is with us—we protect our own above all else."

"Yeah, you're not all alpha-beta-omega-y, are you?" I laughed, my tea rippling from the movement.

Wren chuckled, readjusting on her chair. "Yeah, nah. We don't buy into that. We'll fight for our clan, but not to expand territory or because we're power hungry. I've heard that the wolf shifters are different, but our heritage goes back to the Fae. I guess that's why we're wired differently."

"Denny mentioned that. She said it might be why Alora has made such strong connections with the other kids."

"She's made a habit of flashing over here, hasn't she?" Wren smiled. "It's kind of cute."

"Only if you're not the one freaking out and doing the drive over on the regular." I groaned. "I was still in my pyjamas the other day."

Wren laughed, spilling some of her tea.

"I just don't know what to do. She clearly needs to be around other kids, but she can't just flash back and forth whenever she wants to. And even with my powers, I can't stop her."

"Does she go to school?" Wren asked.

"Um, no?" I replied, the corner of my eyes creasing in confusion. "I think she'd stand out just a little too much at the local public school." The question felt below Wren's intelligence level, which left me a little worried. *What a ridiculous idea.*

"Not the local school," she clarified, giving me a slightly insulted look. "I meant, like, home school or something. A couple of the families here run school sessions together because it's easier than worrying about the kids shifting in a human school."

"That's a good idea," I murmured, my mind suddenly moving a million miles a minute. *This might be the perfect compromise.* "Do you think they might be open to having Alora join?"

One of the Faoladh kids suddenly shouted from where they were playing some kind of chasing game within the play structure. The reason was as clear as the teal gleam of scales in the sun as Zane tried to fly from one end of the play structure to the other. He made it, just, but it had set off some arguments about whether flying was cheating.

It wasn't a decision that should be left to a group of children, in my experience—and Wren's, from the look on her face.

"Zane!" I yelled, unwilling to let whatever skirmish was about to play out to get a foothold. "No flying. It's not fair to the others."

Zane started to protest in a voice much whinier than usual. He was probably tired from all the playing. Hopefully, a nice, long nap would be on the cards when we returned to Halfling House.

"Zane, no flying. If you can't do what I say, we will leave." His whining stopped instantly, and he lowered himself to the ground and joined the game with the others again. I wasn't surprised. Alora might be the one who flashed here all the time, but Zane also loved having friends to play with.

"Thanks for that. The kids can be quick to make a mountain out of a molehill," Wren said, the exasperation clear in her voice. "As for the school, I could run it by the other parents and see if it's something they might be open to."

"I'd really appreciate it. I'll start looking into the home-schooling thing too, I guess. My childhood was full of lessons, though nothing as structured as what they have today. I'd assumed that was enough for Alora and Zane, but maybe it isn't."

I can't believe I haven't thought about this sooner, I chastised myself. It reminded me how disconnected my life as a Goddess had been from that of the mortals or halflings I was around. Some things were so ingrained that even I found myself surprised when they popped up.

"To be fair, that was a long time ago," Wren said. "What, two thousand years? Three?" She smiled as she guessed.

"I am not telling you how old I am, Wren!" I said indignantly. "I'd never hear the end of it."

"You can't blame me for being curious."

"I can, actually," I laughed before taking a sip. "You should know better than to ask a Goddess her age. It's rude."

"Only because you don't want to answer the question. I've already told you that I'm thirty-three. See, easy!"

"Wren, when you enter triple digits, I'll think about it. How's that?"

"Fine," she sighed and leaned back in her chair. "You can be so boring sometimes, you know."

"That's not what Mason says," I teased, knowing it would spark her interest. I took a long sip of my tea and sat back. I didn't have to wait long for her to take the bait.

"Ooh, how's that going?" Wren grinned, her eyes lighting up. "I still can't believe you managed to snag the top-gun of the Rural Fire Service! That man has been on every woman in Briarmoor's most eligible list for years."

"It's going well, I think," I told her. "He just catches me off guard sometimes. It's easy to fall into our usual rhythm, and then he'll go and say something about my eyes or how beautiful I am. I'm not used to that."

Wren just stared at me. "You're a Goddess. How can you not be used to that?"

"The Goddess of pity, mercy and compassion. Most of the humans I came across weren't thinking about how I looked. I can guarantee you that."

"Ah, yeah. That kind of makes sense. Still, you're no Medusa."

I shot her a reproachful look. "That's harsh. She got the rough end of the stick, you know."

Wren laughed, "It's so odd to know someone from a different Pantheon. All the stuff we never thought much about before is, like, actually relevant now."

I looked over at the kids, who were still playing together with only the slightest reduction in enthusiasm. Although, whether that was because we'd been out here for a while or just a natural depletion, I wasn't sure.

"It's definitely an interesting experience. I've spent a lot of time avoiding my Pantheon but not really engaging with the others, either. Less attention was better. Now though, with the kids, I'm really feeling like I need to be making connections so they can know some of their own kind. I mean, look at Storm." I gestured at the ball of chocolate fur bounding around Alora's legs to the laughter of the others. "She's thriving."

"She really is." Wren nodded. "We've always had each other, so we haven't really gone looking for others either. Denny's set on keeping us separate because it feels safe, and it has been. The most exotic we've gotten is Declan and Emrys' mother. She's a witch, but that's as far as it goes. None of us would have ever guessed we'd be making friends with a Greek Goddess, let alone a teen bogeyman, a toddler dragon-shifter, or a genuine Fae."

"I must admit, opening our world up terrified me at first," I told her. "Engaging with anyone other than Mason seemed like asking for trouble. The truth was, trouble was going to come looking for us anyway, and it was the people I'd been afraid to connect with who were the ones who helped save us."

The truth of what I was saying hit home as I watched the kids continue to play, unaware of how special this moment was, even in my immortal lifetime of moments.

"I guess sometimes you have to trust that there is good to be found in everyone," Wren said.

"I wouldn't go that far," I chuckled, placing my empty mug on the small table between us. "But maybe not everyone is out to get us. Especially you all."

"Well, thank you for that kind assessment." Wren grinned and stood up from her chair. "More?" She motioned to my empty cup.

It felt almost treasonous to turn down another cup of tea, but a quick check of my phone confirmed it was past twelve. Zane would be an absolute nightmare if I didn't get him home for lunch and a nap soon.

"I'm going to have to pass, unfortunately. I have to get the kids back home before they turn into uncontrollable gremlins for the rest of the day."

"I get it," Wren laughed. "It's part of why I enjoy being the babysitter and not the parent. Rile 'em up and send 'em back—guilt-free!"

"You're a little evil, you know?" I smiled.

"Shh, don't tell anyone," she said in a stage whisper before turning around to the kids. "Time to wrap it up, guys. Let's all head inside."

Her announcement was met with a resounding chorus of complaints. They still did what she said though, which impressed me more than I wanted to admit. For someone with no kids, she sure knew how to keep them in line.

"Alora, Zane, it's time for us to go," I told them, their complaints growing louder than the others. "Thanks for having us, Wren."

"Anytime," she replied, herding the Faoladh kids into the house.

"Tomorrow, can we come?" Alora asked.

I caught Wren's gaze, and we both laughed.

CHAPTER FOUR

"Oh, Gods! What a day." I collapsed on the chaise end of the couch next to Clara. "How come some days go so fast they could give you whiplash, and then others crawl past at a snail's pace?"

Clara laughed loudly from her spot in the corner, where she was curled up with a book and a stemless wine glass. "Come on, the kids weren't that bad."

"I thought as they got older, it would be easier, but convincing Alora not to flash whenever she got annoyed with me required a politician's level of negotiation, and then throw in toilet training Zane." I sighed. "Did you know he can poop five times a day? Five times!"

I rolled onto my side and propped my head up with one arm. I looked at Clara. I could tell she was enjoying this.

"I seem to remember that you were the one who thought it was hilarious when he was raining poop on me. Not so funny now, is it?" She smirked, raising a brow.

"I surrender, toilet-training sucks."

"Says you and every parent there ever was."

I rolled my eyes. *She was enjoying rubbing this in way too much.*

"Ugh, I need a wine." I sat up and leant on my knees. "Do you need a top-up?"

"I'm good. I just need to finish this chapter. Go get your wine." Clara shooed me away.

"Don't worry, I can tell when I'm not wanted." I grabbed a cushion off the couch and threw it at her, careful to miss the wine.

"Agh!" Clara exclaimed, "You're such a pain in the ass sometimes."

"So are you," I replied as I headed into the kitchen.

Dinner had left the kitchen looking like a war zone, and Clara would only drive me crazy if I didn't let her finish the chapter. I cleaned up the mess and then got the wine from the fridge—our usual Moscato-Sauvignon Blanc blend. It wasn't even close to the deliciousness that Dionysus could concoct, but it did well enough. The thought triggered the memory of my mother, Nyx, and Thanatos. Even though emotions were my power, I couldn't quite understand the mixture of anxiety, need, and hope that welled within me. I'd spent hundreds, if not thousands of years avoiding them, and yet, after seeing them the night the Animus attacked, and being saved by my mother—it felt like it had changed something.

A splash of cold wine on my hand made me realise that I'd gotten caught up in my thoughts. I grabbed a tea towel and wiped up the mess.

I took a deep breath in and out before picking up my glass and heading back into the lounge. Clara was sitting, nursing her wine, but her book was closed, so it seemed I was out of the danger zone.

"I'm glad you didn't want any more. I managed to spill half of the wine on the bench," I admitted a little sheepishly.

"Trust you to do that," she laughed.

"Was it good?" I gestured to the book resting in her lap as I sat down at the other end of the couch.

"So far. I'm not finished yet," she told me, "But whoa, chapter fifty-five had me holding my breath."

"Sounds pretty good," I replied. "The usual?"

"Yeah, you know me. If it's not about witches, vampires, or Fae with wings, I'm not interested."

"Reasonable, I guess. For you." I smiled. "Every time I see you with a book, it reminds me of when your powers came in."

Clara laughed loudly. "Oh my gosh, I try really hard not to think about that."

"Oh, don't worry, I remember clearly. You were obsessed with that vampire book with the sparkly guy. I came up to say goodnight, and instead of you, I found a very pale, sullen, dark-haired girl whose name rhymed with Ella."

Clara's face flushed red at the memory. "I was a teenager. Everyone loved that book."

"Not enough to actually become the character," I laughed.

"The worst part was it took forever for me to work out how to drop the glamour. I swore I was going to stay home forever if it didn't go away," Clara admitted.

"That probably would have been a good thing. You do not want to know how much fanfic that book inspired."

"Don't even get me started on that, El!" Clara groaned.

"Okay, okay, I surrender." I took a sip from my glass. "Ah," I sighed. "This is what I've been waiting all day for."

"That's *definitely* healthy." Clara rolled her eyes. "How was the visit with Wren?"

"Good, the kids had a blast. No news from Gabe or Farron. Zane napped for over an hour when we got home. Alora and I did some gardening. Nothing major. She did ask me what we did with the old sunflowers again, but I just distracted her."

"Yeah, the last thing we need is for her to know that Gabe chopped them down. She takes it so personally."

"Exactly. What did you get up to?" I asked.

"I checked out the bookstore in Briarmoor. The owner, a lady named Olive, runs it, and she was really helpful. I managed to find what looks like some genuine spell books, and one on the history of witches as well," Clara told me, her gaze turning wary as she waited for my reaction. "I think she might be a witch too."

I kept my expression as neutral as possible, even though a part of me had already started worrying.

"I'm starting to feel less surprised when a new magickal pops up here. Briarmoor seems like a magnet for them. Did you ask her?"

Clara was so keen to find someone like her that it made me worry she would miss the red flags even if they were thrown in her face.

"Do I look like I'm trying to cause problems?" Clara exclaimed. "No, I did not ask the kind store owner if she was a magickal being."

"I'm not going to answer that." I winked at her. "Well, Wren mentioned today that Emrys and Declan's mother is a witch, so there are definitely some around Briarmoor. It might be a good place to start? With someone we know, sort of?"

Clara took a sip of her wine, holding my gaze. "Is that something you'd be okay with?"

"I understand that you want to connect with others like you, I really do." I sighed and wrapped my hands around my glass. "I just want you to be cautious. Not every witch is a good one. There's a lot of grey area out there, but I trusted Declan and Emrys enough to put our fate in their hands. It gives me a little more confidence that their mother would be a trustworthy place to start."

"I get that." Clara nodded. "I know it's hard for you, but I don't want to spend my whole life scared of reaching out to others like me just because there are some who are bad."

"And I understand that I can't stop you." I gave her a small smile. "I don't think I *want* to stop you. I just wish I could wrap all of you up in cotton wool and keep you safe from everything ever." My throat closed over, tears pricking at the corners of my eyes. It wasn't sadness that had created them but a weight in the pit of my stomach that formed knowing that, even as a Goddess, I couldn't protect them from life.

Life would come for them, give them happiness, serve them sadness, and deal them every experience in between. That was the joy and pain of being alive.

"Hey, El. Look at me." Clara scooted over and grasped my forearm. "You've been the best mother I could have had. You've protected me and kept me safe, and given me the chance to work this stuff out. At some point, you've gotta trust that there's more good in this world than bad. And even if I find the bad, you've taught me how to deal with it."

"Plus ..." She trailed off.

"Plus what?"

"Plus, if it all goes to Hades, I can always call you for help." She grinned, leaning over to give me a squeeze.

I laughed. "Glad you have your backup plan sorted then." I wiped the tears in the corners of my eyes. "Ugh, it's good to know that getting my powers back hasn't made me any less of a crier."

"You know, for someone who used to complain about losing your powers, you spend an awful lot of time worrying about losing your humanity now that you have them back again," Clara observed.

"Sometimes it's hard to see the good when you're in the middle of it. It's only when you think you could lose it that you really know how much it means to you," I told her.

"That's deep." Clara smiled. "We might need another bottle of wine."

I leaned my head on her shoulder. "You might be onto something there."

The loud buzzing of my phone woke me from my deliciously empty sleep. It was one perk the return to my Goddess status had given me—no more nightmares. I was only at the mercy of my memories if I let myself be. I was in control again.

No more tasty snacks for Shade from me. Not that he wanted anything to do with me anyway.

I reached for my phone, but the buzzing had stopped. A quick look at it told me it was Mason who'd interrupted my beauty sleep. At least it was a pleasant change from the kids waking me up. I checked the time—six-forty a.m.

Ugh, I didn't need sleep anymore—immortality did that—but I still really liked it. The absence of all the mortal aches and pains I'd experienced meant that I could enjoy my beautifully expensive mattress without distraction. Usually, anyway. The butterflies in my stomach had already chosen Mason over the luxury of my bed, so I sat up and swung my feet over the side and into my slippers. Reindeers, this time. Cream fluffy puffs of wool with golden ears that moved when I walked.

I grabbed my phone and hit his name, putting the phone between my shoulder and ear so I could walk and talk. If I had to be awake, I'd be damned if it wasn't with a cup of tea in my hand.

Mason answered after the first ring. "El, you up?"

"The fact that I'm calling would be a good sign." I headed down the stairs toward the kitchen, a smile forming at the sound of his voice.

Mason laughed. "Feel like company?"

"Only if it's yours," I replied, cringing at my awful attempt at flirting. *I was so out of practice it was embarrassing.*

"I'll be there in ten."

"I'll be waiting." I hung up the phone and flicked the kettle on. The sound of it boiling was always a welcome one. Two sugars, a splash of milk, and a long-steeped English Breakfast tea were just what this Goddess had ordered. I leaned against the bench top and crossed my arms as I waited for my tea to reach the perfect dark amber colour I loved.

A loud, dragging sound from the basement distracted me for a moment. *Shade*. He was probably rearranging something. Every couple of weeks, he got bored with whatever configuration he had and gave something new a shot. I wanted to offer to help, but he'd told me, clearly, to leave him alone.

Or, more precisely, to *keep my immortal ass the Hades away from him.*

It wasn't my instinct to listen to a bogeyman teenager, but I also knew he needed to feel heard, even if it meant letting him hate me for a while. Fortunately, I didn't have long to dwell on the situation as Mason's knock at the door stole my attention.

"No coffee?" Mason asked as he walked into the kitchen, shooting me a mischievous smile that emphasised the strong line of his jaw. He placed his work jacket over one of the dining chairs. We were still two seat cushions short, but I'd had more important things to focus on.

"For you, I could change that." I smiled shyly. We'd been at a bit of a stalemate ever since the night the Animus attacked, almost as though what we'd gone through was too intimate to reverse out of but going forward felt just as odd.

Mason's cheeks flushed, his brown eyes shining brighter. "Thanks, El."

"Hard night?" I knew that would have been an understatement. It was the back end of the Australian summer, and bushfire season was having one last hard go at it before autumn stole its power away. The Rural Fire Service were at the front line of it all, and being the Leading Firefighter meant that Mason was the boss who had to make the hard decisions between lives and livelihoods.

"Yeah, we lost a good chunk of the national forest. Burnt a path straight through it. A couple of Jervis Bay locals lost their homes, but everyone was evacuated in time. It looks like we'll be on it for a few more days though," Mason explained as he settled into one of the chairs with a cushion.

"It's just awful." I finished stirring his instant coffee and added a bit of milk. Too much, probably. Coffee was just *so* bitter.

"The coffee or the bushfire?" Mason chuckled.

It wasn't the stellar brew that Shade could whip up, but I'd done my best. I placed the coffee in front of Mason and sat beside him.

"The fire." I rolled my eyes at him. "Why would it be the coffee? It's in date. I checked."

"You can't stand making it, can you?" he asked. "The nose wrinkle gives it away. You could change a nappy, and you'd make the same face."

"I don't mind making it." I defended myself. "It just smells horrible. It's even worse now that Shade is using the new machine. I swear he makes it so that it wafts through the whole house. I have no idea how you like it more than tea."

"It's an acquired taste." Mason smiled. "Kind of like a certain Goddess I know." He took a sip and didn't choke while I felt a blush work its way up to my cheeks.

"Just like a Leading Firefighter I know," I shot back with a grin. "It still weirds me out when you say that."

"It weirds you out," Mason said with incredulity in his voice. "In one night, I drove my car into your house, fought with shape-shifting warriors, and met your mother—who made another God bring you back to life. I think I'll be processing that for the next forty years."

"I'd suggest not taking that long," I teased. "I'm the immortal one, remember? You don't have that much time to waste." *And I don't want to miss a minute with you.* A sharp, quick pang reverberated in my chest, a wound once healed but suddenly reopened. *I'm not going there.*

Mason laughed, grasping my hand and squeezing. "I guess I'll have to work on getting over it fast then." The butterflies in my stomach returned, drowning out my doubts.

"I'm definitely on team Get Over It." I stood up and moved in front of him, gently lifting his chin so that I could bend down and kiss him. "We have better things to focus on."

"Gross, that is!" Alora announced her arrival in the kitchen with a bang. "Hungry, I am. Mama E, breakfast time it is." She wandered over to her usual chair and jumped up, ready to go. The good little soldier I am, I headed over to start the morning routine.

Zane followed quickly behind Alora, his overnight nappy still secured even as he flapped his way into the room, about a foot off the floor. "Gross, gross, gross," he chirped, repeating Alora's declaration all the way to his seat at the table.

"Dirty, you are." Alora directed her next judgment at Mason.

"Good morning to you too, Alora, Zane." Mason smiled. "I just got in from work, so I still need to shower, but I thought I'd come visit my favourite people."

"People, you're not my favourite," Alora replied. "Mama E, my favourite people, is."

"I. Love. Love. Love. Clara," Zane declared, hitting his hands on the table to emphasise each word.

"Well, at least you two let me know where I stand," Mason chuckled as he stood up and grabbed his work jacket from the back of the dining chair. "By the way, El, is there any chance you might bring some old blankets or anything like that to the station?"

"I could probably rustle some stuff up," I agreed. "What's it for?"

"We have a Park Ranger working with us to manage the injured animals we're coming across, but we're running short on blankets and things. Really just anything soft and fluffy will do," Mason explained.

"Of course, I'll try to bring some things down later." I smiled.

Mason took his coffee mug to the sink, near where I had started the morning breakfast assembly line.

"Thanks for the nightcap," he told me before placing a kiss on my forehead and turning back to where Zane and Alora sat at the table. "I better head off. You kids be good for El and Clara, alright?"

The two of them grinned but didn't agree.

"I did my best," Mason quipped before leaving the kitchen behind. I heard the front door close quietly and turned my attention to the kids.

"Okay, so what's it gonna be this morning?"

CHAPTER FIVE

THE AFTERNOON SUN SHONE brightly as I parked on Main Street in the heart of Briarmoor. After a busy morning tag-teaming, Clara had let me loose for some kid-free time, so I'd taken the chance to head into town and buy some extra supplies for the animals Mason had wanted donations for. After collecting most of what we had at the house, I realised some of it wasn't even really fit for anything except the trash. I figured I could enjoy some retail therapy while getting better quality blankets for the rescue animals.

I grabbed my purse and jumped out of the car, heading straight to the coffee shop a few stores down from Denny's pet shop. Tea was my first love, there was no doubt about that, but a well-brewed hot chocolate was a close second. Only when I was out though—I couldn't make a decent one at home if I tried.

I lined up behind a couple of people before placing my order. "One large hot chocolate with full cream milk and two marshmallows, please."

The barista plugged it into the register. "Five dollars and sixty-five cents," she told me. "Name?"

I tapped my card. "El."

"Wait over there. We'll call you when it's done."

"Thanks." I smiled and headed to the bar counter, where a few others were waiting. I didn't recognise anyone, which made a faint shiver of nervousness run through me. I'd been working on getting more familiar with the town and its people after everything that had happened, but it was still a work in progress.

Leaning awkwardly against the counter, I waited for the feeling to pass. Except it didn't. It slowly morphed into something else, closer to fear. Only, it wasn't mine.

I felt for the thread of emotion, covertly looking at the people in the coffee shop in the hopes of identifying the source. My powers hadn't been this strong in a very long time—hundreds of years, really—and getting used to them again was as challenging as losing them had been.

Try as I might, I couldn't narrow it down. The surrounding faces gave away nothing, and my powers couldn't decipher a single connection with the fear in the coffee shop.

"El," the server shouted. "Large hot chocolate's ready."

"Thanks." I collected my order and took a quick sip. *That was better.*

Casting another brief look around the coffee shop, I headed out the door and slowly headed up the street to Denny's pet store. Walking up to the door, I saw my reflection and the chocolate moustache I'd created as I drank my hot chocolate on my way over. I wiped the top of my lip and went inside, the bell dinging loudly as I entered.

"Hey, El," a deep male voice called out, catching me off guard.

"Emrys?" I replied. "I wasn't expecting to see you here."

"Denny's dealing with a bit of an emergency, so I volunteered to man the shop for her." He shrugged, although the crease in his brow made me think it was more of a family emergency than an individual one. It triggered the memory of what Mason had said earlier.

"Is everything okay?" I asked, walking over to the counter where he stood.

"Yeah, I think so. Or it will be anyway," he answered, more vaguely than I expected. *That was odd. There is definitely something going on that they don't want to share.*

"Oh, that's good then. I'm just picking up some blankets for the rescues coming into the fire station from the bushfire," I told him. "I can sort myself out. I'll be back in a few minutes."

"All good." He nodded and turned away to fiddle with something on the bench top behind him.

I rounded the display shelves and pretended to stare intently at the various pet blankets and rugs that lined them. Instead, I was searching inside myself for the thread of fear I'd felt at the coffee shop earlier. It was almost as though I could pull on the thread of emotion that my powers responded to. Where the connection had been vague before, it was clearer, more defined, and strongly coming from Emrys, although it felt too powerful to be just *his* fear alone. I could feel the weight of it as though it was a physical thing. My powers pushed back, knowing that they could ease the fear I was sensing. *Needing* to ease it. I'd forgotten how insistent they could feel when I hadn't used them in a while. I gathered a large bundle of the blankets and rugs and walked back over to the counter, determined to see if I could find out something more from him.

Emrys looked at the pile and then at me again. "That's a pile and a half. How many rescues do they have at the station?"

"I'm not sure, but I figure there's no such thing as too many blankets."

"That's a good call." He nodded as he scanned them through the register.

"Look, Emrys, I don't want to seem like a busybody, but are you sure that everything is actually okay? It feels like there's something pretty big bothering you, and I'd like to help if I can."

Emrys' eyes narrowed. "Your powers?"

I shrugged. "The curse of being a Goddess. Or this Goddess anyway."

"Don't say anything," he warned, eyes darting back to the front door of the shop. "We've been waiting for some family to arrive, but they haven't come. Denny thinks something odd has happened, so she's taken off for Sydney to check it out."

"No wonder you're worried. Is there anything I can do to help?"

"A little pick me up?" he asked with a wink. "I'm sure it's just some stupid scheduling problem or something, but Denny leaving to investigate has given me the heebie-jeebies. I could do without it for a few hours."

I gave him a look before letting out a sigh. "You know I don't usually do this, but my powers have been niggling at me for a chance to do something. It's a one-off, okay? And only because you're helping Denny out." I placed my hand on his and focused on the thread of fear that connected him to me, pulling it into my body while I sent the warm, glowing sense of mercy and compassion flowing back into him. It was over in a moment, the difference clear immediately as I saw the tension leave his face and a small smile return.

"Thanks, El."

"It's okay, Emrys. Now, if you wouldn't mind ringing me up, I was hoping to find a bookstore Clara found the other day. She said it had some good magickal stuff in it, so I wanted to have a peek myself."

"That comes to four hundred and seventy-six dollars and thirty cents. Card?"

"Uh-huh." I tapped my card and entered the code. *Goddess knows how I remember it.*

"Sweet, all yours. You should definitely have a look at the shop. If you head all the way up Main Street and then turn left down the last laneway, it's the store at the end." He handed me two bags full to the brim with blankets.

"Thanks. I didn't pick you for a reader," I replied.

"Nah, I'm not. My mum runs it, so we were always hanging around there as kids."

"I guess I better go put these in the car and get them to the station." I smiled at him. "Thanks for the tips. And don't forget to let me know if I can help—if it turns out to be anything major."

"Will do," Emrys replied with a mock salute.

I headed back out onto the footpath and made my way back to the car. A few minutes later, I was taking the corner of the road the fire station was on. It was nearly impossible to miss, the lights illuminating it from a mile away. Usually, the view was comforting, but the bushfire loomed ominously in the background of the mountains, the sunlight interrupted by shades of red, orange, yellow, and even purple, painting the sky in impossible colours. I'd been around for a few Australian bushfire seasons, and they just seemed to get longer and longer with each one that passed.

It was easy to wonder if the Gods had abandoned the world when I saw the damage that just one bushfire wrought on the land it consumed. The humans had stopped worshipping, but the Gods had stopped protecting too.

I had stopped protecting them. Did it matter which one came first?

I shook the thought from my head. I didn't need to bring more family drama into my life. I was here to drop off blankets and do my bit for our animal community. It only took a few minutes to park outside the fire station and load myself up with the donations I'd gathered from Halfling House and the store. I headed to the front door and used the one finger I could get free to press the doorbell, hoping someone answered quickly, given the precarious nature of the load I was carrying.

A young recruit whose name I couldn't remember appeared and opened the door. "Can I give you a hand?"

"That would be great, thanks," I accepted quickly.

"Blankets for the animals?" he asked, leading the way down the corridor to the main recreation area.

"Yeah, Mason mentioned that it's pretty bad out there—for the animals, and you guys." I could sense the stress and pain as soon as I stepped inside. It hadn't been that bad in all the time I could remember being at the station.

The recruit, Ortiz, if the name on his uniform was correct, just nodded. "It's difficult, that's for sure."

"Well, just let me know if there's anything else I can do to help," I offered. *You could always use your power.* The thought wove its way through my head.

"Will do, ma'am," he replied. "You'll find the boss in here." I blanked for a moment as I took in the 'ma'am' comment. *How old do I look?*

I had little time to process the fact that I'd been called 'ma'am' *after* my powers had returned and I'd stopped aging again. Ortiz entered the recreation area and placed his load of blankets down on a folding table that was set up near the entryway. A few more were scattered throughout the room, with various useful things loaded on top of them. I followed suit and placed everything I had in my arms on top. "Thanks for your help."

"Anytime, ma'am," Ortiz responded before disappearing back down the corridor. There was that word again.

Arms empty, I decided to leave *that* word alone and focus on finding Mason. The room was busier than usual, but given the current crisis, it was to be expected. Briarmoor's fire station wasn't designed to run multiple active firefighting crews twenty-four-seven, so they'd had to call in some nearby stations for help. I wandered around for a few minutes, avoiding unfamiliar faces, until I spotted Mason across the hall in the kitchen, a cup of coffee in his hand, talking animatedly with some of his mainstay crew and someone in a uniform I didn't recognise.

"El!" Mason called out as I approached. "Everyone, El. El, everyone."

"What a useful introduction." I shot him a reproachful smile.

"Well, you've met Mac and Erik before." The two firefighters in question smiled and nodded hello, which I returned. "And this is Kirra." He gestured to the dark-haired, brown-skinned woman in the unfamiliar uniform. "She's our liaison from the local Wildlife Rescue Unit."

"Nice to meet you, Kirra." I put my hand out, and she shook it, giving me a tight smile.

"Good to meet you too. Just wish it was under better circumstances," Kirra said.

"Me too," I replied. "I know it's not much, but I brought in a few blankets and things, so hopefully that will help a bit." The stress was clear on all their faces, my power edging toward the emotion as though it wanted to smooth the discomfort over. *Not a bad idea, really.*

"It will, thanks," Kirra answered. "We have a lot of scared wildlife out there that doesn't know what direction to run. The best we're seeing is dehydration, although there are a lot more burns coming through the longer the fires last. Then there are the ones who don't make it ..." She trailed off.

A sharp pang of pain hit me in the chest. Not my pain but Kirra's. Instinctively, I reached for her shoulder and connected with her pain, absorbing the edge off it and replenishing it with a little more calm and peace. Hopefully, it would help her focus better if the pain wasn't so present. And take the edge off the urge for me.

"You're doing your best," I told her. "You all are." I addressed the rest of them. "If there's anything I can do to help, just let me know."

"Except make coffee, right?" Mason teased, lifting his cup to his lips.

"Ugh. You can line someone else up for that job." I grimaced. "I think I'm going to head off and let you all get back to business. Can I steal your boss for a second before I go?"

"He's all yours," Mac told me. "Let's take five, and then we can go over the plan again, everyone."

With that, the four of them wandered off while Mason led me into his office and closed the door.

"Miss me?" he asked, pulling me close to him and placing his hands on my waist in a way that sent a shiver—*the good kind*—up my spine.

"A little," I answered, playing with the edge of his collar. "Maybe more if you kiss me."

Mason didn't need another invitation, taking charge and kissing me until I was out of breath and I'd almost forgotten my real reason for getting him alone.

"How about now?" he asked, a twinkle in his eye.

"Definitely missing you about a million times more." I grinned cheekily. "But ..."

"But what?"

"My power is itching to come out," I told him. "And this place is swamped with stress, pain, and frustration."

"Are you asking what I think you are?" I couldn't read the look on his face.

"I think I can take the edge off. It might help my power back down a touch and give you all a bit of peace and calm, rather than operating off adrenalin and nerves," I explained.

"Will it help?" he asked warily. "Is it safe?"

"I'm a little rusty, but I wouldn't offer if I didn't think it could make a difference. A good one," I clarified.

Mason nodded. "Then do it. I trust you."

Those three words made my breath catch in my throat. They both warmed my heart and chilled it. That was a lot of responsibility. *Was I ready for it?* Did that matter?

"Okay, here we go." I moved back and placed my hands one under the other, palms facing upward, closing my eyes and turning my focus inward. I took a deep breath and then released it as I started to connect with the power within me. My mind reached out to the magickal energy channelled throughout my whole body, harnessing it within my mind, ready to wield.

With my power ready, I sought out the pain and stress running rampant throughout the fire station, my mind's eye seeing the emotions as pure energy within the people there, their whole beings consumed by it. This time, when I breathed in, my power began absorbing the anguish and strain from all the surrounding people, spreading further and further until everyone within the fire station had loosed their stress and pain and it had found a new home inside me.

I gasped, the flood of overwhelming feeling almost bringing me to my knees. I was vaguely aware of someone—Mason—grabbing a hold of my waist and holding me up. I let go of the breath I was holding, laden with their pain, and released the mercy and compassion they needed. Its strength nestled within the space where their anguish and strain had been moments before. It only took a few seconds—although it felt far longer to me—before the exchange was complete, and I collapsed completely into Mason's arms.

"Thanks for the catch," I told him, my voice shakier than I expected it would be. "It took a bit more out of me than I thought."

"I couldn't tell," Mason quipped as he moved us to the couch opposite his desk, pulling me onto his lap. I let my head fall against his chest and closed my eyes, breathing in the heady yet comforting mix of leather, wood, and smoke that made up his scent. *I could stay here forever.*

It had really taken it out of me to use my power on so many people at once. Still, I could already tell that the steady diet of pain and stress they had been subsisting on for the last few days was gone, and that the compassion and mercy that had filled its place would help them get through the next round of challenges they faced.

"I think I'm alright now," I murmured, my eyes still closed as I stayed nestled into him.

"Good, you had me worried there for a bit." Mason placed a gentle kiss on my forehead as I opened my eyes. I tilted my head up so that I could rest a kiss on his lips.

"It's been a while since I used my powers on so many people at once. Hundreds of years, in fact."

"Well, I'm grateful that it's us you chose to help."

"If it helps you, it helps me," I admitted. "So I guess it might have been a little selfish."

"That's definitely not the word I'd use to describe it, El." He smiled at me. "I should get back out there and make sure everything is on track," he said, giving me a squeeze.

I squeezed back. "Me too. I promised Clara I wouldn't be long, and I still want to drop by the bookstore." I slid off his lap and stood up, feeling surprisingly solid, given how I'd felt a few minutes ago.

"The bookstore?" he echoed, arching his brow.

"I just want to make sure that everything is on the up and up, no big deal." I shrugged nonchalantly. "It'll be fine. Clara won't even know, and I'll feel a lot better about it all. It's a win-win." *Especially if the witch who Clara ran into is Emrys and Declan's mother.*

Mason nodded, the crease of his brow shifting to his typical concerned look. "If you say so. Do you think you could do me another favour?" Mason asked, his smile enough that I'd probably have agreed to send a thousand ships to Troy for him.

"Chilling out the entire station wasn't a big enough one?" I chuckled.

Mason grinned. "This one's a lot simpler. I had a few missed calls from Gabe and the others, but I haven't had a moment to get back to them. Do you think you could check in on them? My gut tells me something's off, but I can barely keep up with this place as it is."

"Consider it done," I agreed, gently planting a kiss on his lips. The temptation to go further heated me from within, even as I did my best to push it back down. "One thing to keep in mind though—all the pain, the stress here—it's gone," I told him. "They should all feel a lot better now, but don't waste it. Make sure you all still take care of yourselves. It's not a second wind. It's a firmer foundation. What you do with it is what will make the difference."

"When you talk like that, it's easy to believe that you're a thousands-of-years-old Goddess with more life experience than this entire station combined," Mason said, his brown eyes reflecting something that looked a lot like admiration.

Maybe even love.

The thought was enough to keep me floating in the clouds all the way out of the station and into the car. I'd forgotten the high that came from using my powers to help people.

Once I got back to town, I followed Emrys' directions to the bookstore. Sure enough, a sign with white loopy writing declared that Page Bound was open. I pushed on the door and walked in, a light, melodic sound alerting whoever was within that I'd entered.

As my eyes adjusted to the dimmer lighting, I realised the bookstore was much larger on the inside than on the outside. Four rows of wooden mahogany shelves stood in front of me while the perimeter was lined with the same wooden bookcases. At first, it seemed like they only had the typical bookstore fare—romance, history, nonfiction, children's, and a bit of sci-fi and fantasy—however, after walking around for a few minutes, I spotted another door marked 'Special Editions' at the back of the store.

"Hello, dear." The unfamiliar voice surprised me, making me jump a little. I turned around to see a short, dark-haired woman with bright purple glasses smiling at me. I could see the resemblance to Emrys and Declan in her straight nose and tanned skin. "I'm Olive. How can I help you?"

Relief slipped over me like a soft blanket over my skin as I realised my suspicions were correct. It wasn't some random Briarmoor witch Clara had encountered.

"Oh." The sound slipped out of me as I realised I'd let my thoughts distract me. "Sorry, I didn't see you there."

"It's a special skill. I don't enjoy disturbing the books if I can avoid it," She smiled. "Are you looking for something in particular?"

"I am, actually. It's more alternative than what I've come across so far," I told her as I pulled myself together.

I cast my powers out and sought whatever emotions I could find, but they only found warmth inside Olive—compassion, mostly, although mercy was strong too. My powers were coming up empty on anything negative, which was reassuring.

Olive gave me a curious look. "You're an interesting one."

Hmm, I wonder if she can tell that I'm a Goddess? Some magickals were better at sensing others. I looked at her intently, waiting to see if any emotions spiked, but nothing came.

"What brand of alternative floats your boat?" she prodded again, waiting for an answer.

"Sorry. I'm more interested in the ... magickal ... variety," I offered, watching for her reaction.

"Ah, is it spell books you're after? A love spell, maybe? Or is it something else, dear?"

I couldn't very well tell her she was what I had been looking for. The rational part of me knew it was time to let Clara reach out to other witches and start discovering her magickal heritage without me holding her hand. The other, less rational, more impulsive part of me still wanted to protect her as much as I could. A side-stop at the bookstore to get a feel for who that might be felt like a good idea.

"Um, yes. Do you have anything useful for young witches? Like, a beginner's guide or something?" I answered.

"Ah, someone preparing for their first Coven?" She smiled excitedly. "I remember mine like it was yesterday: a beautiful full moon, the citrus scent of flowering lemon-myrtle trees, and, of course, the chanting. Oh, it was just glorious! Is it local?" Olive looked at me expectantly.

"Local? N-n-no," I stuttered. "Not local." *I do not need anyone connecting these dots.* Maybe if I came back with something helpful or supportive, it would keep Clara's curiosity sated a little longer.

"Follow me." Olive threaded her way through the bookshelves and led me into the Special Editions section, which ended up being as much a maze as the first part of the store. Eventually, we stopped at a shelf with pretty, shining crystals and a variety of books—some closer to my age than I expected—before she picked one up that was relatively new. "This. Is. Perfect," Olive declared, handing me the book.

'You're a Witch. Now What?' the cover said, etched on a lavender hardback decorated with a silver rectangle, accented with delicate flourishes in each corner. "Are you serious?"

"As a natural disaster, dear. It's a good one. I gave each of my young ones an earlier edition before their first Coven."

Hmm. I turned the book over in my hands and looked at the back before turning to the front again.

"I'll have to take your advice then," I agreed. Another thought popped into my head. "Actually, do you have any moonstone crystals?"

"Of course, dear. What would you like, necklace, bracelet, earrings, or are you after something for an altar?" Olive asked. "The jewellery is at the front counter." She turned and led me back out to the main store.

"A bracelet would be nice," I answered as I followed. Olive pulled a display of bracelets out and placed them on the counter when we got to it. I knew the right one immediately—a thin gold bracelet with three elegant raw pieces of moonstone connected at the midpoint. I pointed it out, and Olive set about putting it in a pretty velvet envelope.

"You have excellent taste," she said before putting the amount through on the register. I tapped my card and finished my end of the transaction.

"Thanks." I smiled. "Hopefully, you're not the only one who thinks so."

"I'm sure I won't be," Olive said in a motherly voice. "Now, if your little witch needs anything else, be sure to let her know I'm here. We're a friendly lot in Briarmoor. Always happy to help!"

I gave her another smile and a polite wave before tracing the path back to my car, my thoughts busy with everything that had happened that afternoon. No matter how friendly the Briarmoor witches were, I wasn't sure I would be ready for the next step Clara took.

It was only when I checked my phone on the way back to the car that my heart dropped. Five missed calls.

And they were all from Denny.

CHAPTER SIX

THE SIGHT OF THE glaring red notifications created a pit in the bottom of my stomach as I settled myself into the car, shutting the door and turning the engine over.

Even with Alora flashing over there so often, it was rare for Denny to call me directly. Even rarer for her to call me more than once.

Five times—that meant that something was really wrong.

Storm.

I dialled Denny's number and listened to the phone ring. I tapped the steering wheel with my fingers, rapping out an anxious pattern with no discernible rhythm. It felt like an age before I heard her voice on the other end of the line.

"Hello," Denny answered.

"Denny, it's Ellie. Is Storm okay? Is everything alright?" I asked in one rushed jumble of words.

"She's fine, love. Happily playing with Conrad and the others," she reassured me.

I sat back against the car seat and let out a relieved sigh. "Thank the Gods. My mind went all over the place for a second. What's going on then? Is everything else okay?"

"That's the thing, dear," Denny started. "We have a problem, and I think you might be the only person who can help."

Curiosity replaced the concern that had overwhelmed me earlier. "What's going on, Denny? Is it something to do with why you were gone?"

"Yes, love. We were expecting a Faoladh young'un with her Ma to arrive from Belfast a few days ago, but they never called when they were supposed to," she explained. "You know what it's like when you're in a new place; you can get all caught up in all the fancy lah-dee-dah things. Forget to call. Wouldn't be the first, won't be the last. We gave it a few days, but still, nothing, and no one back home had heard from them either."

I could hear the edge of worry in Denny's voice.

"So, you went to Sydney to try to find them?" I asked.

"That was the plan. I didn't think it would be too much more than just a couple of overwhelmed wolves in a big city. But it was so much worse, darl ..." She trailed off, going quiet.

I let the silence sit, a wave of her pain reaching me even through the phone. *Oh, Denny.*

"Ellie, when I got there, I found out they never made it to the hotel. They'd been in a bad car crash, and the coppers were still contacting their next of kin. The long story short is that the young'un is missing, and we have no way of finding her."

"What happened to her mother?" I wasn't sure I wanted the answer to the question, but I asked anyway.

"Her Ma passed, in front of her, it seems. That's where it starts to get a little hazy. The cops only found her Ma at the scene, in human form. Rowan—the young lass—had shifted into her wolf form, so they tranquilised her and shipped her off to an animal holding facility while they sorted the whole thing out. Only ..."

"Oh, Gods!" I gasped. The thought of what the young girl had gone through pierced straight through to the core of my heart. Places like that were awful—sterile, cold, and the last thing a traumatised child should be exposed to. "Please tell me they didn't keep her there?"

"No, love, they didn't. She shifted back to human form and scared the bejesus out of the people on shift. They let her out and called the cops, but she took off before they got there, and no one's set eyes or ears on her since."

I couldn't say it was unexpected. In my experience, the Faoladh didn't seem to take kindly to being contained or restrictions of any kind, really. That was why they'd settled on the large acreage in Briarmoor. It very literally gave them the room they needed to run.

"That's awful, Denny. She's just a kid, isn't she?"

"All of seven years old, darl. You know how we are though. She looks like a teenager, and that's only if she's in her human form." Denny's voice cracked, the sadness seeping through.

"How do you think I can help?"

"Well, we're assuming she's on her way here. We're the only Faoladh nearby, and she'd have to be terrified. The boys—Emrys, Declan and Farron—are out looking for her, trying to use a scent from some clothing I could grab in Sydney, but the fires are throwing a spanner in the works. Even with their heightened sense of smell, it's no use. The smoke is overpowering everything. But I know you can *feel* someone's pain, their fear—it's how you know who to help, isn't it?"

"Yes, that's how it works. Sometimes, I'm just drawn to them. Other times, I pick up on the emotions first," I explained. "Although, I've never tried to use it to find someone in a shifted form before."

"Emrys told me what you did for him at the store," Denny said quietly, "So it's not just finding her that's going to matter, dear. She's going to be in a lot of grief, and if you can help lessen it a little, I think that would make a big difference."

"You have my help, however you need it. You're family to us," I told her, my throat tightening as I thought of how much kindness and generosity they had shown us after the Animus attack and the long road to repairing Halfling House.

"Thank you, darl." The relief in her voice was palpable.

"So, do you have a plan, Denny?" I asked. "Or any idea where we need to look?"

"Now, that's where I was hoping you might rope your handsome gentleman lover into helping."

I couldn't help but laugh. "You can just call him Mason, Denny."

My mind was still whirring with the information Denny had imparted during our call when I pulled up to the house and headed inside.

The smell of disinfectant and bubblegum-scented bath wash greeted me when I walked inside. I put the bag from the bookstore away in the storage cupboard under the stairs and followed the cacophony of sounds coming from the bathroom. From the squeals and shouts, it sounded like Clara was having a Hades of a time getting Zane and Alora through the rigours of bath time.

"Guess who's home?" I sang out loudly as I climbed the stairs.

"Oh, thank the Gods!" Clara exclaimed, popping her head out from inside the bathroom door, her hair shining bright white against the colour of the hallway. White meant stressed. A whole head full of white meant she was completely overwhelmed.

A loud plop, punctuated with a splash, reached my ears a few seconds after hers. Clara's head disappeared, and a giant sigh echoed off the tiled walls.

"Zane," Clara and I said simultaneously, although her tone was more resigned than mine.

I entered the bathroom just in time to see Zane grin, flutter a couple of inches above the bath, and release another pellet straight into the water. Alora, sitting on the other side of the tub, cringed and started crying.

"Yucky, Zane is," she let out through the tears. "Out, out, please."

Her reaction only excited Zane more, the grin turning cheeky and his eyes mischievous.

"No, Zane," I told him, using my serious voice. "No more pooping in the bath." I grabbed a towel and scooped Alora up, turning around to Clara. "Why don't you and Alora go and get her all nice and clean and in her pyjamas? She can even use my special moisturiser, the one that smells like the flowers she likes."

"Thanks, El," Clara agreed. "I swear he just does it because it gets a reaction out of me."

I nodded. "I hate to say it, but I think you're right. You've either gotta fake it until you make it, or we're going to be in for a Tartarus level of toilet training."

"Ugh, that is not what I want to hear. Have I ever told you that being an adult sucks sometimes?"

Laughter erupted from me. "Well, as someone who's been an adult for longer than most civilisations have existed, I can confirm that you are, in fact, correct."

Clara pulled a face at me and then headed down the hall, Alora perched on her hip. I turned to see Zane still hovering above the bath water, an expression of intense concentration on his face.

"You okay there, Z?"

"No poop," he exclaimed, disappointment in his voice.

"Ah, you've run out, have you?"

The scales around his face shimmered under the warm bathroom lights as he nodded.

"That must mean its time to clean up then," I told him. Zane's wings stopped flapping, and he fell into the bath, the water softening his fall but splashing out onto me and the tiled floor. It wasn't exactly a surprise that he wasn't keen on the cleaning part of his escapade, but if I'd learned one thing since taking in halflings, it was that natural consequences were often the best consequences.

Clara had tried to spot clean as Zane tortured her, but her success level was debatable. So, much to Zane's chagrin, we spent the next half an hour cleaning up his poop and then the bathroom, followed by the two of us having a wash as well. After what felt like a lifetime, bath time—and the cleanup—was over and done with.

All dried and clean, I sat down with Zane on the bathroom floor and took his two chubby little hands in mine, capturing his attention.

"What have we learned today?" I asked in a light-hearted voice, moving his hands slowly back and forth to keep him focused on me.

"To poop!" he replied enthusiastically.

"Yes!" I praised him, "You can poop! But where do we poop, Zane?"

"In the bath!" He giggled, and I shook my head at him, turning my smile upside down.

"Nope, not the bath. That's where we get clean. Can you guess again?"

"On the floor," he tried again, his cheeky smile giving him away.

"Yucky, that doesn't sound fun. You'd just have to pick it all up again. Do you want to do that again?"

"No, no, no." He shook his head.

"There is one place that is hungry for your poop though!" I told him excitedly. "The toilet!"

Zane let go of my hands and looked at me warily. "The toilet's hungry?"

"It is!" I told him, plastering an overexcited grin on my face. "Just look." I grabbed a couple of squares of toilet paper and popped them into the toilet before flushing it.

Zane's eyes widened. "The toilet growled!"

"It did, because it's hungry for more," I explained to him. "Do you think from now on you could try feeding the toilet your poop?"

"Yes, yes, yes! I want to feed the toilet!" Zane fluttered a few inches off the ground, excitement colouring his face a blush of pink against his shimmering scales.

See, I thought to myself, *I've got this.* This time, my smile wasn't forced as Zane decided to give the toilet a good meal before bed.

Clara took over for bedtime, thankfully, so I stopped in for a quick kiss goodnight. Alora was settled in her bed while Zane lay amidst too many blankets to count, his chubby hands wrapped around a toy car and plush bunny, respectively.

"Sweet dreams, Z." I dropped a kiss on his forehead, the smooth sensation of his scales caressing my lips. I moved over to Alora and did the same. "Dream big, baby girl."

"Early night?" Clara asked from her spot sitting on the floor between the two of them.

"Not a chance." I rolled my eyes at her. "I'm in need of some trash TV and wine." I backed away from the door and started down the hallway.

"Don't watch that dating show without me. I want to see who gets eliminated!" Clara shouted from behind me.

"I won't," I promised as I headed back downstairs.

It couldn't have been more than half an hour later that the sound of Clara's voice pulled my focus from the TV, the pitch nearly making me jump out of my skin.

"You have got to be joking, El!" Clara was the kind of furious that turned her skin a mottled red and her hair a flaming ruby colour. I'd only seen her that angry twice in her life before.

But that was the first time I'd ever felt her anger—and pain—to that degree the entire time I'd known her. And there was only one thing I could think of that would make her so frustrated.

Not the bag, please, not the bag from the bookstore.

"I can't believe you went to the bookstore behind my back! All your talk about being okay with me investigating my heritage is rubbish. You couldn't even trust me enough to let me be the one to do it. You had to go and stick your big nose in it!" Clara ranted, the colour of her hair pulsing with each breath she took.

I touched my nose. *It's not that big,* I thought self-consciously. *Greek noses are strong and firm, like the women that wear them.*

"Really?" Clara stopped pacing and stood before me, hands planted on her hips. "Everything I'm saying, and you're going to worry about your nose?"

"I'm not worried about my nose," I replied. "I'm not going to apologise for going to the bookstore. I wanted to see what it was like. And I figured it couldn't hurt to meet the woman you thought was a witch. It's my job to look after you."

"El, it's your job to look after the *kids,*" Clara emphasised the last word with some dramatic mouth movements. "Not me, El. You're treating me like I'm Shade, like I'm a teenager. I'm old enough to walk out that door and never come back—*if I wanted to.*"

Suddenly, it felt like my heart dropped to my feet. She said the words as though it wasn't the first time the thought had entered her mind. *Oh, Gods.*

"You really feel that way?" I asked, my voice sounding smaller than I expected.

Clara sighed. "Just because you've lived for a million years or whatever doesn't mean you get to treat me like a kid forever, El. You're not giving me any space to be who I want to be." She sat down at the end of the couch. "I can't live that way."

"I-I'm sorry," I breathed out. "All I've ever wanted to do is protect you. I never wanted to make you feel that way, Clara. And I really never meant to make you feel you needed to leave." I put my head in my hands. "I really am sorry. I thought I was doing the right thing. You've been through enough in your life, and I just wanted to do everything that

I could to make sure you wouldn't get hurt. Some humans—some witches—are great, Clara, but others ... others ... They're really not."

Clara scooted over closer to where I sat. "Do you honestly think I don't know that, El?" she asked. "Do you think I've forgotten what we've gone through trying to find a home? I *know* bad people exist, El, and I haven't forgotten the damage they can do."

"I don't want you to feel you need to leave," I told her, ignoring the prick of tears in the corners of my eyes. "You always have a home here. Even if I have to work on being less of an overprotective pain-in-the-butt."

"I said that because I was angry. You know what it's like when I get angry," she explained. "I'm not going to say I haven't thought about it because I have, but I think everyone does at some point. Sometimes it feels like the only way you'll be able to accept that I need some independence is if I leave."

"I knew you wanted to be involved and be treated more like an adult, and I thought I was doing better, especially after the whole Animus thing. I guess I kind of slipped back."

"And I need you to realise that. Going to the bookstore just to snoop on me—that's going too far, El. Maybe if you asked for us to go together, I would have considered it, but you know this is something I want to do for myself and *by* myself."

"I didn't just go there to 'snoop' or whatever you called it," I explained, lifting my gaze to meet hers. "I wanted to get you something to show you I support you."

"This?" Clara held up the book I'd bought for her. "'You're a Witch. Now What?'—I'm not sure if that makes it better or worse."

"I figured starting from the beginning might help."

"I don't think I'm that much of a novice, but I appreciate the thought." She gave me a wry smile.

"That's part of it, you know. I don't know what you know—what you remember from what I taught you or what you've found out on your own. It's like it's a part of you that you won't share with me, and I think that makes it even harder to step back." I found Clara's hand and gave it a squeeze. "It's always going to be easier for you to follow your path than it will be for me to let go. You're the first one, and I think that means it's going to be the hardest for me."

"Look, let's make a deal," Clara offered. "I'll be more open with you about what I'm learning and how I'm going about it all, but only if you promise to work on giving me the space to do it. And no more snooping behind my back."

I nodded. "It's a deal."

Clara leaned over and wrapped me in a hug, one I returned with the biggest squeeze I had in me. It felt like I'd come close to losing her, and that had sent terror screaming through my brain. She eventually pulled away, but not without a final squeeze from me.

"Now, will you let me give you the other half of my present?" I asked.

"Other half?"

"I told you I wasn't just snooping." I gripped her hand and then let go, getting up from the couch to find the bag from the bookstore. "Did you leave the bag where it was?"

"Um, nope. It's on the dining table."

"Okay." I disappeared into the kitchen and collected the bracelet in its pretty packaging. I walked back into the lounge a minute or two later. "Close your eyes."

Clara did as I said, and I placed the bracelet in her hands. "You can look now."

"Oh," she gasped, holding the bracelet in her hands. "Gods. It's stunning! What stone is it?"

"It's moonstone," I told her. "The Goddess Selene created moonstone by storing the light of the moon inside the gem. She blessed them to be imbued with the power to help you harness the moon's feminine energy. It's supposed to help your intuition guide you toward your destiny."

"It's beautiful, El," Clara said in awe. "The bracelet and the meaning." She looked up at me, placing her wrist out so I could do it up. "Thank you."

I smiled at her. "I love you, and I'm proud of you. And I will do better, I promise."

Clara stood up, and we hugged again. "I love you too, El."

"Just do me a favour," I asked as we pulled apart. "Keep the bracelet on, okay? It should help you sense the right path to take."

Clara laughed and held her wrist up, the bracelet hanging delicately on it. "I'd roll my eyes at you, but I think I can handle compromise when it's this pretty."

"That's good, because I need to tell you something. I had a phone call from Denny on the way back over. It sounds like they could use some help." I gave her a rundown on the details of our phone call and their missing Faoladh, Rowan.

"How horrible," Clara gasped. "No wonder the poor thing was all over the place. You leave for a holiday and lose a parent. She must feel so alone."

I nodded. I'd seen enough mortals suffer loss in my immortal life that I knew it changed them, no matter how it happened. The younger, the worse it was. No one stayed the same.

"You know you're the right person to help her, yeah?" Clara told me, moving closer again. "This is what you do. You find lost kids and give them a home. Sure, this time, you're literally trying to 'find' her, but it's not that different. Denny was right to call you." She squeezed my hand, catching my gaze so I could see the sincerity reflected in her eyes.

CHAPTER SEVEN

One thing about immortal sleep was that it never really got all that deep, so once I heard the rooster crow on a nearby farm, somehow laying on my luxurious bed lost most of its appeal. I'd started to find at least a small amount of joy in the earlier hours when I could sneak in a cup of tea without a kid hanging off me, flying, or flashing around me. After a quick change, I headed to the kitchen, where I started steeping a French Earl Grey tea that was like drinking warm flowers without the grittiness of *actually* consuming flowers.

"Did you enjoy it? Using your powers again?"

A familiar voice asked from the entryway, surprising me. It could only belong to one person, or God, should I say. *Thanatos.* I turned around to look at my brother. Chin length black hair framed the strong lines of his tanned face, deep mahogany eyes reflected back at my own. When I'd first seen him, he'd still been wearing his traditional black chiton, but his time in the mortal realm must've been rubbing off on him because today he had on a loose black shirt and cargo shorts.

"Well, did you?" he asked again.

"Yes, of course I did," I answered him. "Although I'm looking forward to when I'm back at full strength and can just teleport myself out of situations like this."

"Does seeing my face pain you that much?" he asked.

"It's not your face that's the problem. What are you doing here, Thanatos?" I sighed.

"Am I not allowed to visit my sister?" he asked, pulling out a dining chair and sitting down. "Is that the 'tea' you've got such an affection for? I'll have some of that, if you don't mind."

I mind. But I made him a cup anyway and took it over to where he sat, placing my own on the table as well.

"We both know that you're not here for a brotherly visit," I said as I sat down, meeting his gaze. "So, answer me honestly."

Thanatos threaded his fingers through the handle of the mug and held it in front of him as though he might very well actually drink it. *Small wonders.*

"You are correct. This is not just a social visit," he admitted. "I have come because I believe Mother is too proud to reach out on her own, even though she has told me she wishes to see you."

"She could have seen me anytime she wished. She chose not to." An ache near enough to ancient swelled in my heart.

"The same could be said for you, Eleos," Thanatos replied, flexing his fingers around the mug.

"*She's* the mother, Thanatos."

"That doesn't mean you must always act the part of the *child,* sister."

I sat back in my chair, crossing my arms in front of me. My desire for my tea started wilting at the edges.

"Neither of you has let go of your pride enough to be the family either of you needed. It has cost her dearly to lose you, and no matter what she says, she wants to have a relationship with you," Thanatos said, his voice soft. "Does it have to be that way for the next thousand years as well? Can one of you not yield some ground?"

His words echoed in my head. My mother's way had always been immovable, bull-headed even. But I had never considered myself much of her daughter in that way. I looked at Thanatos, and the sincerity etched into the lines on his face told me he believed what he was saying.

I gnawed at the inside of my mouth. *Was it really stubbornness that had kept us apart? Was I just as much to blame?* But it was the thoughts edged with hope that were the ones that stung the most. *Could it be different? Could we be different?*

"I suppose just because it has been this way doesn't mean it always has to be," I answered cautiously. Maybe it wasn't the only thing that could benefit from a different approach. "Although, if I am going to reach out, as you suggest, then could you perhaps help *me* with something?"

Thanatos' eyes sparkled with interest. "Perhaps. What aid is it you seek?"

"Shade. He's a young bogeyman halfling I've been caring for," I said. "I'm not his favourite person at the moment. I think I'm cramping his style—"

Thanatos' brow creased, appearing confused.

"I think he thinks I'm stopping him from letting him take on more magickal responsibility," I explained, "when all I'm trying to do is help him understand himself better before he goes out into a very unforgiving world."

"It sounds somewhat overprotective, Eleos," Thanatos smirked.

"Only to Gods who are used to abandoning their young at their own whim, Thanatos." I hoped that the seriousness in my voice made my feelings clear. "If I'm to make an effort with Mother, I need your help with this."

Thanatos' dark eyes stilled momentarily until he nodded. "I agree to your deal."

"Thank you," I replied, uncrossing my arms and leaning forward on the table. "So, am I on the most wanted list on Mount Olympus?"

The change of subject might have been sudden to Thanatos if his raised brow was anything to go by, but it had been on my mind.

"You care for their opinion?"

"I'm more curious. I also don't want to get any other sudden, uninvited visits." I let a sly smile form as Thanatos processed the shade I'd thrown his way.

"Only a few know. Those that Mother trusts. Zeus hasn't uttered a word of the deal the two of you wrought from him, lest the other Gods and Goddesses see it as a weakness on his part."

I was right. Zeus' ego was too big to let the others know we'd bested him.

"The same for Briarmoor being a Sanctuary?"

"If returning your powers was a sign of weakness, declaring your home a Sanctuary would be the equivalent of signalling his vulnerability to the entire Pantheon. Only Mother, Asclepius, and myself know, and Zeus will keep it that way. His rule of Mount Olympus is tremulous, and he will not risk weakening it further." Thanatos's eyes flickered with something that my power sensed as compassion.

Compassion? I'd felt it from him many a time, though it was usually for someone we tended, not for me.

"You are safe, sister. Your home is protected. And I will help with your youngling," Thanatos reassured me, returning to his typical stoic manner.

"Halfling," I said softly. "Are you staying for breakfast then?"

"I've had worse offers." Thanatos grinned widely. "Although I do believe there is another feast to be held on Mount Olympus that I must get to. Another time, perhaps?"

"Sounds for the best. We'll take a rain check. You'll come back to see Shade?"

"Within the next few days, I shall return and meet with your child." He dipped his head in agreement.

My child.

I didn't correct him—Shade might not be my blood, but he was my family in all the ways that mattered. And I needed to try something different to reach him and show him that. Hopefully, Thanatos would be the olive branch we needed to get past this.

Thanatos stood up, leaving his full cup of tea on the table. "I'll be going now, sister."

"You're not going to finish your tea?" I asked, raising my brow. "I made that just for you."

He winked before disappearing right in front of me. I let out a sigh of annoyance and stood up from my seat, collecting his cup and emptying it in the sink.

What a waste of tea.

Once Thanatos left, the morning passed in a flurry of toilet-training Zane for me and convincing Alora not to flash to the Faoladh house for Clara. Shade had appeared momentarily, taking the last of the new pack of Froot Loops down to the basement with only a grunted greeting. I'd debated bringing up my conversation with Thanatos, but it wasn't the right time, given I'd have had to chase him to get a word in before he disappeared.

Fortunately, after lunch, Zane fell asleep on the couch while Alora was immersed in a fairytale Clara was reading to her next to his sleeping form.

"Now that everything is a bit calmer, I think I'm going to head into town and see if I pick up a few things. Do you think you could manage while I pop out and grab some groceries?"

"Sounds like a good idea," Clara said. "We should be fine as long as you're back before nap time is over."

"Mission accepted." I left while I had the chance. I'd run out of a couple of my favourite tea varieties, plus there was no such thing as enough milk and bread in a household like ours. Before I headed back, I picked up a few other bits and pieces.

My quick trip to the store had escalated from a couple of items to a good dozen more than I'd anticipated, so it took a couple of trips from the car to the kitchen to get everything inside. It wasn't until I'd unpacked and made my way into the lounge that I realised Alora and Zane were no longer napping. In fact, the only one getting any shuteye was Clara, who'd spread out on the couch—all six feet of her.

I nudged the Converse hanging off the edge of the couch and waited for her to respond. *Nothing.* I tapped her foot again but had no luck, so I tickled the end of her nose instead. Sure enough, it worked, and she sat straight up before her eyes had even fully opened.

"Looks like you were having a nice nap there. So, are you going to tell me where you hid the kids?" I looked around, but there was no sign of them. In fact, I hadn't seen Alora or Zane since I'd walked in the door.

Clara's eyes widened slightly, and she sucked in the side of her lip. "In the basement. With Shade and …"

I raised my eyebrows. "And …?"

"With Shade and Thanatos," she squeaked out, pushing herself further up the couch, away from me. "Don't kill the messenger! He arrived while you were gone, and the kids got really excited, so I just let them be." She held a cushion in front of her.

It was a good idea because I grabbed another and threw it at her.

I wasn't worried about what Thanatos would do. The Sanctuary meant that no one from the Greek Pantheon could harm anyone in Briarmoor.

Even then, what many people—even Gods and Goddesses—didn't know was that my brother, Thanatos, the God of death, was kind. Kinder than most could expect and far kinder than some of the other death Gods and Goddesses from other Pantheons that I'd had the misfortune to encounter in the years I'd wandered the world.

He just wasn't well versed in how to manage kids or what you could, or should, tell them. However, the sight I came upon as I descended the stairs into the basement—into Shade's bedroom—was something entirely unexpected and unlike anything I'd seen in my entire long lifetime.

"To the left! To the left, T!" Shade shouted from his bean bag, his eyes glued to the enormous TV screen a couple of metres in front of him while his headphones hung around his neck. Next to him, Thanatos—all seven feet of him—squashed the other bean bag, tiny balls of foam popping out at the seams as he moved with the controller, trying to nudge out another cartoon race car on the screen. Zane sat happily on his shoulders, bouncing in time with Thanatos' movements, every so often a squeal of joy escaping his smiling face.

Alora sat between Shade and Thanatos, holding her own controller, although my keen eyes spotted that it wasn't connected to the console beside the TV but tucked in behind. Not that it seemed to bother her at all, as she waved the controller around enthusiastically.

"I cannot make it go that way! It's not working," Thanatos exclaimed before a banner flashed across the screen, and the littlest kids exploded with shrieks and laughter.

"Alora won!" Shade picked her up and tickled her. "You beat us both!"

"I didn't lose?" Thanatos questioned, his deep voice rising at the end of the sentence.

"You lost, mate," Shade whispered out the side of his mouth as he kept tickling Alora, much to her delight. "But these two don't know that, so we might as well let them have some fun with it."

Kind. The thought returned to the front of my mind. *It was something that Shade and Thanatos had in common, no matter how much either protested it.*

"Oh," Thanatos acknowledged, pausing briefly as he watched Shade playing with Alora. "You're more like your mother than you think, Master Shade."

"My mother's dead," Shade batted back, a glare flickering across his face.

"You are fortunate. You have had more than one mother in your life," Thanatos said solemnly. "I never had these moments with my mother, my own siblings."

"Never?" Shade settled Alora on his lap as they both caught their breath.

"Never," Thanatos repeated. "And neither did Eleos."

Shade met Thanatos' gaze. "So, this ..."

"This is her first family, Shade. You are her first son. And just like you—like me—she is learning what that means."

For a split second, there was silence before Zane started jumping on Thanatos' shoulders and shouting for them to play another game.

"Let's start with teaching you how to *lose* then, T." Shade smirked, moving past the moment's intimacy and back into his normal mode.

"I am the God of death. I *will* win." I could swear I saw Thanatos puff his chest out. "Let the challenge begin."

As I reached the bottom of the stairs, I stopped just out of sight and watched them all for a moment longer as I absorbed the conversation I'd overheard. I wanted to capture this picture in my mind perfectly. The reflection of Thanatos' and Shade's faces on the TV, smiling while they fought against each other in whatever cartoon racing game it was, with the kids playing right alongside them.

It was something innocent, pure, and joyful, and I could feel it in my heart and my power. I quietly retreated up the stairs, leaving them in their little bubble of camaraderie and fun, my heart full in a way I least expected. Things might not be fixed with Shade, and it was possible they'd never be perfect again, but somehow, perhaps I'd work out what I needed to do to find a happy medium we could both live with.

It was an idea that would benefit from a steaming cup of tea and a comfortable spot on the couch. *But then,* I thought, *what idea wouldn't?*

CHAPTER EIGHT

"STORM."

I grinned and dropped the kids' bags I was holding. I knelt down as she raced across the backyard to try to bowl me over. The way she was growing, it probably wouldn't be much longer before she did. I chuckled as the coarse roughness of her bright pink tongue licked at my cheek, the sensation almost ticklish. She tried to climb me, her beautiful fur lush and silky against my skin. I stood up and ruffled the fur on her head. "Gosh, you are growing so fast, baby."

"She really is," Maree said, standing a few feet away with a soft smile on her face. "It's so lovely to watch, especially now that she and Conrad have found their feet as siblings."

"That's so good to hear. I can't thank you enough for giving her the home she needs, Maree."

"Oh shush, she's a blessing," Maree dismissed good-heartedly, picking Storm up as she raced back to her. "Aren't you, honey?" Storm licked her face, then leapt to the ground and took off toward the other Faoladh kids.

Warmth flooded my body at the sight of such affection between them. It's what I wanted for all my halflings, and while I hoped I came close to giving it to them, I could see the difference when they were with their own kind.

But that's not possible for all of them, I reminded myself. *Sometimes, the family you find is better than the one you come from.*

Clara's voice sounded from behind me, warning Alora and Zane to behave themselves before they ran past Maree and me at full force.

"Ugh, those two are a handful," Clara groaned, her hands on her hips. "They're lucky that they're cute, I swear."

"That's what the first ten years are all about. They're cute long enough to sucker us in and make us love them so that we can persevere through the teen years," I chuckled, although my mind flickered to Shade. Things were still so tense between us, and I hated how it made my heart ache for how things used to be when we could converse without a confrontation. I'd written him a note and signed it off with love before we left but it didn't feel even close to enough. Hopefully, Thanatos could help us find a way forward.

"Now that's true," Maree giggled. "I grew up with five brothers. My poor parents."

"I can only imagine," I agreed. "Are you sure you'll be okay watching the kids while we head off to meet with everyone?"

"I'll be fine. Sean's going to give me a hand, as well as a couple of the others who do the homeschooling. We have a handle on it."

"Have you warned her about Zane's flying poop?" Clara asked cautiously.

"I gave Maree the full rundown. She also knows all about Alora's flashing, although I doubt that will be a problem now that she's here. And I've told both Zane and Alora that if either of them misbehaves, they won't get to come back for two weeks."

"Oh no, not two weeks!" Maree said, feigning horror.

"I know, I know. But I guess when you're a kid, two weeks can seem like forever, or at least you would think that from the way they reacted. Honestly, I don't know whether to be grateful or insulted that they want to be over here so often." I chuckled.

"Consider it a compliment that they feel safe enough to leave because they know you'll always welcome them back," Maree quipped.

I looked at her, squinting a little in the sunlight. "That was deep, Maree. I'm going to keep that one up my sleeve. I like it."

"So do I," Clara chipped in. "But we should get moving. The kids look like they're having fun, and the sooner we get a plan together, the better."

"You're right," I sighed. "We better go. You have my number, so just call me if there are any problems, Maree. Thanks again."

Maree waved it away. "It's all good. No need to thank me. I'll see you when you're back."

Clara and I walked back out to the car and jumped in, making the short trip to the fire station in comfortable silence. The kids had made sure that the house was buzzing all morning, so it was a welcome break from the noise. It only took a couple of minutes to park, and then we headed into the station, buzzed in by the recruit at the front desk and directed to a meeting room opposite Mason's office.

When we got there, it was clear that we were the last to the party. Mason was already inside, talking with Denny and old Jack, while Declan and Emrys were in the back of the room with Olive, their mother, serving themselves all up some coffee or tea.

Gods, I could do with a hot tea. I made a mental note to make my way to the back of the room as soon as I could.

Wren was sitting at the table, a mug in hand, talking animatedly with one of her assistants. I wracked my brain for their name—Ever—that was it. Farron sat a seat or two over, staring intently at his phone.

"Hi, guys." Clara greeted everyone and headed up the back toward Declan, Emrys, and their mother. *Hmm, interesting.*

I waved 'hello' to whoever was paying attention and went to join Denny and Mason. "Already in talks, are we?"

Mason beamed at me as he leaned over and planted a kiss on my lips. "We don't have much time. It's still pretty full-on out there. I'm not sure how long I can stay away."

"I understand," I said. "Whatever you can do to help would be great. It felt dangerous sending people out to look with the bushfires between us and Sydney."

"It was a good instinct. The last thing we need is more people caught up in them."

"Not to mention that they're probably scaring the hell outta the young lass," Denny interjected. "Fires like this aren't common in Ireland. She'd have to be beside herself, wolf-form or not."

"It takes our young ones time to master their shift, and if she's not coping, she may not find her way back to her human form," Jack explained. "Emrys watched one scary movie when he was eight and wouldn't shift back to human for a week."

"That's a good point. There's a high chance that she's not thinking clearly with everything that's happened," I agreed.

"Alright, well, let's get this party started then." Mason turned away from us, walked to the front of the room, and stood in the middle, letting out a whistle that silenced the chatter and brought everyone's attention straight to him. "Find your seats, people. We need to get to work on this."

It was like a switch had flicked, and the separate groups came together at the table, their focus shifted. I sat down next to Denny and waited to see who would take charge.

"Great, thanks everyone. Now, I'm going to give the floor to Denny, and we'll go from there." Mason perched on the edge of the desk at the front and gestured to Denny.

Denny stood up and faced the group. "Thanks for coming, all of you. Now, would you mind doing a round and introducing yourselves? I'm too old to be expected to remember you all." A small chuckle worked its way around the room.

The introductions were quick and fast. I didn't pay much attention to the ones I knew, but I was still observing Ever. It was the first time I'd seen them outside of Wren's vet clinic, where all the personal protective equipment they wore practically doubled as a Halloween costume.

Ever had short, dark blonde hair with shaved sides, slightly pointed ears, an oval-shaped face with freckles smattered under bright blue eyes, and an eyebrow ring above them. The blue of their eyes was reflected in the colour of the tattoos that covered their arms, all the way to their wrists, disappearing under short sleeves before reappearing at their chest and stopping just below the jawline.

"I'm Ever, and I'm your resident pixie, at your service," they introduced themselves. "Wren asked me to come and help today because I have some skills that might be useful."

Wren grinned. "Mainly their ability to enchant humans—I figured a little magickal coverup will probably be needed."

"What can I say? I'm charming and here to help," Ever quipped.

There were nods all around the table. As magickal prowess went, the room was pretty full—but besides Clara's ability to use glamour magick, there wasn't much to help hide the search from the mortal world. The last thing any of us needed was the wrong kind of attention.

Briarmoor might be considered a Sanctuary by the Greek Pantheon, but that was only a slice of the pie when you considered all the others—magickal and mortal—that could decide to take an interest in our small piece of the world.

The thoughts continued to swirl around in my head as the rest of the introductions were made, with Mason and I going last.

"You didn't tell me she was a real life Goddess," Ever hissed under their breath, nudging Wren, who just shrugged cheekily.

"The Greek Pantheon? What an interesting life you must've led! We must chat after all this." Olive clasped her hands together in excitement.

Clara rolled her eyes and shot me a glare. I didn't need an interpreter to know she wasn't keen on that cup of tea catch-up.

"You all know why we're here. One of our own is missing. Rowan O'Connor. She may not be from our clan, but she is one of us, and she is out there and scared. It's our job to find her." Denny pulled us all back on track, picking right back up where she'd started.

A sombre look was exchanged between the other Faoladh at the table. They didn't need to know this girl, Rowan, to care about her.

Clara raised her hand halfway into the air. "Do you have any idea where she is?"

"She was in Sydney, but that was a couple of days ago. We Faoladh have something of a homing beacon within us for our kind. Given that we're the main clan within the country, I have to assume she's headed here."

"Without the fires, it would have been a clear run, as long as she was sensible enough to avoid the threat that the traffic posed. Plenty of wide open land once she cleared the metro area, but the fires have changed all of that," Mason said.

"Where are they now?" Declan asked, a deep furrow clear in his brow. "The smoke has been messing with our ability to scent out anything. I can barely smell dinner, let alone a bloody wolf."

"The current wave is just past Wollongong. It's cut off most of the mountain roads from Sydney, including Mount Ousley, so there's no real traffic at the moment except for our trucks and the emergency services. Jervis Bay has also been hit hard, although if you can find her before she gets too far past Briarmoor, that won't matter. The southerly winds are strong, which is what is keeping that line of fire moving, and that's why you can't smell a damn thing," Mason explained.

Emrys patted Declan on his back. "See, bro, you're not losing your touch."

Declan glared at him in response.

"If scenting's not working, we need another way. That's why I asked Ellie to use her powers to help us," Denny said, giving me a nod.

"I'm still getting the hang of things. Until Nyx returned them, I hadn't used them at full strength for a very long time." I didn't want to get their hopes up.

"How long?" Wren piped up, a wide grin on her face. *She's never going to give up, is she?*

"Hundreds of years, if you must know, Wren." I rolled my eyes at her. "Anyway, the point is I can sense pain or grief, any sort of combination of that, from a while away. By the sounds of it, Rowan is consumed by both. I'm hoping that if we can get close enough to wherever she is, I'll be able to pick up on it and narrow down our search area," I explained, running my hand through my hair, my curls falling to the side.

"Olive—Declan and Emrys' mother—has also offered to help with a scrying spell." Denny gestured to the woman from the bookstore. "That should help to identify the area we want to focus on and help Ellie narrow down to where she needs to look."

"That would help, I'm hoping that Rowan's emotions stand out from the others in the area, but with the bushfires, there may be a lot of mixed feelings running loose."

"Just a question," Mason interrupted.

"Go for it," I said.

"Have any of you actually done a search before? Identified a search area? Designated a grid? Allocated teams and shifts?"

Each question was punctuated by a definitive silence from the others in response.

"I've had some experience." I tilted my head as I raised my hand slightly. "It was a while ago," I paused as Wren made a sarcastic coughing sound. "I had, um, more *help* then and knew the geography pretty well. That's not the case here, so any help you can give, we'd appreciate it."

"Mmm," Mason said, scratching the back of his neck as though in thought. "I kind of guessed. I'd help, but I can't run an active bushfire response team and this search. I might know someone who could though, especially if you could offer some help in return."

"What kind of help?" Denny asked warily.

"Kirra." Mason tilted his head toward me. "Ellie met her a few days ago. She's the Head Park Ranger of the Wildlife Rescue Unit, and she's coordinating all the wildlife identification, search, and rescue for the bushfires. I asked her to stick around because I thought you might work out a bit of a tit-for-tat thing?"

"And, my dear, how do you suppose we explain that we're looking for a wolf?" The white of Denny's brows knitted together and created layered wrinkles in her forehead, the obvious concern in her voice reflected in her tightly pursed lips and sharply spoken words. "They're not native here, and it's not like any of us owns a zoo."

"Kirra's not like that. She won't ask questions. As long as your focus is on helping *all* the animals, she'll work with you. There's not a lot of personnel in her unit. They're all volunteers."

"So, if we boost her team by," Wren counted under her breath, "eight people, including a vet and a vet's assistant," she looked at Ever, who nodded back, "that would be a pretty big win for her?"

"Nine," Denny interrupted, annoyance clear in her voice and how she spat the word out.

"Eight, Gran," Wren repeated, her voice soft. "You know you can't be anywhere near the bushfires with your asthma. It'll only trigger an attack, and then we'll all be focused on you and not Rowan. Is that what you want?"

Denny shot Wren a look that would have shrivelled me up from the inside out, but she said nothing after that. *One point to Wren, zero to Denny.*

"Yeah, it'd be tripling what she has now. If you're open to it, it could work well for both of your causes. What do you think?"

Farron was the first to voice his concerns. "Do we really want to risk pulling an outsider into this whole mess? We have options that don't involve dragging humans into this. Can you flash, Ever?"

Ever shook their head. "Not my brand of magick, Farron."

"Well, what about Alora?" Farron asked.

"What *about* Alora?" I snapped.

"She can flash. Why don't we use her to flash through the forest until you find a trail?" he said. I could see the challenge in his eyes, daring me to refuse to use one of my own to help them this time. "Or you. You've got your powers back now. Can't you do it?"

"It will be a cold, dark day in Tartarus before I will pull a child—which she is, if you remember correctly, Farron—into a search and rescue for a traumatised wolf at the edge of an active bushfire," I spat back at him, standing up and crossing my arms. "And if I could do it, don't you think I would have suggested it already? My powers are back, but not at full strength, and I don't know when they will be."

It was all I could do to tamp down my power and not thrust more compassion at him than he could handle, all at once, so he could get a taste of it. I wasn't much for anger, but the flare he lit within me was quick and strong. Mason caught my gaze for a second, but I was too frustrated to hold it. The tension in the room hung heavy, like the sea air on a humid, hot day.

Olive cleared her throat. "I'm not trying to speak out of turn, lovelies, but aren't we here trying to save a child? Bringing another one into this seems counterproductive, doesn't it, Denny?"

Denny looked over at Olive for a beat, and then she looked at me before answering. "We've asked Mason here for his help, and he's giving it. Alora is off the table. Ellie has made that clear. If he thinks Kirra is our best bet, we follow his lead."

"What if she alerts the cops or thinks we're off our tree?" Farron ran his hand through his hair before leaning forward, focusing on Mason. "Then we're screwed before we even start."

"Kirra's first loyalty is to the land, to the animals. She's not shy about it, and she's not the type to go dibber-dobbering to the nearest police officer. If you don't mess with her, she won't screw with you," Mason answered. "I'm not saying it's the only way. I'm just saying it might be the easiest way. This is literally her job, and there's nothing saying she won't find Rowan before you do."

That shut everyone up.

"Do we really want this Kirra stumbling across Rowan before we do?" Declan asked the group, gesturing to everyone. "Who the hell knows what could happen, especially if she's completely out of the loop."

"I'm with Declan," Wren confirmed. "If someone unfamiliar with Faoladh sees her, there's every chance they'll shoot rather than ask questions. Australians aren't used to wolves in their bush. One bad reaction, and we lose Rowan for good."

Ever and Emrys were in obvious agreement, along with Wren. Olive didn't give much away with her expressions, although I could see concern growing in her eyes. She'd had two boys who had to grow up with the threat of that kind of accident their whole lives. Denny's face reflected a similar consternation; her forehead lined with worry, and her eyes darkened with the same tension that had her knuckles white as she held her hands in front of her.

"You all can go back and forth on this forever. We're taking this to a vote, and if you can't decide, loves, I will," she announced. "All for working with this Kirra girl?"

Six hands went into the air. "There we go, Mason. See if you can get the girl to give us some of her time."

Farron frowned. He was the only one who didn't raise his hand. It didn't surprise me. Farron had a serious issue with newcomers. *Hades, it had taken me dying—and coming back again—for him to even come close to trusting me.*

I still wasn't one hundred percent sure he trusted me completely, but I didn't have the emotional energy to invest too much worry in that. We were in a better place than we'd been, and with him, I had a feeling that was probably good enough.

"I'll be back shortly," Mason said before leaving the room to get Kirra.

I leaned back in my chair and took a deep breath in, then let it out slowly. It still felt so odd to be working with a team of people again. It reminded me of my early days in Mount Olympus when it felt like we still had purpose and meaning as Gods and Goddesses, rather than just turning humans into figures on a chessboard.

I kind of liked it.

The chatter in the room picked up the longer Mason was gone. I kept quiet, watching as everyone interacted. My attention was unavoidably drawn to Clara and Olive, who sat near each other, with Declan and Emrys close by. They seemed deep in conversation, although I couldn't hear what it was about. A stab of jealousy surprised me as I watched them talk. I was caught off guard by the feeling. I wasn't often jealous, so I had little in my arsenal to deal with it, and sitting with it, well, sucked—a lot.

The good news was I had little time to dwell on it because Mason showed up with Kirra just then.

"Kirra, this is the family I was talking to you about. Everyone, this is Kirra. She's the Head Park Ranger for the local Wildlife Rescue Unit," Mason made the introductions.

"Hi there," Kirra greeted the group, waving her hand. "I hear that I may have a group of willing volunteers?"

I bobbed my head up and down, as did most of the people around the table, except for Farron, who still looked like he was carrying his doubts in his eyes.

"We're hoping that by helping you, you could help us, darl." Denny took the lead.

Kirra's eyes clouded at the 'darl.' *Not a fan, clearly.* "My focus is on saving as many native animals as I can. If that's something you can be on board with, then we can work together. If your priorities are elsewhere, this might not be a good fit."

"That's the thing," Mason replied, his tone measured and even. "They're looking for an animal that isn't native. A young wolf, to be exact. She got loose during a transport, and all reports have her heading this way."

"Are you serious?" Kirra's eyes widened. "So now there's not just a bushfire out there threatening wildlife, but an imported wolf that's getting a barbecue smorgasbord of injured native animals." She took a deep breath and released it slowly, pacing the front of the room. "This was not what I was expecting when I walked into this room, Mason."

"I know," he replied, "but you're also the only one who can help, and this gets you the help you need too."

She sighed. "But there are rules. We do this *my* way. There's one thing you all need to understand. This is my operation. *I* am in charge. You will follow my orders. My people, the indigenous people of this land, have cared for this land since the dawn of time. This land is my land, and I know it like the back of my hand. If you want to find your wolf, I *will* help you, but these are my rules: like them or lump them," she said as she stopped her pacing and placed her hands on her hips, waiting for an answer from a room full of people that weren't used to doing things anyone else's way.

"You have our word," Denny answered, putting her hand out to Kirra. "We'll do things your way. We'll help you find your creatures if you help us find ours."

Kirra looked at Denny's hand momentarily before reaching out her own.

"It's a deal."

CHAPTER NINE

"WELL, THAT WAS ONE hell of a meeting," I said to Clara as we returned to the car. The others had already headed off in their own directions. We'd waited a few more minutes so I could say goodbye to Mason without a crowd—not that Clara had minded the extra time talking to Olive.

Deep breaths. This is a good thing. She's nice. We need her help.

"You can say that again," she replied. "Although at least we have someone who knows what they're doing. For all the military training that Declan has, if it weren't for Emrys and Olive, he'd already be out there trampling all over everything."

I got in the car, and Clara followed suit.

"Do you think we're going to find her? That bushfire is terrifying. I can't imagine anything making its way through it, let alone a kid wolf."

"I have to," I answered. "If I didn't, I don't think I could help. And that's what they need right now, Denny and all of them. They need hope, and the best way to give it to them is by helping."

"Sometimes you're really intense, you know," Clara smirked. "For an ancient, eternal Goddess anyway."

"You're lucky I'm driving," I said dryly.

She just grinned back at me, enjoying the small win as she wound down the window and leant back in her seat, breathing in the coastal air with the tang of sea salt and smoke travelling through the car.

It was moments like these when I felt I could still see the child inside her. Usually, it would make my heart ache, but at that moment, I felt like I could see the adult she was becoming—the adult I had to step back and *let* her become without my interference.

We were back at the Faoladh house in no time, the peaceful drive disappearing as quickly as the joyful shrieks of the kids replaced it. Once we were in the house, it was a hive of activity, and I couldn't stop the smile from spreading across my face at the sight of all the kids seated at the large table, chowing down on tofu dogs covered in tomato sauce and mustard. Even Alora's golden-laced forehead wore it.

Maree was marshalling them all, organising plates of seconds—possibly some thirds, if Zane's distended stomach was any sign—all while keeping things relatively calm. Her husband Sean was manning the grill outside, keeping the food coming for the hungry crew, which now seemed to include mostly everyone from the meeting at the fire station.

"Maree, what have you done to these kids?" I asked, a snort escaping. "They're having entirely too much fun."

"The usual—lots of sugar, no naps, and strict instructions to make your life hell when they get home," she joked. "Honestly, they've just been playing around, chasing each other 'til the cows come home. Rounding them up for lunch was an awful lot like herding cattle, now I think about it."

"I have no doubt, but somehow, you make it look easy."

"Skills," she said with a sarcastic glint in her eye. "Some people can fight monsters. Others can magick up spells or do Goddess-y stuff. I can corral kids like a cowboy in a field of cattle."

I watched her, taking in the subtle downward tilt of her mouth and the gentle furrow of her brow behind the smile she wore.

"You know that all of that is momentary, right, Maree?" I placed my hand on her arm cautiously. Not everyone liked being touched. "What you're doing now—what you're doing every day—making these kids feel loved, that's what makes the biggest difference in the long run. Trust me on that."

She looked me in the eye, and I watched the tilt of her lips change, the furrow disappear. "Sounds like you're speaking from some kind of experience."

"A few thousand years of it, give or take," I joked. "Just don't tell Wren. I like to keep her guessing."

"Well, from one less-than-loved inner child to another, I appreciate the reminder." Maree murmured, her gaze flickering back to the rambunctious lot at the table as she grabbed the wipes from the kitchen bench. "Duty calls, and so do dirty hands."

"Let me help," I offered, grabbing a handful from her before diving into the mammoth task of cleaning up the kids with her. Their resistance was persistent, although futile; even Zane eventually submitted to a cleanup after a quick attempt at flying away. The force was strong in that one. Maree kickstarted round two of outside play, bribing the kids with putting their plates in the sink in exchange for free time in the backyard.

It was amazing how motivated the kids could be with the right incentives. I made a mental note to look into getting some proper play equipment at Halfling House.

"Whew, I'm glad that is done," I announced as I walked out to the backyard, where the rest of the adults gathered around the grill and a couple of picnic tables. I sat down on one of them, next to Farron, who at least gave me the decency of not cringing. "Sean, your wife is a legend."

"You're not tellin' me anythin' new," he chuckled as he poured a beer onto the grill and continued cleaning it. "You don't let the good ones get away, do you, Maree?"

On cue, Maree stuck her head out the door, "You got that right, honey. I'll be out in a sec."

I chuckled and leaned against the table, taking in the natural camaraderie of the Faoladh amongst their own. *Almost our own, I guess.* They'd slowly become part of our family in their own way.

"Sorry," Farron said, his voice low enough that only I heard it. He lifted his gaze from his food to meet mine.

"For volunteering one of my children to the fire-front?" I raised my brow at him, a frown instantly forming on my face.

"Yeah. That. It wasn't right," he acknowledged before taking a bite.

"It wasn't. Do me a favour, and if you wouldn't let a pup do it, don't expect one of my kids to." I let the silence sit. Farron nodded and bowed his head slightly, the Faoladh way of saying sorry.

"So, you ready?" Farron asked a couple of minutes later.

"I think so. I'm just hoping we find her fast. The idea of a kid out there in that, I don't like it." I gestured to the plumes of smoke coating the tops of the mountains. "You?"

"I'd be out there already if it weren't for the whole schtick Mason pulled with the wildlife ranger," he grumbled. "It's a waste of time. We should be out there now."

"Denny's with Kirra planning the grid search for tomorrow. The fire crews are working on keeping the lines stable. And we're getting ready, preparing ..." I paused as I looked around at the others around the table and then back at Farron. "Even if that looks a little different from what you'd expect."

He stared at his beer before taking another swig. "Maybe."

"Do you think everyone will hold up under the conditions? It's getting pretty smoky even here?"

"Our wolf forms would hold up best, but we're still hardier than your standard human in our normal forms. We can heal from smoke inhalation and burns faster than humans. It only becomes a problem for Denny and Jack. Asthma's kicked Denny's ass the last few years."

"How bad is it?" I asked, a trace of worry weaving its way through me. "Will the coordination hub for the volunteers be far enough away from the front for her to be okay?"

"Bad enough that even shifting doesn't help, but I mean, she's a couple of hundred years old, so ..." Farron shrugged. "She's got inhalers and stuff. It's the best option. There's no way she'll stay away. And at least if we leave Jack with her, he'll monitor her."

"I guess that's the best we can do then," I agreed, but it didn't ease my concern.

"What about you?" Curiosity filled Farron's voice.

"I'm an immortal Goddess. My powers are back, even if they're not full strength. I should be fine. My body purges toxins straight away. I don't even have to think about it. I'll be fine."

"Good," Farron said with a surprising softness in his gaze before returning his focus to finishing his food.

The next hour passed quickly. I made my way between the kids and the adults, checking in with both but not feeling particularly a part of either. It wasn't an unfamiliar feeling. In fact, it had been how I'd survived for as long as I had, abandoning the world of the Gods and wandering the mortal world but not truly being a part of it. The thread of worry and fear that wove its way through the Faoladh was less all-consuming for me when I felt separate from it, and less tempting to solve with my powers when I wasn't carrying the full weight of it. It was a hard balance to strike, the line between helping and hindering.

Humans and Gods alike needed pain to understand pleasure, sadness to understand happiness, and grief to understand gain. The power to take away one meant I had to bear the responsibility of the other.

The barbecue wrapped up not long after. Clara and I rounded up Alora and Zane from the rest of the Faoladh kids and grabbed their gear from the entryway.

"Thanks for today and for tomorrow," I said to Sean and Maree. "Few people would volunteer for another day of this."

"You're family, and you're helping our family. We appreciate that," Sean said, Storm settled on his hip.

"But don't worry, we'll add it to the tab," Maree chuckled, Conrad hiding behind her legs.

"We'll trade you a date night when this is all over," Clara promised, carrying Zane to the car. "We'll see you all tomorrow at the crack of dawn."

"Yes. Fire station at eight am, so we'll be here by seven-thirty."

"With any luck, you'll all be home by sundown, with an extra in tow," Maree said, her eyes clouding over as I felt apprehension spike within her.

I gave them a tight smile and turned away.

By the Gods, if it was within my power, Rowan would not spend one more moment scared and alone than she had to.

"Alright, people, let's get some order in here," Kirra shouted across the meeting room, where our haphazard group and a few others we hadn't met had gathered. "My understanding is that we'll only have about twelve people today, so we're going to have to cover more ground in teams of two. Do I need to pair you up like kindergarteners, or do you think you can sort that out yourself?"

"I think we can manage," I answered.

The pairings were sorted quickly. Farron and Gabe, who'd been caught up with a job yesterday, and Wren and Ever, who were the obvious ones. Olive, Declan, and Clara were back at the bookstore, working on a scrying spell to narrow the search area down, although we kept that from Kirra. That just left me, Emrys, and Denny.

"Gran, you're not stepping foot out there." Wren narrowed her eyes at Denny. "You've got to be kidding me. You might think you're fit enough to deal with all that smoke, but there's not a chance in the world you'll come outta that without a hospital stay."

Relief and gratitude hit me at the same time. I was glad that it was Wren voicing my thoughts because it meant I didn't have to.

Denny shot Wren a look that Medusa would be envious of, only Wren wasn't lucky enough to be turned to stone. "*I'll* decide what *I'll* be doing, young lass. That'll be the end of that."

"Uh, Denny?" Kirra interjected. "I haven't accounted for you in the field. We need someone at the site coordination hub who knows the area, someone local, who can help mark the areas that we search as we go. I'm sure you're handy with a radio. They're more reliable around here than phone service with the fires." Kirra punctuated her explanation by handing Denny one of the black walkie-talkies, her dark brown eyes tightening in the corners as she waited to see if she would take it.

"I'll stick around and help too," Jack volunteered. "You know this lot will get turned around on themselves without someone at the helm."

Denny released a heavy sigh through gritted teeth and accepted the walkie-talkie. "I'm not here to argue. I'm here to find Rowan. If making sure you lot don't waste time in an area twice over matters, then it's best left to the only one left with two brain cells to rub together."

It felt like the whole room relaxed with her insult, as though no one minded being called dumb if it meant that Denny got to save face and stay safe.

I'd had the barest glimpse into what it was like to age, and only for a remarkably short time, but it was enough for me to imagine what it would be like to have my body fail me long before my mind. The Faoladh lived a long time, but a long time wasn't forever, and they were as vulnerable to everyday diseases and disasters as most mortals were too.

Protecting her might hurt her ego, but it would also keep her alive.

On the plus side, I would be paired with Kirra or Emrys. And while I knew Clara had said not to pry and to give her space to explore her witch heritage—and I'd promised I wouldn't—a little casual conversation with Emrys during a grid search wouldn't qualify as prying, surely?

CHAPTER TEN

IT TOOK ABOUT HALF an hour for Kirra to give us the basic volunteer induction, followed by laying the law down as far as risks were concerned, and then another half-hour for us all to be equipped with protective gear. We'd all come prepared in boots, long pants, and long-sleeved shirts, but Kirra got us lined up and started handing out masks, gloves, a walkie-talkie per team, as well as backpacks with water, a basic first aid kit, some blankets, and a GPS tracker in case we went off course.

My thoughts wandered to Mason as she went over the various risks and got everyone to sign safety waivers as they took their equipment. He was on the opposite shift but still found the time to send me a good luck text before he crashed for the day—or until his phone rang and he was brought back in. He wouldn't hesitate to run straight into the station, ready to help wherever his hands were needed.

Sometimes, the compassion inside him was so strong I wondered how a human body could hold so much, yet when he shared it with me, it energised me. Most humans were fuelled by ambition or desire, but he was pushed forward by a need to quell the pain he saw in others. I'd been around a long time, and humans like him were so very rare because others usually sucked the goodness out of them, taking until there was nothing left. Mason was an example of what happened when compassion was met with kindness and love from those around him.

The movement in the line brought my thoughts back to the present. A sliver of optimism swept through me as Kirra gave us the main coordination point, and the volunteers started driving there. She'd explained that we'd be leaving our cars at one of the local parks where the field volunteer efforts were being coordinated out of, and we would go on foot from there. We weren't allowed in the fire's direct path, but we were allocated the search areas where the risk of smoke inhalation was low and in turn, where the wildlife was most likely to be fleeing.

Frustration resurfaced within me. If I had my full powers, I could easily flash from place to place, searching kilometres of bush at an unfathomable pace, but that wasn't the case, so we were stuck, searching like humans for a young girl who was anything but.

It was a solemn drive over. Our group was split between my car and one of the Faoladh's four-wheel drives. Finally taking action and starting the search for Rowan sent warmth through my body, lighting it up and banishing the feeling of not doing enough. I could feel the tension that had worked its way into my bones, tethering me to the same undercurrent of anxiety and fear that ran within the Faoladh.

Whatever the day held, hopefully, part of it was finding Rowan.

The good news was that it didn't take long for us all to be assigned our grid sections and for Kirra to let out another whistle to draw our attention back to her.

"Alright, everyone. I know we're all keen to get started, but remember the basics—stay hydrated, check in every thirty minutes, and if the smoke starts blowing your way, it's time to head back. One case of smoke inhalation is one too many. The same goes for fire. If you come across an active fire spot, you retreat immediately and call in a report." Kirra paused briefly, moving her head from side to side as she took in all the volunteers. "We have one job and one job only—to find at-risk or injured wildlife and call it in. We're lucky enough to have some experienced volunteers and even a veterinarian with us." She nodded at Wren. "So make sure you leave any handling of the animals to them. These animals are scared, they are in distress, and they may lash out at you, so caution is the name of the game."

"Remember, above all, you are not firefighters. You are not wildlife rangers. You do not put yourself at risk because then we have to worry about you *as well as* everything else. Do not become a liability. Be an asset. Any questions?"

Silence fell. I wasn't sure if it was supposed to be a pep talk or a warning. Or a little of both. Either way, it had done the job of pulling everyone into line before they even thought about stepping out of it.

"Good. Let's go!" she shouted, her tone less 'doom and gloom,' and more 'you can do this!'.

With that, everyone set off to their designated areas. Farron and Gabe were to the left, while Wren and Ever were to the right. Emrys had joined up with one of the other volunteers, which left me disappointed over losing the chance to learn more about Olive and her coven. Maybe even *his* coven? Instead, I was paired up with Kirra, whose walkie-talkie blasted off every few minutes, even as we started on our first section of the grid. We all had sections of about half a kilometre each to search and report back.

For the first hour, we didn't really talk, our eyes and ears trained on the ground and the thin veil of trees that edged the start of the forested area. The smoke was much stronger here, every breath heavy with the dryness of the fire in the air. The longer we walked, the easier it was for me to ignore, although I could tell that wasn't the case for Kirra, who's breathing steadily became hoarser through her mask. I could only hope the Faoladh weren't feeling the same way.

I took a breath in and turned my attention to where it needed to be—Rowan. I divided my focus between what I could *see* and what I could *feel*.

The connection between the Faoladh and I still thrummed with the same tension as earlier, surrounded by a weaker stress level that I figured was the other volunteers. Kirra held her own higher frequency fear that emanated from her, unrestricted, flowing as though she couldn't contain it within herself. My power instinctively wanted to take some of it away, like I had before, but my conscience fought back. This was a different type of pain. I didn't know Kirra, not well enough to know the cause of her pain or if relief from it would help her or harm her. I cast a look in her direction as we continued trudging forward, the distance between us meaning that I couldn't read her expression well enough to tell whether she was anywhere on the spectrum of actively distressed. Mostly, all I could tell was that she wasn't sobbing, which didn't narrow it down all that much.

My power itched to be set loose, but I refused to use it on her. I needed to keep everything I had for Rowan.

I pushed a low tree branch out of my way and tried not to think about it. Instead, I cast my power out further, trying to see if anything else spiked, if I could pinpoint a direction or something. If I could *feel* Rowan. But it was a big blank sea of nothing. Animals of the non-shifter variety didn't register for my power, so I couldn't even help Kirra with the wildlife. That was just all eyes and ears and good, old-fashioned observation.

I groaned louder than I intended. *You did not get a body like mine from regular bushwalking.*

Kirra veered closer to me, her head tilted in concern. "You good? Smoke inhalation getting to you? Do you need to head back?"

"No, I'm fine. Honestly, I'm just not used to exercising like this. Gets me a bit stuck in my head," I told her as I kept walking.

"Keep your focus on the bush, and you'll be out of your head before you know it," she replied, her breathing heavy even as she strode forward. "It has a way of healing you without you even realising it."

The words she spoke sunk in, through my ears, through my skin, and into my heart. "That's why you're here, isn't it?" I asked. "Taking care of this place."

Kirra nodded. "It's my people's land. Always has been, always will be. It's what I was born to do, so I do it. And it takes care of me in return." She started moving back to where she'd been tracking, the conversation over. I let the magick of what she'd said sit with me as I continued looking through the bush, searching for anything, or anyone, that could be helped. I took a moment to text Clara for an update.

How's it going? Any luck? x

I slipped the phone back into my pocket and kept moving, only a step or two behind Kirra, although she was a few metres to my left.

Everything looked much the same as we trekked our way through the first section. Eucalyptus half-stripped, their bark hanging down as though peeled like a banana; broken branches and twigs crunched underfoot, a thick layer of dried leaves harmonising with the sounds of cicadas and the other small insects that hurried across the ground. The air hung heavy in the sky, thickened with the smoke from the fire every so often as a gust of wind carried through. Occasionally, some animal scat made an appearance, but aside from the birds flitting from tree to tree, there wasn't much sign of anything else.

My phone vibrated. *Finally.*

Not yet. Close though x

Not what I wanted to hear. I sighed. I could hear Kirra's walkie-talkie buzz every so often. Usually, it was just another team checking in. Her voice carried—cool, calm and collected, if a little hoarse—but not a crack or a stutter to give away whatever was bubbling away inside. Maybe this place was enough to keep the pain inside her in check.

We broke for lunch around midday and met back up at the main coordination hub, where we all lined up for sandwiches and fresh bottles of water. Maree had also sent us off with a cooler full of soft drinks and baked slices. Most of the Faoladh were used to her baking on the regular, but I still hadn't gotten past the drooling stage. I collected my sandwich and water and sat at the picnic bench where Emrys, Wren, Ever, Farron, and Gabe had set themselves up.

"I think that's literally the deepest I have ever been in the bush." I blew air upward out of the corner of my mouth, moving the stray hair that had fallen in front of my eye.

Gabe chortled. "You haven't been here long enough then."

"Yeah, we've seen every inch of this bush," Wren grinned. "Remember when we used to take off at sunset and then camp up at the ridge?"

Emrys, Gabe, and Farron all caught her gaze, shooting each other mischievous looks. "Denny almost killed us more than once for that," Farron joked.

"Almost killed you for what?" Denny interrupted, her own sandwich and water in hand. I thought I caught a faint tremor in her hand, but it was gone before I was certain.

"Nothing," the four of them replied in unison. I could almost picture them as the pain-in-the-ass kids I was sure they'd been.

"Whatever it was, I'm certain you lot deserved it," she said, a little out of breath, as she sat down beside me, her body sinking heavily onto the seat. "How's it going out there? Any closer to finding Rowan?"

Our silence gave her the answer that our words didn't. Farron stared intently at his sandwich as though it held the answers to life while Gabe took a swig of his water, the sweat on his face joining with the water that spilled out of his mouth before he wiped it away.

Wren was the first to speak. "Not yet, Gran, but we're still looking. We're not giving up. Have you taken your inhaler? You don't sound too good."

Denny shot her a look that would have made me wither inside but didn't deign to answer Wren's question.

"It's only day one, and every place she isn't gets us closer to the place she is," Ever chimed in, trying to diffuse the tension.

"I like your optimism," I said. "Plus, we're still waiting on Clara and the others to finish the scrying spell. That'll help us narrow it down."

"Mm-hmm," Denny agreed, her mouth full of what looked like a cheese sandwich. She used a serviette to wipe around her lips. "We can't rely on it though; witchcraft can be finicky." She took a deep breath, aware of Wren's eagle eyes on her. "You all just have to keep your eyes open and your senses alert. I don't need to remind you that it's important we find her soon." The sentence seemed to take most of her breath, her chest puffing in and out faster than usual.

"It's all we're thinking about," Gabe said. "We're working as hard as we can." He took another bite of his sandwich and cast a quick warning look at Farron, whose frustration was a little less effectively contained if the pulsing vein in his forehead was any sign. At least I wasn't the only one who annoyed him.

"Gran," Wren said again. "Your inhaler, you need to keep it up. Please," she added gently, as though the pleasantry might prevent Denny's scorn. Not that it worked.

Denny ignored Wren, but I could feel the edge of panic eating at her thoughts. She knew she wasn't well, but she wouldn't admit that to anyone.

"Alright, people," Kirra shouted from a few metres away. "Anyone who doesn't feel up to the next round, let me know. There are no winners if anyone goes down in the bush." She paused, but no one spoke up, even though I caught the furtive glance that Wren shot at Denny. "Alright, let's wrap it up. Ten minutes to finish your food, grab some more water, and find yourself a toilet. Time to get back out there. We've cleared a good section, but there's *a lot* more to go."

With that, the movement around the hub sped up quickly. A few volunteers went around collecting the rubbish from lunch while everyone started moving to collect water. There was only one thing I needed. "I'm just going to head over for a quick bathroom break if anyone wants to join me?"

The Faoladh looked at each other and laughed at some inside joke before shaking their heads and saying various types of no.

Denny tsk-tsk'd at them and nodded, which they took as some sort of permission before they headed off into the denser bush to the left of the field, leaving Ever, Wren, Denny, and I by ourselves.

"Did I miss something?" I asked, my brows knitted together in confusion.

"Love, they don't need four walls and porcelain to see to their needs. I don't think I've seen that lot wait for a loo in all my life," she chuckled, ending it with a dry cough.

The blood in my body suddenly rushed to my face. *Of course*. "Uh, that, that was not what I was expecting. I think I'm going to walk away now."

"I'll come with you," Wren said, jumping up from her spot at the table.

I could hear Denny still chortling—and coughing—even as we put distance between us. "She's enjoying this a bit too much."

"Yeah, she can be like that. Gran enjoys giving people a little shock here and there."

"I've noticed. She's got a cheeky streak in her, that's for sure."

"You can't even imagine. She had us believing all kinds of things as pups. I'm still not sure if the Loch Ness monster is real," Wren giggled, shaking her head.

I joined her. "Well, I can't help you on that one. Not my Pantheon, not my business," I said as we joined the line for the toilets. Another question popped into my head, and I spilled it out without thinking.

"Why didn't you go with the others?" I asked as the line slowly crept forward.

Wren's face clouded over instantly. *Oh, Gods, that was evidently not the right question to ask.*

"I'm sorry, Wren," I said immediately. "I didn't mean to say the wrong thing. I shouldn't have asked."

"Yeah, nah, it's okay," she mumbled. "I just don't tell people. Or I haven't *had* to tell anyone for a while." Wren started twisting her fingers in her hands, taking a few steps forward as the line kept moving. "I'm not like the others. Even though I'm full-blooded Faoladh, I've never been able to shift. Or at least, not since I was a small pup."

"So, toilets?" I gave her a small smile, watching her face to see her reaction.

Wren gave me a wry smile in return. "Yep, toilets. And honestly, I'm a big fan of toilet paper."

"Me too. Try living over two thousand years without it. Or worse, rags." I shuddered at the memories.

"Over two thousand years?" Wren's eyes widened. "Did you just tell me how old you are?"

"I don't know, did I?" I winked as it reached my turn in line and headed into the nearest cubicle.

The rest of the afternoon passed by a literal step at a time as everyone continued the grid search throughout the bush. I stayed paired with Kirra, and we kept to our section of the grid, our search turning up nothing more than leaves, twigs and branches, and the insects that ran up my leg every so often. The smoke in the air didn't shift as much as it had earlier in the day, choosing instead to sit in one place and overwhelm the surrounding air. I made sure to cough occasionally behind my mask so I didn't seem suspicious, but Kirra's coughing was very real.

Ugh, I hate bugs. Animals I was good with, but anything that had an exoskeleton or more than four legs, I was not a fan of.

Every so often, I'd push my power out again, hoping to find something that might lead us to Rowan, but it came back empty. The pent up tension of the volunteers remained, as did whatever the Hades it was that lay within Kirra, but aside from that, there was nothing. Nada. Zip.

It was just more walking, looking, searching, and more acrid smoke-filled air. From one section of bush to another. Again and again and again. The eucalyptus and paperbarks blended together, as did the bushes and the scrub, the dirt and the leaves, and the branches and the trees—just one big, empty bunch of bushland and no Rowan.

Kirra's walkie-talkie went off again, almost making me jump out of my skin. As the day had stretched on, so had the shadows, and a part of me still saw an Animus waiting around every thick tree trunk or tall bush. It was completely irrational, given the Sanctuary status that Briarmoor had now. Still, I knew we had to be near the edge of it, and even Goddesses weren't immune to a little anxiety or post-traumatic stress reactions.

Or at least, not this Goddess.

"Good news," Kirra called over. "It looks like they've found a koala and her baby. The mother has some superficial burns, but they're taking them in now."

"That's good. Not the burns part, but the finding them part. Superficial means she should be okay, right?"

"Generally. Especially if she gets hydrated quickly. It's not an easy recovery, but it's a recovery, and that's a win," Kirra explained as we continued trudging through the brush.

"It's not an easy job you've got."

She shrugged. "Honestly, it's worth it. People are full of crap. Animals, they're always straight with you. You're either their friend or their prey. No mucking around."

"I get that. It's like kids. They're so uninhibited. It's kind of freeing. Much easier than adults."

Kirra laughed. "They say don't work with kids or animals, and here we are, working with both."

"Eh, what do 'they' know anyway?" I chuckled.

After that, we went quiet for a while, clearing each section as we walked. No matter how many times I sent my power out searching for Rowan, it continued to come back with nothing. Fortunately, as the sun started to descend, two more teams called in rescues—a dehydrated possum and a pair of young kangaroos with superficial burns, just like the koala. By five-thirty, Kirra sent out a blast on her walkie-talkie to wrap it up for the day and head back to the hub. We walked back, silence hanging between us until Kirra broke it.

"Disappointed?" she asked, her voice raspy from the day amongst the smoky bush.

"Yeah," I replied. "I was hoping that we would find her today."

"Her?" She looked at me curiously. "Does she have a name?"

"Rowan. I know it sounds odd, but it's all a bit unusual anyway. She's important to Denny and her family, so I know they'll be hurting going home without her tonight."

"They're an odd bunch, I'll give you that, but they seem to be a goodhearted lot. You've just gotta remember that the search isn't over. It'll keep going until you find her. And I'm going to be here every day anyway," she reassured me as we joined the others returning from their section. "My job isn't over until the fires are gone and the land—and the animals—are healing again."

"This place is lucky to have you, Kirra."

"Funny, Mason told me the same thing about you." She smiled before waving me off and heading over to join the other bigwigs at the hub.

I stopped to watch her walk away, surprised at what she'd said. Not so much that Mason had said something kind or sweet because that was pretty on-brand for him, but that he thought Briarmoor was lucky to have me when I'd always felt I was the lucky one.

Either way, it made me feel a happiness that warmed my soul.

CHAPTER ELEVEN

JUST LIKE THE REST of Denny's house, the lounge was warm and cosy looking, even though it was easily double the size of ours at Halfling House. Couches lined a half-wall that separated the lounge from the dining room; they were mismatched, but both wore a similar shade of brown, thick and plush, with blankets layered over the top half. On either side of the couches were wooden side tables with small, orb-like lamps that cast a warm yellow light around the room.

At each end of the room was an assortment of bean bags, high-back chairs, and plush armchairs. The floor was hardwood planks, with their fair share of scratches and well-worn grooves, not that you could see too much given that the floor was covered in different rugs—some shaggy neutrals, others colourful and thin, with more than a couple wearing holes I suspected were from one or two teething pups.

"That was useless." Farron threw himself onto a couch, his pale skin a light shade of red, even with all the sun protection he'd worn. Gabe dropped down beside him, placing a hand on his thigh.

"It might feel useless to you, but you'd be surprised how much ground all you young ones covered today. Near on half the town," Denny said, her tone encouraging.

"I wouldn't have thought you lot'd have it in you, but you proved me wrong," Jack grinned as he found himself a comfy spot in an armchair, a glass of whiskey in one hand and a roll of licorice in the other.

"That's something, I guess," Farron admitted, closing his eyes and massaging his forehead. "Is there any aloe vera sun gel here?"

"Of course, son." Denny gestured toward the kitchen, and Gabe disappeared briefly before returning with a bottle full of bright green gel. "Don't overdo it, or you'll end up stuck to the couch," Denny warned him. Farron nodded as Gabe got to work applying it on his reddened skin.

"Do you know when we'll be hearing from Declan and that coven of his?" Denny directed his question at Emrys, who shrugged in response as he chugged down an ice cold beer, the condensation dripping onto the floor.

"Clara just messaged to say that she's on her way here," I piped up from my spot on one of the high-back chairs across from Farron. "I can only assume that Declan and Olive will be following too."

"Any news on the scrying spell?"

"Clara said they were close, but that's it. I kind of assumed it would be a quick thing, but then, I'm no witch."

"Scrying's a pain in the ass when you have nothing that belongs to the person. They're trying to locate someone they've never met in a place the person's never been while they're in shifted form. It makes it nearly impossible. If they get anything from it, we'll be lucky," Emrys explained.

"Oh, that makes sense then," I said, feeling slightly chastised.

It was easy to think that I should know pretty much everything after being alive for a few thousand years, but I'd spent a good chunk of them in shock, wandering the world after abandoning the Pantheon. I hadn't exactly been studying up on my witch lore or fae customs, that was for sure.

"Even a Goddess can't know everything, El." Gabe met my gaze. I gave him a small smile in return for his reassurance. I still couldn't help but feel like I should though.

"Any progress is progress, right, Wren?" Ever filled the awkward pause, casting a glance at Wren.

"Ever's right. Even if we didn't find Rowan today, we managed to save five animals that wouldn't have made it otherwise," Wren added. "I'm used to seeing them come into the clinic, but after today, I'm thinking of signing up to their regular volunteer roster."

"I think that's a good idea, love," Denny mused from the armchair she'd settled into. The way she'd sunk into the cushions told me more than the strangled fear that sat within her—although I couldn't tell whether it was for Rowan or her own condition—only that it was there, and it was real.

Denny sighed, her face as weary as I had ever seen it, the day's tiredness etched deeper than the lines at the corner of her eyes and around her thin, pale lips. "Now, who's going to make me a tea?"

A frantic look passed between the Faoladh.

"Not it," Farron called out quickly.

"Nope, I stuff it up every time." Emrys put his hands up in surrender.

"You're so full of it," Wren said frustratedly. "That's just weaponised incompetence." She rolled her eyes and caught Ever's gaze.

"I am not getting in the middle of this," Ever chuckled.

"Still incompetence though," Emrys countered, a grin on his face.

I snickered at their exchange, enjoying the release of tension it brought. "Alright, calm down, I'll make the tea. Any other takers?"

"Not a chance," Gabe said. "The others should be here soon, so I'm going to hit up the fridge for some beers. First in, best dressed."

"And wine!" Wren piped up. "Bring out a couple of wine glasses too."

"Please." Ever interrupted.

"Please," Wren repeated, deadpan.

"With manners like that ..." Gabe laughed and followed me into the kitchen, where I set the kettle to boil and pulled two mugs out, one for Denny and one for me. It had been a long day, and I didn't have the patience to steep anything.

Gabe raided the fridge, finding a few more beers and the bottle of wine that Wren wanted. The clatter of glass as he collected the wine glasses, combined with the building shriek of the kettle boiling, made hearing anything else impossible, which was why I nearly jumped out of my skin when I heard Clara's voice near my ear.

"Miss me?" she asked cheekily, cackling loudly when I almost flew two feet into the air. Maybe it was more like a centimetre or two, but still. "Clearly not enough to have a wine ready for me?" She cocked an eyebrow at Gabe, who pulled another glass down and handed it over to her before opening the wine and filling her glass. "Thanks, Gabe. I've been looking forward to this."

"You're not the only one, Clara." Gabe grinned before taking a swig of his beer and loading his arms up with the drinks for the rest of them.

"What about you?" she asked me, eyeing the boiling kettle.

"Tea for me. It was a long day, and we still have kids to get to bed, so I'm holding off," I said as I loaded the mugs with sugar before pouring in the boiling water, mixing the tea as I went. "Milk?"

"Here you go." Clara went to the fridge and passed it over. "Speaking of, where are they? It's insanely quiet for almost seven o'clock."

"Ladies, excuse me." Gabe interrupted, passing between us to take the beers and wine out to the lounge.

I poured the milk in and gave the bottle back to her so she could return it to the fridge. "Maree offered to keep them over at whatever passes for the schoolhouse here, playing games so we could have a moment to debrief and prepare for tomorrow. She'd already given them dinner, so they just think they're getting away with staying up late."

"Gotta be some perks, I suppose."

"We should head back out there. Denny's keen for her tea, and I think we'd all like an update on what you, Declan, and Olive managed today." I picked up the two mugs and led the way out of the kitchen. "Emrys was explaining that you guys were pretty much trying to achieve the impossible. I didn't realise what a big ask it was, to be honest."

"I didn't either," Clara answered as she followed me, the swish of wine in her glass growing less at risk of a spill with each sip she took. "It was a really long day. Every time it felt like we were getting somewhere, we'd end up back at square one. Olive was amazing though. I think I learned more today than I have in years."

"That's what you needed, isn't it? You're practically glowing right now." I smiled at her, even though a part of me was still hesitant. "Which is mildly inappropriate given that Rowan is still missing, now I think about it."

"It's awesome, really. And I'm trying not to seem too excited, I promise. It's just hard when I've been thinking about all of this for so long, and now there's someone who's happy to teach me," Clara explained, her voice low. "Anyway, we have an idea to help with Rowan overnight, at least."

"Now that's amazing news. No time like the present," I said as I walked into the lounge room, Clara only a step or two behind.

"Here you are, Denny," I announced as I placed her mug of tea on the table next to her before returning to my spot on the couch, which had somehow stayed free even though Declan and Olive had settled themselves in. Clara plopped down next to me, squeezing between me and Declan.

"Thanks, darl." Denny lifted the tea up to her lips much faster than I had set it down. *A woman after my heart.* She took a big sip, ignoring the steam rising from her mug. "No whiskey?"

"I thought we'd start with the soft stuff and work our way up." I grinned, careful not to spill my tea. I noticed a couple of inhalers had appeared beside her while I was gone. No matter how tough she appeared, the conditions were getting to her.

"Alright, now we have everyone here." She took a deep breath. "Clearly, the search didn't bear any fruit." Denny started the debrief, looking around the room. "Olive, do you have an update for us?"

Olive adjusted her bright purple glasses before speaking. "We spent the day working on the scrying spell, trying to narrow down where Rowan might be, but it just kept blowing up."

"It was like that time Mum tried to cook a tofu roast." Declan nudged Emrys, the two of them bursting into laughter. "Just black smoke everywhere."

"Yes, Declan Jamison Quinn, it was exactly like that. And that might have been funny *if* we weren't trying to find a young Faoladh missing in the forest, in the middle of a bushfire," Olive reprimanded him, pushing her glasses back up her nose again.

The room fell silent. Declan and Emrys had the good conscience to look remorseful, their gazes lowered and laughter cut short.

"The scrying is challenging because we have nothing of Rowan's. It's like looking for a needle in a haystack, literally, but we haven't given up. I've left a cauldron simmering with some fur that Declan so kindly volunteered," Olive explained.

"Happy to help where I can." Declan rubbed the back of his neck as though there was still a sore spot.

"Hopefully, that will at least allow us to scry for Faoladh, and then we can rule out those we know, leaving what's left to be Rowan. I think that will bring us some more success."

"That's a solid idea," Wren agreed. "Most species share enough common DNA that it might work. We know all the Faoladh in Briarmoor. It should be easy to narrow it down."

"In the meantime, Clara had another idea. We could cast a protection spell, not specifically for Rowan, but for the wildlife caught in the bushfire or nearby," Olive said, looking to Denny for agreement.

Denny nodded, her grip white-knuckled around an inhaler, and looked between Olive and Clara. "Do you think it might help?"

"The spell I found in one of Olive's books was pretty niche, but it couldn't hurt to try?" Clara answered, giving a little shrug. Seeing her confidence at a novice level was odd, but I could tell from the upward turn of her mouth that she was happy to have a way to help.

"Then I think it's worth a shot, love." Denny agreed, a small cough escaping her.

"Wait a second," Wren interjected, her face flushed red and lips down turned into a frown. At first, I thought she was about to read Denny the Riot Act, but I couldn't have been more wrong. "If you have a spell like this, Olive, why haven't you used it before? We lost so much wildlife in the last season of fires. I put at least twenty animals to sleep. And now you're telling me you could have protected them?" The fury in her voice was barely contained as she stared Olive down.

"It-it doesn't work like that, Wren," Olive replied, twisting the gold ring on her finger. "Witchcraft is about balance. All living things have a time to live and a time to die. When we interfere, we change the course of what is meant to be, and there are consequences."

"But you're willing to face the consequences this time for Rowan," Ever piped up, squeezing Wren's hand tightly as though speaking the words for her. Wren's eyes sparkled with unshed tears. "You know what Wren goes through when she has to put an animal to sleep. Is it not worth it?"

"Not when the cost could be your life, Ever," Olive answered quietly. "Or mine. Or my sons. Is there a single one of you that wouldn't risk your life for Rowan today? Who hasn't already?"

The room went quiet. Wren blinked away her tears, sharing a look with Ever. "No," Wren replied for the group.

"And would you do that every year, for any animal, with no worry for the cost?"

"No," Jack said, meeting Olive's gaze with a solemn stare. "We couldn't. Not without losing what matters most to us. No matter the pain, Wren, we could never risk losing our family just to interrupt the sacred cycles of life. Not without having good reason. And Rowan is good reason."

Wren looked at Jack and gave a small nod before looking away again.

"Back to the spell." Denny picked up the conversation without missing a beat. "What do you need us to do?"

"The firepit has a view of the mountains and the bushfire, doesn't it?" Olive asked.

"Yes, it does," Denny said.

"Perfect. If we can use that and some kindling, that should be enough. I've brought along my own dried rosemary and sage. Other than that, I think it's a good idea for Declan, Emrys, and Clara to perform the spell with me. The more power we can channel into it, the more chance it will work and work well." Olive clasped her hands together, a smile working its way across her face. "At least we can do something to help the poor little one."

"We'll take all the help we can get, that's for sure," Denny said. "This meeting is over. The rest of you, go get some food in you and then get yourselves to bed. It's going to be another early morning. Olive and the rest of you kids, do what you need to do and then take the same advice." She stood up slowly, the empty mug in her hand, looking around at everyone gathered. "I don't need to tell you that if we don't find Rowan tomorrow, things are going to start looking a lot bleaker." Denny drew in a shaky breath, her eyes darkening as she continued, "She's been in shifted form for too long already. If her wolf takes over, we may never get her back, no matter if we find her. It's not a fate any of us want to see again."

A quick look around at the faces in the room made it obvious they were all clear on the high stakes game we were in. Jack shuddered and finished his whiskey in one big gulp, staring at the glass as though it would refill itself.

Shifted too long? Denny's words echoed in my mind. *What did that mean?* I had heard stories of shifters that never returned to their human form, but it varied whether it was by choice or not. Maybe it was the same for the Faoladh?

I made a mental note to ask someone when the mood lightened. It only took a flicker of my power to sense the strength of the emotions crowding the room—fear, anger, sadness, frustration, hopelessness, determination, and optimism—all battled it out for dominance without a chance to actually win.

Denny left the room, her movements slowed by what I could only assume was tiredness. I didn't dare offer a hand, mainly because I was certain she'd chew it off if I even slightly challenged her independence. A spike of fear, followed by a wall of terror, hit me out of nowhere, its distinct edge bringing only one name to my lips.

"Denny!" I gasped at the same time as I heard a loud crash in the hallway she'd just headed down. "Call an ambulance!" I shouted as I leapt up from the couch and ran in her direction. It only took me a second to recognise her crumpled body lying on the hallway floor, her face a ghostly pale white that made her lips, tinted an ugly purplish blue, stand out in the most awful way.

The furious rise and fall of her chest made it clear that she was in the middle of an asthma attack, and no amount of inhalers was going to help this time.

"You're gonna be okay, Gran. It's your asthma. We'll get you to the hospital, and they'll get some oxygen in you, quick, fast." Wren appeared from behind me, reassuring her. She gave her a quick once over before grabbing my attention and whispering under her breath, "The ambulance will take too long. Jack's getting the car so we can run her to the Emergency Department. Can you help me lift her?"

"I can hear you, you know," Denny pushed out through gritted teeth. "I'll be fine."

"Your definition of fine and my definition of fine are very different, Gran," Wren griped. "On three?" Wren looked at me.

I nodded, but before I could help, Gabe appeared and took over. Farron quickly replaced Wren on the other side, and they got Denny up and out of the hallway. Jack had already pulled the car to the front door, and they had her inside within seconds.

"I'll go with them," Wren told us as she climbed into the backseat next to Denny. "We'll call with an update when we know anything."

"Make sure you do," Gabe agreed.

"We'll hold the fort down in the meantime," Farron reassured her. "Just make sure she's okay." Wren gave him a sharp nod as Jack put the car into gear, and then they were gone.

The whole Faoladh clan and the rest of the group had made their way to the door. My heart clenched at the strength of the distress that ran through them all at the thought of losing Denny. We'd become a live audience to the consequences of a day in the smoky haze of the bushfire. The same bushfire that we would be going back to tomorrow because if we didn't, it wasn't just Denny that we would risk losing.

Gabe was the first to break the silence a minute or two after they left.

"Who's up for some bubble'n'squeak? We have some left over from the tofurkey last night. I can have it ready in fifteen." A murmur of agreement passed through the room, sending Gabe off to the kitchen to create whatever concoction that was.

Ever caught my eye and grinned half-heartedly, "If you're as confused as you look, I'm worried."

"Bubble'n'squeak?" I lifted my hands, palms up. "It sounds like a bath wash, not food." I clearly didn't say it quietly enough because the rest of them started laughing as though I'd suggested something ridiculous—although I suspected it was more just to release the tension that had wedged its way inside them at the sight of Denny, their matriarch, vulnerable.

"It's leftover mashed potato mixed with vegetables, fried up and put on toast," Ever explained, keeping an almost straight face, somehow. "Not my favourite, but then it relies too much on salt for me to enjoy it."

"A pixie afraid of salt, I never." I gave them a small grin.

"Afraid's a strong word," they joked. "But on that note, I better make sure Gabe doesn't forget."

"And I have kids to collect, so we should probably all get moving. I appreciate the explanation though," I said. "Please let me know how Denny is as soon as there's an update."

"Of course. She's tough, but I've never seen her go down like that," Ever said, their brows knitting together worriedly.

I caught Clara's gaze. "It looks like you have some more work to do."

"No rest for the wicked. It helps Rowan and I get to do a new spell, so I'm not complaining. Plus, it will take my mind off the whole Denny thing." She stretched her arms out wide before bringing them in, using one to stretch each shoulder out, left, then right. "It feels a lot more dire than it did this morning, somehow."

Clara looked over at Declan so quickly I was sure she thought I didn't notice, their eyes connecting, before she gave me her attention again. *Hmm.*

"Okay, well, I'm going to go check on Maree and the kids. Hopefully, they'll be happy enough to keep playing with the others. Maybe we can stick around? I'd rather be here when the news about Denny comes through. Otherwise, do you think you could get someone to drop you back to the house?"

"Declan will drop me back afterward, I'm sure," Clara confirmed.

"I'm certain that he will." I winked at her before she could say anything. At least someone was getting some butterflies in amongst all the craziness. The emotions around here were only getting heavier, to the point where I could practically touch the fear and anxiety in the air. I headed out the back door to another cluster of buildings to the left of the main house where Maree had said the kids would be.

As I walked, I thought of Mason and how intense it had been since the fires started. *I missed him more than I'd expected. More than felt safe,* I thought. Falling for a human felt more dangerous than I could admit to myself. *He was so vulnerable to everything. Literally, everything.* The fire had nearly taken Denny out, and she wasn't even anywhere near it. He was right in the thick of things, with no powers or healing or anything, just a weak human body that could break down at any obstacle. I shook my head as though it would dislodge the uncomfortable thoughts from where they were wedged in my mind.

I'd been so consumed by my thoughts that I didn't realise I was at the rooms used for the schoolhouse until I heard the sounds of a movie mixed with the noises of happy kids. I looked in the window, watching briefly as I saw Alora and Zane's heads peeking out of a blanket fort along with Conrad and Storm while they watched a cartoon on a projector.

Contentment spread throughout me as I took a moment to enjoy their happiness at such a simple thing. *No wonder Alora never wants to leave. She has friends. Real friends.*

The door to the right of the window opened quietly as Maree slipped out, closing it behind her gently.

"It's pretty adorable, isn't it?"

"More than that. Sometimes, it feels like my heart's going to burst seeing them like that, having friends. Not hiding all the time," I confided to her.

Maree put her arm around me and squeezed, giving me a hug I hadn't realised I'd needed. "The world's a little bigger for all of us, and that's a good thing."

"You're right about that. Did you hear about Denny?" I asked cautiously.

"News travels fast. The boys said she looked bad," she replied quietly. "You were there. Do you think she's going to be okay?"

"I hope so." I couldn't imagine the Faoladh without her. "Do you think the kids might be okay for a little bit longer?"

"What, you mean the kids who are so engrossed in the movie they didn't even see me sneak out?" Maree snickered. "Leave them be for a moment. They're happy. Why don't we just chill out here for a bit? Sean's got it covered." She gestured to the two chairs a little further down the patio. "We're only going to be staring at the phone waiting for an update on Denny anyway."

"I suppose it can't hurt. Clara's helping Olive, Declan, and Emrys with a protection spell for Rowan, so it'll mean she can head home with us. Saves Declan the trip anyway."

"Not that Declan would mind." Maree's eyes twinkled briefly. I could see why Sean had fallen for her. The way her eyes lit up with every emotion she felt, and her wide smile and hooded eyes made for an unusual but beautiful combination.

She just felt so much that I could feel it without even trying, let alone letting my power free, just like with Mason. Most humans were guarded, wary, and untrusting, but not them. They reminded me of the best of what humans could be.

"I wouldn't say I'd be surprised if there's something there, but I'm not sure if it's him or the magick she's falling for. She's been wanting to explore all of that for so long. Now that it's happening, I think she's almost giddy with excitement," I elaborated. "Not that the situation isn't serious, or that she isn't taking it seriously; it's just the first time she's had the chance to connect with other witches."

I held back a little, trying to ignore the threads of guilt that were winding inside me as I realised I was part of the reason she'd been kept from all of that. As though saying their names had summoned them, we watched Clara, Declan, Emrys, and Olive as they walked from the back door of the main house, the boys with their hands full while Clara and Olive were deep in conversation.

"Things happen when they're supposed to. I have to believe that," Maree answered. "Maybe she's finally ready to face the challenges that come with knowing the other side of herself."

"I hope so. I sometimes wonder if because I've seen so many horrible things, I forget about the beautiful things that can happen too." My phone buzzed. *Denny*. Fear flashed through me as I pulled my phone out, flicked the message open, and saw Wren's name at the top.

Grans ok. On oxygen and steroids. Hospital for the night. Drs will review in the AM

Thanks for the update. Give her our love x

Relief flooded through me, and I handed my phone to Maree so I didn't have to contend with the rock in my throat or the tears that threatened to fall. *Denny was okay, for now, at least.* Maree took a deep breath as she read the text and handed my phone back to me.

"Thank the Gods." Maree glanced up at the night sky and made a small gesture. "There's always beauty—goodness—in the world, Ellie. Those kids in there, that gorgeous woman you've raised over there, Denny being okay—they're proof of it. And as long as there is hope, it's all worth it."

"Oh, Gods, Maree, I might need to keep you around as my personal pep-talker if you keep this up," I chuckled.

Maree joined in. "I'll settle for being your friend. How's that sound?"

"Well, I did have a question to ask. Especially if you're my friend." I hesitated a moment. "I was wondering if Alora might start coming to school here?"

"I don't see why not." Maree shrugged. "She fits in well with the kids, and she's rocking up here often enough anyway. Might as well make it official."

I breathed a sigh of relief. "Thank you!" I leaned over and hugged Maree. "You have no idea how much help that is going to be."

"I suspect I do." She paused, her eyes shifting to the direction the others had gone in. "Can you hear that?"

We both stopped talking, and I focused on other sounds, picking up a slow but melodic chant. "I think that's the protection spell they're doing for Rowan," I whispered to Maree. We sat back in our chairs and listened to the spell as the four of them wove it around the firepit a few hundred meters away.

"Earth, water, wind, and fire,
Carve your path as you desire,
All we ask is that you keep our kin safe,
And leave them unscathed in your wake.
As we will, so it shall be."

I felt the pulse of power as it was released into the world, unleashing into the nighttime sky something as magickal as the energy that ran within my veins. It was like the world took a breath and released it all at once.

"Wow." Maree's eyes widened. "Did you feel that? I don't think I've ever felt so much power come out of one spell."

"I've only been around a few witches in my time, and to be fair, most of them were in hiding. Or so voraciously vicious that I was busy dealing with the victims, not the power source."

"You have a weird way of saying yes." Maree chuckled. "Although I'm definitely down for some story time another day. I wonder if it's because it's the four of them together. It must amplify stuff or something."

"That sounds right." I rubbed the back of my neck gently and looked out at the stars, twinkling high above the trees, entire sections now obscured by the smoke from the bushfire. "I just hope that it works."

"So do I."

It wasn't long before three of them left the firepit behind, burning brightly, while someone, either Declan or Emrys, stayed behind, sitting on the ground, feeding it. As they got closer, Clara waved goodbye and headed over to where Maree and I were.

"It looks like that was a success," I said as she approached. "We could feel the burst of magick from here. Wren just texted to say that Denny's okay. In hospital, but okay."

"Oh, El." Clara hugged me tightly. "I'm so glad."

"Me too." I hugged her back. "At least the spell went to plan."

"Something had to. I'm not sure if casting a spell is always that way. I think I'll ask Olive about it tomorrow. It's left me buzzing, that's for sure."

Maree peered into the window and sighed as she checked on the kids. "End credits. Looks like it's time to wrap it up, ladies," she announced, standing up.

I was glad to be heading home. Not just for the sleep, although it was still a human novelty that I was not willing to give up. Not yet anyway. No, mostly I wanted to watch Alora and Zane fall asleep in their cute pyjamas, all safe and tucked into their beds, and just feel that feeling, the one that told me everything was okay, or that it would be okay, or it had been okay—just all the okays.

I needed it tonight when I knew someone else's baby was out in the woods, alone and literally scared out of her human form.

"Let's take these kids home," I agreed, wrapping my arm around Clara in a side hug. "I'm proud of you."

CHAPTER TWELVE

Bedtime hadn't been the smoothest we'd ever had, so I'd given in and let them play until they grew tired enough to snuggle with me and read a story. By the last page, Alora was snoring lightly in Clara's arms while Zane was trying his hardest to keep his heavy eyelids open. A moment or two later, he nuzzled his snout into my arm and fell asleep. I wasn't too far behind him.

The morning dawned too soon. I'd checked in on Shade briefly when we got in, much to his disdain, before we'd settled the kids to bed in their room. Clara had snuck away at some point in the night to enjoy the luxury of her own bed. I'd stayed in the nest of blankets that made up Zane's usual bed, only this time, it was Alora, me, and Zane all tangled amongst them.

The kids were still asleep when the sun started poking its rays through the window, so I extricated myself as quietly and gently as I could and headed downstairs to boil the kettle. When I walked into the kitchen, Clara was already sitting at the dining table, cradling her own cup of tea. .

"Beat me to it, did you?" I asked, surprised.

"I'm *still* buzzing from the spell last night," she exclaimed. "I don't know what it is. It-it's like I can just feel the magick all around me."

I poured myself some tea and sat down next to her. "Maybe the more you use your magick, the more sensitive you become to it?"

"Maybe. I'm hoping to catch Olive and ask a few questions before everything kicks off this morning. Any updates about Denny yet?"

"Still the same. Wren texted me not too long ago. Olive's probably a good place to start," I agreed, taking a sip of my far-too-hot tea. "Ooph. Hot." I fanned my mouth, even though it felt pointless.

"Yeah, I made it hot. Wanted it to last, sorry." Clara gave me an apologetic look.

"It's okay. I'll probably need a full pot before we head out ..." I hesitated before continuing. "I think I'm going to reach out to my mother. She might help with finding Rowan ... and I kind of promised Thanatos that I would start trying a little harder."

"Is that why he's been hanging with Shade?" Clara said. "I thought that was odd."

"I asked him to. I figured that the two of them probably had more in common than we did, and maybe that would help him more than I could. Something's gotta work at some point. I don't want him to sit by himself with everything he's feeling."

"It's not a bad idea. Just interesting that you'd accept something with strings attached." Clara raised her eyebrows. "The Animus thing really did a number on you, didn't it?"

"I wouldn't say that." I grimaced. "I'm just trying to make progress, become a better person—Goddess—whatever. I mean, look at me, letting go and trusting you with running your own life. I'm practically a new person already," I said with a dramatic flourish.

"That's, that's—I don't really know what to say to that, El. Progress, for sure. I'll drink to that." She took a gulp of her tea. "I'm going to go get the kids up so we can head on out."

"And if you happen not to be here if Nyx shows up, that's just coincidence, right?" I smirked.

"Total and complete coincidence," she said sarcastically. "I'm not saying your mother is terrifying, but, well, she is. Good luck!"

Clara disappeared quickly, leaving her mug on the table, a little ring of condensation joining the other marks from the many mornings before. I took a sip of my tea and breathed in, then slowly released my breath. I got up, headed to the basement door, and knocked loudly before opening it.

"Shade, we're heading off to Denny's place in a few minutes. Do you need anything before we go?" I called down. A minute passed, so I yelled down again. "Shade, did you hear me?"

A cross between a grumble and a growl greeted my ears, turning into something resembling normal speech. "Got it. I'm good."

I waited a moment to see if he would say anything else, but it was radio silence, so I shut the door. That was the best I was going to get out of him. I looked around the empty room and realised I couldn't procrastinate any longer. Even being a Goddess wouldn't get me out of it.

It was time to call her.

I closed my eyes and focused inward until I could feel the ether that only our Gods and Goddesses inhabited, somewhere between our souls and our powers, where we could find one another. I sent the call out to my mother and then retreated, returning to the mortal plane and opening my eyes again.

Now it was time to wait. She'd either answer or not. I'd done my bit.

I glanced at Clara's mug and sighed. I might as well clean up while I waited to see if she turned up. *I probably should have gotten dressed before I called her,* I realised as I looked down at my stained shirt and two-sizes-too-big sweatpants. *Too late now.* It's not like anything short of a chiton, and at least a kilogram of gold would please her anyway.

A cursory glance around the kitchen gave me nothing more to procrastinate on. It wasn't a surprise, really; we'd barely been home with everything going on. I took the moment of quiet to finish the rest of my tea, now that it wasn't going to scorch my tongue. Even immortals hated that.

"Ellie!" Clara shouted for me from upstairs, making me spit the last sip of tea out, adding another stain to my shirt. I dabbed at it quickly and put the mug in my sink in the same movement before heading to the stairwell.

"Geez, did you have to scare me like that?" I yelled back. "What's wrong?"

Clara stuck her head out of the doorway of the kids' room. "Did you tell Alora that she was going back to Denny's house today?"

"No. Did you?"

"No. And that explains why she just flashed out of the bedroom."

"Oh, Gods, not again." I shook my head.

"Yep. Again. Maybe it would have been a good idea to tell her last night so that she wouldn't pull this disappearing act again." Clara stopped just short of saying, 'I told you so.'

"Hindsight is twenty-twenty, Clara. Can you call and check that Alora made it there safely? We might as well just get our stuff together and head over anyway. There's no point chasing her now, just to leave as soon as we get back."

"I'll take care of it. Has Nyx shown up?" Clara asked tentatively.

"No, not yet. I'll head up in a minute to get dressed, and then we'll go. She'll be able to find me if she wants to."

"It appears you spoke too soon, Eleos." The silky, dark sound of my mother's voice caught my attention, and I looked to the doorway of the kitchen. I swallowed the breath down that she'd startled out of me. There was no doubt that she knew how to make an entrance.

"She's here, Clara. I'll be up soon," I shouted the warning up the stairs, not expecting a response. It was clear that Nyx had left a lasting impression on her the last time.

"Mother," I greeted her cautiously. Somehow, she managed to look ethereal and yet threatening all at once, and perhaps especially so in a mundane mortal kitchen. Anxiety clouded my thoughts for a second as I processed the fact that she'd actually shown up for me.

"You called," she stated, standing with her arms crossed elegantly over the black chiton that fell from shoulder to knee, held together with gold clasps that shone like the stars while a golden thread held tight to the line of her waist, emphasising her figure. Thick black curls fell gracefully on either side of her face from a pile intricately braided to sit atop the crown of her head. She was every inch the Goddess she appeared to be and probably a million times more powerful too.

"I did," I answered, walking past her and into the kitchen, where she followed behind. I swallowed the lump in my throat and reminded myself that this was just a normal mother-daughter chat. Humans had them all the time. Surely I could manage one without an argument? "I wanted to check in. See how you were."

Nyx glowered at me. "You? My darling, you haven't done that in thousands of years. Not that I've minded. You always were terribly needy, but this kind of ruse is entirely unnecessary."

"I guess I thought I'd try a different way." It might have been a half-truth, but at least there *was* some truth in it. She eyed me warily, accidentally brushing past the bench, which sent a flicker of annoyance across her face.

"And?" she asked, her brow furrowed.

"And ... we have a missing Faoladh—a young girl trapped in her wolf form. I was hoping you might help." I looked up and caught her gaze. "I've tried using my power, but with the bushfires, it's flooded with just about every negative emotion you can imagine. I haven't been able to narrow down where she is."

"That sounds like a problem for the Celtic Pantheon," Nyx answered, the wariness in her eyes turning to steel.

"I'd like to think it's a problem for *everyone*, mother. Not just the Pantheon of her kin. She's a young girl, is she not? As a wolf, she is an animal, also our charge. And the bushfires are destroying the very wildlife our Pantheon is responsible for. That sounds like an *us* problem to me."

Nyx sighed. "We are not the only Gods of these charges. We are not even truly the Gods of this land. The Gods of this land are still here. How are we to know our interference will not be viewed as malicious?"

"Malicious?" I repeated, frustration pushing my lips into a thin line. "That's grasping at straws, Mother. Saving a child—saving Rowan—is worth the risk."

"Is this really the route you want to go down, Eleos?" She met my gaze, her eyes black as night yet swirling with starlight.

"Mother, if we can help this girl, it will be worth it. You and I both know that these bushfires wouldn't be threatening any of us if our Gods and Goddesses were doing their jobs instead of gallivanting with Zeus like it's 1999."

"You are correct. Our Pantheon is a mess of hedonistic, selfish Gods who have forgotten their duties to the mortal world." She sounded aggrieved, which surprised me. Not because she'd noticed, but because, for the first time, she seemed bothered by it. "I will speak with Artemis—this is her domain and her responsibility."

"Thank you, Mother." I gave her a tight, nervous smile. Artemis wasn't my favourite Goddess, but Nyx was right. This was her domain.

Nyx nodded and then lifted her hand, a movement I recognised as her preparing to depart.

"Wait, mother, just a second." I moved closer to her, raising my hands to stop her.

"Yes, Eleos?" She looked at me questioningly.

"Will you come to dinner next week sometime? Have dinner with us, with my family?" I asked, feeling as though I'd just torn the band aid off a huge gaping wound that had never healed in my heart. Her gaze held mine as I watched her process what I'd just proposed.

"Dinner?" she repeated, almost speechless. "I-why-I-I suppose I will join you and your *family* for a meal," she answered, the stutter in her voice appearing to surprise her as much as it did me.

"Look, I shouldn't have asked—" I started before I realised what my mother was saying. *She said yes.* "I-uh, um. Thank you, Mother."

"Farewell," she declared, and then with that, she disappeared completely.

I leant back against the nearest kitchen bench and let go of the breath I hadn't realised I'd been holding. Not only was she going to help us, but she was also coming to dinner. *Dinner*. With me. With the kids. All of us.

What in the Hades did I just sign up for?

"Is the coast clear?" Clara shouted down from the stairs, interrupting my disturbing train of thought. Thankfully.

"As clear as it'll ever be," I answered, heading back out to the entryway and then up the stairwell. "I'm going to get changed, and then we can head over."

"Go for it," Clara said, her outfit already suitable for the public. "Zane needs a toilet break, so I'll cover that."

"Fingers crossed it lands where it's supposed to." I grinned at her and then dashed into my room. It didn't take long for me to get presentable—a quick brush of my hair before slapping it into a ponytail, and then some pants and another long-sleeved shirt had me ready to go. My mind wandered to Denny and how she was doing. Maybe a quick call-out to Asclepius wouldn't be a bad idea.

"I did it! I did it! I fed the toilet." I heard Zane squeal excitedly through the door, distracting me. I smiled at the sound as I pulled the cover up the bed.

"You did. What a smart little boy you are, Zane! I'm so proud of you," Clara exclaimed, which only made me smile more widely.

Clearly, it had landed where it was supposed to.

It didn't take long from there to get all of us rounded up and into the car. Zane didn't need any convincing, that was for sure. If I were more self-conscious and insecure, it might have made me wonder how horrendously boring we were. Then I remembered they were kids, and these were their first friends.

Whether it was on purpose, we'd given them something that had been entirely out of the realm of possibility a year ago. *Friends.* And not just other deserted or abandoned halflings thrown together out of necessity. *Real friends.*

Gods, even Clara and I had found real friends.

A smile crept across my face. The muscles that had been stuck in a near constant, stressful line while the worry for Rowan, and now Denny, hung over my head somehow relaxed enough to let the little ray of happiness show on my face, bringing some relief to the tension in my heart.

"Alora's all good. Gabe's giving her breakfast as we speak," Clara confirmed as she secured Zane in his car seat.

"That's good. Thanks for checking."

"I don't know whether that's your 'happy' face or if you've lost your actual mind, and that's a 'gateway smile to hysteria' type of face," she joked, her gaze wary but optimistic as she slid into the passenger seat.

"Happy." I laughed, leaning my forearms against the steering wheel loosely. "Hysteria involves a lot more eyebrow movement and hyena-like laughter. You won't be able to miss it, I promise."

"What are you so happy about then? It's not like we have any good news on the Rowan front," she asked, doing her seatbelt up.

"Did you ever think, when we came here a few years ago, that we would have friends? That the *kids* would have friends? It just blows my mind sometimes," I explained, locking eyes with her.

"Not all of us were as pessimistic as you were, El." Clara smirked and rolled her eyes. "But would I have thought it would turn out like this? Maybe not. So, I guess you kinda have a point."

"Thank you. I can feel how hard it was for you to admit that." My thoughts flickered back to the dangers we were heading back into today—to Denny, in the hospital, and Rowan, still lost in the bush, and to the group of us that would face the bushfire conditions to find her. "It's not all sunshine and rainbows, so I mean, the downside is that there are more people to worry about."

"There it is." Clara shot me a wry smile. "What's the opposite of seeing a silver lining?"

"Go, go, go!" Zane interrupted us, his wings flapping against the back of his car seat, marking each word with a gentle thud of wings on fabric and plastic.

"Alright, alright, I get the message." I looked at him in the rearview mirror. I was glad that we'd kept the kids clueless as to why they were getting to spend so much time with the Faoladh. It was not going to be fun when things settled back down to normal, and they had to get used to being home more often, but I pushed that thought away quickly.

I needed whatever dopamine boost I had that morning to last as long as possible.

CHAPTER THIRTEEN

We were still parked when the familiar sound of Mason's truck caught me by surprise. I looked up to see him pulling up near the front verandah. A second later, Mason jumped out, dirt and soot covering nearly every inch of him, from his forehead to his steel-capped boots.

"Looks like you have a visitor," Clara said in a singsong voice, a grin spreading across her face.

"Would you mind taking Zane over and getting him settled? I feel like I haven't seen Mason in forever, and I'm sure I can get him to drop me off. I won't be long."

The click of her seatbelt unbuckling was all the permission I needed.

"Thank you, Clara. You're the best!"

"I know, I know. You owe me one," she told me before hopping out of the car and heading around to the driver's side.

I undid my own belt and got out of the car, only stopping long enough to let Zane know that I'd follow soon, though he didn't seem all that fazed by it. Clara jumped in the car and waved, and I waved back, shouting goodbye as she drove out the same way Mason had come in.

Before they were even out of sight, I felt Mason's muscular arms wrap around me and pick me up, turning me to face him in one smooth move. I twined my arms around his neck and enjoyed being close to him for a moment, resting my forehead on his chin and closing my eyes.

"I've missed you," he whispered, the movement of his lips against my skin sending a pleasant shiver down my spine.

"Me too," I whispered back, lifting my face so that I spoke the last word against his lips.

Mason took the invitation without a second thought, kissing me deeply as he turned us around and pressed my back against the body of his truck so that his hands were free to push my curls back and caress my face. The deep brown of his eyes made me feel as though I was freefalling but, in the best, most delightful way, as though when I hit the ground, he would be there to catch me.

Mason's lips left mine as his hands slipped through my hair, dislodging my ponytail, pulling me close to him and kissing the top of my head, just in time to let me catch my breath. "I needed this more than you know. Something real, something beyond the smoke, the fire, the disaster." He held me tight to him. "I needed you. You remind me that there's good in the world, and I need that right now."

My heart nearly shattered with those words, both because I felt the love he said them with and the surge of love I had for him within me at the same time. It was overwhelming in a terrifyingly amazing way.

"It's bad," I stated. Underneath that love was pain, sharp and fierce, piercing him like a thousand knives.

He nodded, and he kissed the top of my head. "I haven't been home since I saw you the other day when I introduced you all to Kirra. It's just been nonstop. Every time we make some progress, another spot fire lights up in a different direction. And then, Gabe told me about Denny, and Mac, he ..." Mason trailed off.

"Oh no, Mason," I murmured, my hands curled into his hair and cradled the back of his head. "What happened?"

"A branch. We-we were at the front, trying to buy some extra time, but an old paperbark tree had gone up, and before we could fall back, one of the branches fell and took him out. Erik and I got him out from under it and got him safe, but it wasn't looking good when they took him into the hospital." His voice broke on the last word. I could feel his pain peaking, tearing at him. Not for the first time, the depth of his compassion reminded me of how unique he was, even among humans.

"I know it will stop at some point, but that point feels very far away." He sighed.

"It'll be okay. Mac will be okay," I reassured him, placing my hands on either side of his face and pulling him back to look at me. "I may not be able to see the future, but I know you, and I know that you're doing everything you can. That's enough, Mason. It really is. You can't fix everything. But you can let me help you. Will you?"

He nodded, his eyes reflecting an ocean of pain. "I don't think I can keep going if you don't."

I closed my eyes and let myself connect with the emotions within him, the pain fresh and raw and right at the top of it all. Taking a deep breath, I absorbed as much of his pain as I could, replacing it with the mercy he needed to forgive himself for leading Mac into danger, even though it wasn't his burden to bear. It was the downside of his compassion.

The tension in his body lessened, telling me I'd achieved what I'd set out to do, even if it wasn't as much as I'd have liked to. Before I cut off my power, I sent a silent plea through the ether of the Gods to Asclepius' mind to help heal Mac and Denny.

Knowing I had done all I could, I pulled my power back into myself and kissed Mason gently on the lips as I felt the dull ache of his pain settling somewhere deep inside my chest.

"I wish I could take more, but I need to make sure I don't wipe myself out in case we find Rowan. I'm still not at full power yet," I apologised to him. "I was able to send a message out to Asclepius for help. I don't know if he'll heed my call, but it was worth a try. There are too many people we care about all caught up in this fire."

"Thank you." Mason met my gaze with an intensity that made me feel as though my entire soul were on display to him. It was exhilarating and terrifying at the same time. "I don't know what I would I'd do without you."

"Definitely not this." I looked at him coyly as I distracted myself from the feelings whirring beneath the surface and lifted his face to mine, kissing him again. "Or this," I whispered, moving his hands from my thighs to my waist, under my shirt.

"No, definitely not," he answered as he kissed me back, leaning into me and holding me in place between him and the truck, the whole moment thrumming with a heat that belonged in the bedroom, not in the front yard. I leaned into him, the smell of smoke and sweat filling each breath, my hands releasing from around his neck so that I could run my hands through his hair.

I knew it was selfish, but I wanted everything to disappear except us. The world, the worries, the search. I could *feel* how desperately Mason needed to forget too, and Gods, how I wanted to give in. But I couldn't, we couldn't.

"I could do this all day," I said as I placed a trail of kisses along his jawline. "But *I* can't, and *you* can't."

Mason rested his cheek against mine. "No, I can't. Although I will admit that being so tired I can see two of you has its perks," he murmured, the feel of his smile against my cheek sending ripples of delight through me.

I wasn't used to being considered beautiful—not many mortals cared if the Goddess tending to them in their moments of pain was attractive or not. It was my power they sought, not my beauty. And yet, the way he made me feel, it was like I was the sun, and he couldn't look away. It was the most thrilling feeling.

Mason gently loosened his grip on me and guided me back down to the ground, his hands slipping from my body to grasp mine in his instead. We stood leaning against his truck for a moment longer, our hands clasped together.

"I guess we have to go back to the real world then," he said with a lopsided grin, brushing his thumb across my cheek. "I rubbed off on you."

"In more ways than one. But the real world calls." I let go of one of his hands so I could trace the buttons of his ash-covered shirt all the way up to his collar—the same ash that now peppered my own clothing. I could almost see the moment that he was finally able to hand over the reins to someone else, and he took his protective gear off, undoing the top couple of buttons as he got far enough away that he could finally breathe in more air than smoke. "*You,* on the other hand, need to go home and join the world of the sleeping—for a good twelve to eighteen hours, at least."

"Mm-hmm, that would sound more appealing if you'd join me, but I'll concede." He squeezed my hand. "Let's get moving."

"Uh-uh." I shook my head and held my hand out. "I'll drive us to Denny's, and then you can either crash there or head home."

Mason handed over his keys without a second of hesitation. "All yours."

I gave him a soft kiss on his cheek and let go of his hand. We both got in the truck, and I started it up, the roaring engine making me jump a little before we started up the driveway and hit the road.

"Maybe crashing at Denny's isn't a bad idea. At least I'll be on hand to find out what happens today. I can't believe that she's ended up in hospital. I feel like I haven't been able to help as much as I wanted." Mason shook his head in disappointment.

"I think you underestimate how much you've actually helped," I reassured him. "You introduced us to Kirra, and she's been great, but most importantly, you've been doing everything you can to control that fire, and that's what's going to make the biggest difference. At the moment, we're mostly just grunts on the ground, hoping to find Rowan before anyone else does."

Mason placed his hand on my thigh, giving me a small smile. "I'm gonna hold on to that."

I put my hand over his and squeezed it gently.

It wasn't a long trip, but it was enough that Mason fell asleep with his head against the window, a loud snore every few breaths confirming it. He wouldn't make it back to his place, not when he was this tired.

"He's a noisy one, isn't he?" a strangely familiar voice piped up from behind me in the backseat, making me nearly jump out of my skin.

"What the Hades?" I exclaimed, nearly swerving from the shock.

"Oh, don't make such a big deal about it. Be grateful I didn't reveal myself when your little human lover was awake." She smirked. "Likely would have lost his marbles, I expect."

"Artemis," I greeted her, trepidation accompanying the realisation. "I assume Mother reached out to you."

"Indeed. Didn't want to call on me yourself, did you?" Artemis' glittering brown eyes met mine in the rearview mirror, their almond shape framed by short eyelashes and thick, perfectly arched brows, the same colour as the straight, dark chocolate hair she'd scraped back into a high ponytail at the top of her head.

"Would you have come?" I countered.

"Probably not," she admitted. "But then, refusing your mother is entirely different to ignoring the call of a deserter." The word sprung from her with a vicious disgust that was so sharp it instantly pierced the veil of shame I'd worked long and hard at keeping from the surface of my mind.

"As different as ignoring the pleas of an old friend, I guess." I let my anger slip past my tongue. "Do you have anything useful, or are you just here to throw barbs and waste my time?"

"Ah, you've grown a bit of a bite on you, haven't you?" She mocked me. "At least the time away has been useful, I suppose."

"Artemis." My patience was wearing thin, and the distance to Denny's was growing smaller. I did not want to be dragging Artemis into that combustible combination.

"The wolf—the girl—she is on this side of the fire. Not far from where you've been searching. You'll find her shortly. Whatever magick your comrades have wielded, it was successful—not one creature was harmed through the night. For that, I'm thankful, though don't think I am unaware of what they lack. Their protection extends only to their own while other creatures die and suffer," Artemis grumbled.

"It used to be the domain of Gods, Artemis, not witches and fae. It's not their lack that you need to be worried about. We left them alone, and they've done what they could."

I defended my friends, casting a quick look over at Mason, who had shifted position slightly.

"Watch what you're saying, Eleos. Not all of us are partying it up in Olympus. Some of us are busy in the regions of the world that these mortals have forgotten—where women and children hold little value, and life or death hinges on the day's hunt. *Some* of us are needed where *others* cannot see us," she said defensively. "You may have turned this town into a cowardly hole for you to hide in, but some of us still have to deal with the real world outside your pretty little bubble."

I paused, taking in her words, marrying them with what my mother had said earlier. I looked in the rearview mirror again, meeting Artemis' gaze. "Thank you."

She raised her brow and then disappeared, leaving only Mason and I in the car as I drove up to Denny's house and parked. With the engine stilled and Mason's snoring the only sound, I leaned back in the seat and closed my eyes for a moment.

Seeing Artemis so close and yet as emotionally far as she could be had shaken me more than I wanted to admit. I was used to the mortal world, and with every appearance of someone from my past, it felt less and less like it was my world and more and more like the two would collide at some point, whether I wanted them to or not.

I waited for the trembling of my hands to stop, taking in deep breaths and releasing them a few times before I felt ready to disturb Mason and head inside. I squeezed his hand gently, but all that did was elicit a louder snore. Leaning over, I moved both my hands to cup his face and brushed an unruly bit of hair aside.

"Mason," I said quietly. "We're here."

He murmured something sleepily that I couldn't make out, but it was something.

"Time to wake up," I told him again a little louder, punctuating the sentence with a soft kiss on his lips.

"Mm-hmm," he murmured, his arm reaching out and pulling me over the console and into his lap, the landing a little awkward but forgotten as I laughed and realised I'd been caught in his trap. "Now, this is the way I'd like to wake up."

"If it was any other day, I'd be right with you on that." I grinned and gave him another quick kiss. "But today, you need to sleep, and I need to go help them find Rowan."

"You sound confident," he commented, tucking my hair behind my ear. "I love how small your ears are," he breathed out distractedly.

"Stop it." I shooed his hand away. "Artemis paid me a visit while you slept on our way over. She said we'd find Rowan today, not far from where we'd been searching.

And that the spell—the protection spell that Olive, Declan, Emrys and Clara cast last night—worked. No one was hurt last night, not in the fire at least—not Rowan or any wildlife."

Mason smiled, a genuine upturn of his lips that I'd gotten so used to seeing before bushfire season hit. It made my heart beat a little faster, and a little harder, to see it reappear again after what felt like so long. "That's the good news we need to hear. Any chance she has a giant bucket she could drop on the whole fire, save us some of those extra resources?" he half joked.

"No, unfortunately not. That's more Poseidon's domain, and he's more inclined to send a flood instead. Reliability is not his strong point."

"Yeah, nah. Been there, done that, last year." Mason shook his head. "I guess I should get some sleep so I can get back out there again then." He splayed his hand across the small of my back and pulled me close to him, breathing my scent in deeply before releasing it slowly. He opened the passenger door, and we exchanged another quick kiss. "After you, my Goddess."

I rolled my eyes at his cheesiness as I got out of the car, but inside, my heart sang a little. I was used to keeping my hopes in check, preparing for the worst, and not even really daring to hope for the best. That day though, between the boost seeing Mason had given me and the confidence Artemis had that we would find Rowan, I felt more optimistic than I was comfortable with. Or used to.

"We better get you inside before you fall asleep again," I teased, jiggling his keys as he climbed out. "You are not seeing these babies for at least another twelve hours."

"You're the boss." He grinned, shutting the door to his truck. "But make sure the windows are up, will you? I don't need to go all 'man versus possum' again."

"Do I even want to know?" He started to talk, and I shushed him. "Some things are better left a mystery. How you got a possum *in* and *out* of your truck is one of them."

"If you think that's the worst part, El, then you're better off not knowing." His lips curved into a wicked grin, and he grabbed my hand as we walked up to the front door. The sounds on the other side of the door were reassuring and a lot less negative than the talk last night. Hopefully, between the scrying spell and Artemis' revelations, we'd have Rowan home with Denny in no time.

"About time! This lot is chomping at the bit to get back out there," Farron answered the door before we had the chance to even knock. He did a double take after taking in

Mason in all his dirty glory and whatever had ended up on my clothes. "What *were* you doing?"

"You really want me to answer that?" I asked with a mischievous smile.

"No, no, please don't. My imagination's curse enough," he said as he let us through.

"I guess the scrying worked?" I questioned, curious about the massive shift in emotions that were coming at me quick and fast.

"That, and Denny's off the oxygen. We just got the news a minute ago," Farron explained as he shook Mason's hand and led us through to the kitchen, where everyone was gathered. It was busy, with most of them shoving a quick breakfast down or a few gulps of tea. Before he could answer, Clara came running at me and gave me a giant hug.

"The scrying worked, El!" she shouted, a few sore heads wincing at the decibel level of her voice. It was all Clara could do not to jump up and down from the frequency she was vibrating at.

"That's amazing!" I squeezed her back, a big grin on my face.

"It's going to be more than amazing if we finally find her today." Clara beamed.

"I need a coffee, so why don't you give us the rundown in the kitchen with the rest of them?" Mason suggested.

I shot him a cautionary look. "You need sleep, not coffee."

"Okay, okay, decaf. Let me hear the news, and then I'll steal a guest room for some sleep if it's all good with ... well, Jack, I guess, given Denny's not here," Mason agreed, putting his hands in the air as though surrendering.

"There's always a bed for you here, mate, you know that," Jack answered, surprising the two of us as we entered the kitchen.

"Good to see you, Jack. Thanks for all the work at the hub," Mason said, giving him a quick thank-you wave.

"Oh, you know I'm only dragging this old lump of mine down there to help with Rowan. Self-serving, the lot of us." He gave him a sly grin. "Plus, Ma would have my throat if I was anywhere else."

He wasn't wrong. I bit a smile back before returning the conversation to the matter at hand. "So, the scrying?" I asked the room, skimming all the usual faces filling the kitchen. Gabe, Farron, Wren, Declan, Ever, Emrys, and Olive were all crowded around as Clara pulled up a stool and perched near me.

"It gave us a few locations," Olive started. "Here was the biggest pull, obviously, and then there were two weaker ones—one closer to Newcastle, and another about thirty minutes northwest of where Kirra had us searching yesterday." Her eyes gleamed with a hope that had been absent the night before. "I'm assuming the Newcastle one is an outlier, but the other one, that's got to be Rowan." She rubbed her chubby hands together in excitement. "I'm just so glad it worked!"

"That lines up." I nodded before explaining my request to Nyx and Artemis' prompt response to everyone.

"You called your mother?" Wren asked, her interest clear in the raise of a brow.

"Uh-huh," I answered, feeling the pressure of my conversation with Denny a few days ago. "But I don't know if anything more than Artemis' help is going to come from it, so don't go getting your hopes up. Speaking of mothers though, is there any chance that this 'outlier'" — I did air quotation marks around the word—"could be Storm's mother?"

"It's possible," Olive agreed. "But what are we to do, love? Go on and drag her back here? We don't even know for sure who she is or if she'd even want to be with Storm."

The tight line of Gabe's mouth twitched as though this was a conversation I'd come in at the end of, not the beginning. I noticed Farron's hand move subtly to wrap around Gabe's waist, although I wasn't sure if he was offering him comfort or helping keep him in place.

"I guess Rowan is the priority right now anyway," I segued, aware of the shaky ground my path of questioning had led to. We'd have time to worry about that later. "Are the kids all sorted, Clara?"

"They couldn't get away fast enough," she chuckled. "Maree's got a bunch of hyped-up kids on her hands today, Gods help her."

"As long as Zane doesn't try his 'pooping' chase game with her, she should be okay." We exchanged our own chuckles.

"What the actual ...?" Farron exclaimed, disgust colouring his face. "Stop! Don't even start, I don't need to know. This is why we're never having kids," he said, grasping Gabe's hand.

"Yeah, that's why. It's not because you consider less than twelve hours sleep torture at all." Gabe flashed a sarcastic smile at me as Farron led him out of the kitchen. I could hear Farron refuting his claims as they walked away.

"Can you imagine if Farron got the trifecta?" I barely held in the laughter tickling in my throat. *Pee, poop, and vomit.* There wasn't a sane soul on the planet who wanted *that.*

"On the other hand, let's not imagine that." Clara reconsidered.

"You, son." Jack looked pointedly at Mason. "Get yourself to a guest room and make sure you shower before you lay a finger on that bed, d'you hear me? I won't be changing anyone's dirty sheets."

"Yes, sir," Mason answered, looking down at his clothes with the realisation of just how filthy they actually were. "I'll get on it." He nodded and obliged, giving me a kiss on the forehead and a quick, whispered instruction to stay safe before he disappeared out of the kitchen and down the hallway.

"Alright, the rest of you lot. Let's get out of here." Jack stood up, simultaneously slipping a weathered, leather-wrapped flask into one of his pockets. "No more dilly-dallying around. Let's go find our girl."

Once we were assembled at the coordination hub, Gabe took Kirra aside for a quiet word to ask for us to have our search grids shifted to the locations that the scrying spell and Artemis had indicated.

Not that he mentioned those reasons, but whatever he said had the desired effect, and we found ourselves paired up with the same people as the day before, only shifted in the northwest direction where we hoped to find Rowan.

"Listen up, people!" Kirra shouted, catching the attention of everyone in a thirty-metre radius, if not more. "We've had some good news overnight. It seems like there has been an influx of wildlife, all alive but some not even injured, which is a miracle in itself." Her gaze drifted to me, but I remained stoic, trying not to give anything away.

It wasn't my work to take the credit for, but if she already suspected me, it made sense to let her think she was right, mostly because it kept her from suspecting too much of the others, especially Clara. Kirra held something deep inside her, an intense comingling of emotions that I didn't understand yet, and it held me back from trusting her completely.

The volunteers gathered let out a cheer, and Kirra's gaze returned to the group as a whole. "It doesn't change the risks we're facing out there though. The temperature is set to soar today, so keep up your water, remember to wear your mask, and don't play hero. Heatstroke is a very real threat. We all have our roles, but none of them work without the other, so keep it safe." She rubbed her hands together, and her suspicious gaze turned optimistic. "Okay, let's get out there, people, and see if we can find some more to add to that number. Remember, every life saved is a win!"

After her rousing pep talk, we all gathered our things and paired up, heading off for our sections for the morning.

"Everyone seems pretty upbeat," I commented as we headed to our search grid to get started. I took a drink of my water, the early morning sun already making me warm in my long-sleeved shirt and pants.

"It helps when there are more saves than losses, but you wouldn't know anything about that, would you?" Kirra asked, throwing a sneaky side-eye my way.

"No, not really," I said in the most neutral tone I could gather. "Mason did say that they were making some progress. Maybe that's allowed more wildlife to get ahead of the fires without injury."

"Maybe," Kirra acknowledged before picking up speed, so she was a few strides ahead of me. "Did he also mention Mac went down? Between him and your grandmother, I'm worried about how today's going to play out."

"He did." I nodded. "And Denny's not *my* grandmother, but it's pretty terrifying all the same. I'm hoping that's the worst of it."

"You seem to be coping just fine though."

"You're not doing too bad yourself," I threw back at her, meeting her gaze straight on.

"Touché," she replied, her smile genuine, before she turned her focus to the ground again.

That suited me just fine, even if it was a tad rude. I didn't need to be under her suspicious eyes any longer than necessary, and from here, our search section looked much the same as it did yesterday. Full of trees, bush, and brush that was devoid of much of anything, but most of all, Rowan.

We didn't deviate from how we operated the day before—eyes on the ground, scanning constantly, while also checking above for any signs of wildlife. Every step was the same routine, feeling more monotonous than useful as the motivation and hype from the morning slowly wore off with each square metre of empty bush.

The buzz of Kirra's walkie-talkie went off every half-hour or so, with someone somewhere finding an animal or false alarms. One volunteer fainted two hours in, so we found ourselves sitting on a fallen tree log while Kirra coordinated the first aid unit to attend and assess.

My heart leapt into my throat, blocking me from speaking—breathing, even—until I heard an unfamiliar name spoken. Even months down the line, I was still learning about the Faoladh and their capabilities. They were a relatively cocky lot, but what was confidence and what was reality wasn't yet clear to me. I didn't know how they coped with the heat and the smoke, in human or wolf form, so anxiety trailed my thoughts as the reports came in, and I waited with bated breath to hear if it was them or not. When it was established that it was a human volunteer with a mild case of heatstroke, they were taken home, and their partner was reassigned at the hub. And I could breathe again.

We got moving quickly after that, but it was only as the sun approached midday that I felt like we were onto something. An undercurrent, stronger than Kirra's, seeped through the bush and called to me, to my power. I picked up my pace instinctively, heading toward the emotion, although whether it was a willing movement by me or the pulling of the being's—hopefully Rowan's—emotions on my power, I couldn't figure it out.

Until, finally, I did.

CHAPTER FOURTEEN

WE'D FOUND HER.

There she was, all forty kilograms of her covered in striking silver and grey fur, stalking around the edges of the burnt forest, her snout buried in the blackened carcass of a bird. The red blood of her prey coloured the edges of her lips, the skin tightening around her gums coated in the same colour, as she growled at us as we came into her line of sight.

I could feel the anguish coming off her in waves. Not the waves that crashed into the shore of a beach, rhythmic and steady. No, these waves were different. They were mountainous walls of water, thundering down unpredictably, as though a tsunami had forced them into being. Pain, suffering, distress. None of those words seemed enough to really capture what she was feeling.

It was agony. *Pure agony.* As though her soul was so caught up in all the devastation. She had no clear thoughts in her mind. *None.* It was something I'd encountered often in my duties, a type of acute post-traumatic stress reaction where the mortal had been trapped, reliving their moments of deepest pain in a constant, horrific loop.

Kirra caught my attention as she pulled up her walkie-talkie and pressed the button. "We've found the wolf. Location -34.805920, 150.591144, near the top of Tullian Creek. I think we're going to need some backup. Rangers, not volunteers." Keeping her eyes on Rowan, she adjusted her stance, planted her feet firmly on the ground, pulled out a small tranquilliser pistol, and aimed it directly at her.

Rowan snarled, baring her teeth.

"Oh, Gods," I gasped. "Kirra, wait! Please!" I moved toward her, my hand out, but at the same time, I got closer to Rowan. "She's just scared." My power stretched at its confines as though begging me to unleash it. And I was ready to let it go, but I needed it for Rowan, not Kirra.

"Ellie, she might be scared, but that doesn't mean that she's not dangerous. Cornered animals don't think, they attack." She jerked her head to the right. "Get out of the way. Now."

"You're the one who doesn't understand, Kirra," I pleaded, edging my way closer to be in front of Rowan. "She hasn't attacked us. She's just terrified. Let me try to help her first. Please, Kirra," I pleaded, clasping my hands together.

She stood still, her grip tight on the pistol. I couldn't read her. There wasn't a flicker in her eyes or an ounce of hesitation in her body.

She's not going to give me a chance. Disappointment slipped over me, desperation rushing in. *Damn it, Kirra.* I closed my eyes and released my power, pushing compassion into her heart and mind, smoothing the sharp spike of fear that had her pulling out her tranquilliser gun in the first place. As soon as I felt her fear ease enough that I thought she would give me the two minutes I needed, I pulled my power back and harnessed it within me. I needed it for Rowan.

"Lower the gun, Kirra," I instructed her. This needed to work. *Was the compassion I'd instilled in her enough?*

For a moment, she didn't respond, holding her ground. And then I saw the finger she'd wrapped around the trigger tremble, her eyes darkening slightly as she lowered the pistol just a fraction.

I didn't waste any time. I turned around slowly and focused on Rowan. She'd kept her distance, snarling and pacing back and forth as though she were wondering what to do with us. I took a step forward toward her, and she let loose a growl, warning me.

"Easy, Rowan," I answered softly. "I'm here to help."

This time she raised her front paw as though to step forward, anger thickening her howl. *She's not going to let me anywhere near her,* I realised. *She has no reason to trust me. To trust anyone.*

All I could do was believe in my power. It sat there, right at the surface, and I reached out, using it to connect to Rowan's pain. I wasn't even hoping to get her back to her human form, all I wanted to do was bring her pain down a notch so that she could listen to reason and not be so terrified. I looked her in the eyes, their youthful bright blue shimmering with unshed tears, while her ears were set flat against her head, her teeth still bared at me. I focused on the overwhelming agony that seemed etched into every part of her being and started to pull some backward to me—*into me*—until I felt a violent shove, severing my focus *and* the connection.

"What the Hades?" I shouted as I lost my balance and fell backward onto my butt, Rowan's paws retreating from where they'd slammed me down. I'd never connected with a shifter in their animal form so intensely before, but I could have sworn she'd just kicked me out of her mind and out of her space.

"Rowan?"

She glared at me. Anger pulled her ears back tight against her head as she circled me.

"El!" Kirra's voice cut through the air as I felt her fear spike sharply. She had her pistol raised and was tracking Rowan with every step she was taking. "Are you okay?"

I turned to look at her briefly, lashing my power out at her to top up the compassion that had kept her at bay before. "I'm fine, but I'd be a lot better if you lowered that gun again, Kirra."

The words had barely left my mouth when I felt Rowan's anger snap like a tightly strung wire, catching my attention again. With impossible speed, she pounced and sunk her teeth into my calf, the burning feeling of her canines as they tore through my skin setting my nerves alight. I screamed with the pain, crushing my eyes shut instinctively. Almost instantaneously, I heard Kirra shoot her gun. As I opened my eyes, I saw Rowan stumbling, her legs collapsing underneath her body as she closed her eyes, her bloodied mouth falling slack against her paws. The only movement coming from her now was the slow rising and falling of her chest.

Kirra put away her pistol and rushed over to check on me as she called in help again. She knelt down next to me, all the while her eyes darting between Rowan and me.

"Show me where she got you," she asked, rifling through the first aid kit in the pack for something. I hesitated. I could already feel the wound healing, the layers of skin knitting together faster than anything any human could understand.

"Don't worry, it looked worse than it was. I'm fine," I told her, sitting up properly and pulling my leg closer to me.

"There's blood all over your pants, Ellie. Show me." Kirra started pulling up the material to see what was left of the bite. Or the graze, which was now becoming a light welt. By the time Kirra looked up at me, her eyes wide, it was gone.

"You're something else, aren't you?" It should have been a question, but Kirra wasn't asking.

"Something else is a good way to describe it." I watched her face for signs of her reaction, although I was getting used to not finding much to give away how she felt. Her poker face was good. Great, even. It made me wonder what had happened in her life for her to perfect it so well.

"There's more to all of this. Isn't there?"

Another statement. I met her dark brown eyes with my own. "Do you want me to lie to you?"

She raised an eyebrow. "You haven't already?"

I pursed my lips for a second before answering. "Point taken. I'm immortal, and she's a shifter. And I'm hoping you're as straightforward as you seem because if I'm trusting you, I need you to trust me."

I let my words hang in the air as I pulled my pant leg back down before getting to my feet, dusting off my clothes and walking over to Rowan. I knelt over her and put my hand on her chest, my worry relieved by the comfort of her steady breathing.

"She'll be okay. It just knocked her out. But I'm guessing the Rangers I just called in aren't going to be the help I thought we needed," said Kirra, who'd come to stand next to me.

"No, they're not," I confirmed, looking up at her. I could feel Kirra's compassion still amplified by my power, helping her to accept what I'd told her. Guilt crowded at the edges of my emotions as I slipped my power alongside it and gently amplified it with mercy.

"Lesson learned, I guess," Kirra said dryly. "I've called it in already, so that horse has bolted."

"Can you call Gabe and the others? We're going to need them to get here fast," I asked as I shifted my position so that I could place Rowan's head on my lap. Kirra nodded and took a couple of steps away, jumping on the walkie-talkie immediately.

I left her to it, returning my focus to Rowan. I started stroking her fur just above her eyes. The pain radiating from her made me want to pull away, to protect myself, but I held strong and kept it up in the hope that it would help calm her somehow.

Emotionally, touching her was like putting my hand into an open fire and watching it burn. My hand stilled, the movement of stroking her fur overwhelming me, even as I tried to focus on accessing my power.

For the last few months, it had been straining at its confines, trying desperately to get me to unleash it as often and as intensely as possible, only being reined in by my own conscience. Yet now, when I needed it most—when *Rowan* needed it most—it was like it was repelled, pushed away, and impossible to coax forward. I'd only ever been in the mind of a shifter—a Faoladh—willingly before, and my powers had worked without hesitation, but Rowan was not a willing participant, and, somehow, she was blocking me from helping her.

Tension filled my body, though whether it was because of Rowan's pain or my power's impotence, I wasn't sure. I only knew that when Rowan woke, this pain would be as raw and as horrific as it was at that moment, if not stronger, so I had to do whatever I could to ease some of it for her.

Wrestling with my power, I forced it forward and into Rowan, the connection unstable but present. Slowly, deliberately, and sluggishly, I felt some of her pain come to me, my hand absorbing it and replacing it with the mercy she needed. It was nowhere near enough to sate the burning agony within her, but I had to hope it would make some difference because I couldn't think of another way to help her out of this torment.

The pain itself was senseless, directionless, pure terror and anguish. It didn't seem to have any purpose except the overwhelming sensation of needing to get out of my skin, to shed the restraints of my humanity and … and … there was nothing, just emptiness.

Rowan had shed her human skin for her wolf form because it couldn't contain her agony. It was the only way she felt she could survive. And now her trauma had locked her in a prison of her own making. My mind raced with possibilities—and concerns—as to why I couldn't get past the barrier she'd put up inside her mind.

Tears welled in my eyes, blurring my vision. I wiped them away before they fell, a voice breaking into my thoughts from a few feet away.

"Ellie? Ellie! Are you okay?" Clara panicked. My eyes filled with tears again even as I looked to find her. Gabe and Farron appeared only a few seconds behind her.

"Clara, she's okay. She's fine," Kirra reassured her but grabbed her arm to stop her from coming any closer. "You need to stay here. It's not safe."

"What happened? Why is she unconscious?" Gabe demanded, confusion ringing clearly in his voice. "Is she okay?"

"The wolf bit Ellie. I had to knock her out with a tranquilliser," Kirra explained. "It's perfectly safe and will wear off in a couple of hours."

Gabe's face was suddenly red, and it sure wasn't heatstroke. He exchanged a look with Farron. "If they're right, we're too late," Farron muttered under his breath to Gabe.

"We need to get her home, Kirra," Gabe advised. "We appreciate your help to find her, but we can take it from here."

"I'm okay, Clara. Thanks for asking, boys," I said as loud as I dared, given that I still had Rowan's head in my lap. "Already healed, so you don't need to worry."

Gabe and Farron exchanged a look between themselves that I couldn't quite decipher, but I assumed it had something to do with how open I'd just been in front of Kirra. "I had to tell her the truth, that I'm immortal and Rowan's a shifter. The jig was up, and she's called Rangers for backup."

"I wouldn't have believed it myself if I hadn't seen that wound disappear in seconds." Kirra interrupted. "But I did. And don't kid yourself. I want a full explanation later, but right now, if you want to beat the Rangers out of here, you've gotta move fast. The Rangers are about thirty minutes out. That's all the time you have. If you're not gone by then, your shifter will be theirs."

Gabe and Farron didn't need another word, the two of them launching into action. "Clara, can you call the others and have them bring the car to the far side, as out of sight as possible?"

She nodded and pulled out her phone, dialling as quickly as she could.

Farron came straight to me and crouched down, placing his hands under Rowan's head as he eyed Gabe, who was at her feet. "Ready?" Farron asked.

"Ready," Gabe confirmed. The two of them managed to lift Rowan from the bush floor, slowly and gently, distributing her weight between them.

"Wren is on the way with the car. She had Ever flash her to the car park," Clara explained with a whisper. With Rowan in Gabe and Farron's hands, I got up and moved over beside Clara.

"They just flashed. In public?" I whispered back so that Kirra couldn't hear, concern tightening my mouth.

"El, it was like from bush to an empty car park, calm your farm," she reassured me.

"I guess we'd have a bigger issue explaining a wild wolf coming out of the bush. Can we help with anything?" I asked Gabe and Farron.

Kirra answered before either of them could. "Why doesn't one of you wave down the car? The other one can go ahead of Gabe and Farron and keep any stray branches out of their way. I'll cover up the blood and tracks and call in a change of location."

"I'll head up to the bush line and get their attention," Clara volunteered and started on her way.

"That leaves you to clear the bush ahead, Ellie," Gabe noted. "And Rowan isn't getting any lighter."

"Yep, just one second." I paused and caught Kirra's attention. "Thanks for doing this."

"It's going to bite me on the ass, you know that, right?" Her words had a bitter tang to them. "I made a promise to you, and I'll keep it, but it's going to make me look like a fool, and I'm not going to pretend to be excited about it."

"I understand, and I'm sorry. Your help won't be forgotten."

"I'm banking on that. I do this for your people. You owe me one for mine. We clear?"

I nodded and shook her hand. "You have my word."

"You better get on with it." She gestured toward Gabe and Farron, who still held Rowan in their arms.

I gave her a small smile and then turned away, walking toward the path Clara had set in the bush. I turned my focus to holding branches out of the way and clearing the path for Gabe and Farron. It made the trek a lot smoother, and we were back at the bush line within ten minutes. Wren and Clara held the back door of the SUV open and had a blanket laid out for Rowan already.

"Let's get her in and then get out of here," Wren instructed, her eyes darting back and forth along the bush line. It was clear for the moment, but there was no guarantee it would stay that way for much longer, and the time before the Rangers would get there was dwindling fast.

Gabe and Farron moved with purpose, easing her into the SUV and onto the blanket so that Ever could gently pull the blanket, and Rowan, further into the safety of the car. Once Rowan was ensconced inside, Ever jumped into the passenger side and shut the door. Gabe took the car keys from Wren, and Farron jumped into the backseat on one side of Rowan while Wren slipped in on the other side of her.

"Are you guys going to be alright?" Clara asked. "At least to get back to Denny's?"

"We'll be fine, Clara. I'll ride here in the back and keep an eye on her vitals while Gabe gets us home, and we'll go from there," Wren reassured her.

"We've got it under control," Farron reiterated before shutting the car door.

I walked over to the driver's side door and caught Gabe's attention. "We'll meet you at Denny's as soon as we can get there. Let us know if there's anything else we can do, okay?"

"There may not be much any of us can do," Gabe grumbled, his gaze distant.

His words made me pause. It didn't make any sense. We'd found Rowan. Everything that came after should be easy, or at least easier than finding a wolf in the middle of a bushfire. My thoughts were interrupted by him starting the SUV. The motor growled aggressively, making me take a step back.

"We'll see you soon," I told him, only a moment before they took off down the track and back to the road.

"It's just us, for the moment anyway." I gave Clara a quick hug. "You should be proud. The protection spell kept her safe, and the scrying spell led us right to her. Can't ask for much more than that." Pride made my eyes mist with tears.

"Well, I'd probably like it better if you didn't have a ton of dried blood on your pants," Clara declared, nudging me lightly as we walked the same path the car had taken. "It's much easier to forget that you're a fully fledged Goddess again when there's blood involved."

"The good news is it's just scary looking. It's not actually scary." I paused to pull up my pant leg. "See?"

"Yeah, if you weren't a Goddess, there's a good chance you would have been six feet under, Ellie. Which is not that reassuring at all," Clara scolded me.

"Alright, alright, I understand. Be more careful. Noted," I agreed.

"Thank you." This time, Clara hugged me.

"But I am a Goddess. I can't die if I have my powers." I wiggled my fingers at her.

"Noted." Clara mimicked me, sarcasm lacing her tone. "I'm going to call Declan and Emrys. I think Olive is with them."

"I'll buzz Jack and make sure he's on his way back too." I pulled out my phone and found his contact. We both stopped for a moment and split apart as we focused on the calls.

"Hi Jack, have you heard the news?" I asked when he answered.

"Yeah, love, I have. Lit a fire under my ass, it did. I'll be there soon," he replied.

"We're just tracking down Declan, Emrys, and Olive, and then we'll be on our way too."

"I've already got 'em sorted," Jack said. "It might be a better idea if you didn't come by, love. This is clan business now."

It was the second time in less than half an hour that one of the Faoladh had made me feel unwelcome. Only this time, Jack was spelling it out for me. The change in attitude was so sharp and sudden that I felt completely off kilter.

"Jack, don't do this. Let us help. I might be the only one who can get through to her," I asked a little cautiously. It was usually Denny I dealt with most, but now that she was out of action, Jack was the boss. We didn't have the same relationship that Denny and I had, but he had never been like this before, not with me anyway.

"Your part is done, Ellie. Please leave it be." With that, Jack hung up, and I was left with the dial tone. I looked at the phone in my hand and tried to make sense of what had just happened.

I'd been dismissed. There was no doubt about that. It didn't make sense because Rowan was very clearly full of agony, and I was the only one who could help her release that, otherwise, it could take years for her to process everything. I couldn't imagine leaving a young girl alone, in her shifted form, to deal with it all by herself.

It didn't make any sense. The phrase echoed in my head, just as it had earlier. I turned around and walked over to Clara, who was wrapping up her own phone call.

"That was *weird*," Clara said, with a bewildered look on her face. "They're all on their way already. There's literally no one for us to let know or to pick up. It's just us." She put her phone back in her pocket and looked at me, crossing her arms.

"Why bother telling us to round everyone up if they'd already done it?"

"Does it feel like they're trying to make sure we take longer to get back?" Clara asked, momentarily distracted by the sight of the Ranger's utility vehicle driving past us. "We should walk a little faster. We don't want to get caught up in all that."

"Well, Jack just flat out told me that we weren't needed anymore. That it was 'pack business' and to leave it alone. It doesn't feel right."

Another influx of utility vehicles showed that more Rangers were arriving, which spiked my anxiety. "Let's get into the car and head over. At least we can try to sort it out from there," I told her. "I hope they don't give Kirra too much hassle over the disappearing wolf situation."

"She's really taking one for the team," Clara agreed as we made it to the car.

"We've used our favour. I'll just have to wait to see what she calls in when it's her turn," I replied as I unlocked the car. Dirt coated the footwells of the car from the dusty ground of the bushland we'd been trekking through. Flicking over the ignition, I reversed out and headed down past the coordination hub and toward Denny's house.

Whatever weird stuff was going on, I was determined to find out.

CHAPTER FIFTEEN

THERE WAS NO DOUBT that we were the last ones to arrive at Denny's house. The others' cars were all parked out front, and yet there wasn't a soul to be seen. I got out of the car, and Clara followed.

"This isn't getting any less weird," she commented as we walked up to the front door.

"I'm with you on that. I wouldn't have thought they'd have been that far ahead of us, to be honest," I agreed. We got to the front verandah and headed to the door. I took a deep breath and loudly knocked a couple of times. A few moments passed, then minutes, and still, silence. I knocked again. Louder.

Same thing. Silence.

"Ugh, let me give it a go. Knocking is not your strong point." Clara started banging on the door with her fist. At first, it seemed like she was going to get the same response as I had until the sound of footsteps approaching broke the quiet.

"Finally," Clara murmured under her breath.

Declan answered the door, his face drawn and sombre—the exact opposite of what I was expecting. *What in Hades was going on here?* My power could sense the confusion, anger, and frustration that exuded from him as though he were consumed by them all.

"Is everything okay?" Clara asked immediately, concern clouding her face as she stepped toward him almost instinctively.

"Uh, yeah, no. Not really." Declan pulled the door tighter to him as though he didn't want us coming inside. *Something was very, very wrong.*

"What do you mean, 'not really', Declan? What's going on?" I demanded. Declan just looked at me like he wasn't sure what to say. "If you're not going to explain Declan, then I'm going to find someone who will."

I pushed past Clara and shoved hard on the door, releasing it from his half-hearted grip and opening it wide enough for me to stride into the house. Clara followed behind me, Declan trailing last.

I turned back around to him when I realised that the kitchen and lounge were empty. "Where are they, Declan?"

"The door at the end of the hall—the garage," he answered, pushing his hands deeper into his pockets. Clara murmured something to him, and they stopped for a moment. I left them behind and headed toward the door he'd indicated.

Come Hades or Poseidon, I was going to find out what was going on.

As I approached the door, I could hear the murmur of voices behind it—not enough to make out what was being said, but enough to work out that it didn't sound like a happy conversation. The same emotions I sensed within Declan emanated even more intensely from those on the other side, amplified by the sheer number of them. I wrapped my hand around the doorknob and opened it, my arrival causing the debate to come to a screeching halt.

The garage was large, tacked onto the end of the house. It could easily have fit three cars, made of brick walls and a plastered ceiling peppered with down lights. Only one of the three bays for cars actually had a car in it—the middle one. The furthest one had been converted to some kind of plywood-framed room, while the first bay that I'd just walked into was lined with cupboards and a wooden bench top littered with tools and various projects, ending with a white fridge just before the roller door.

Most of the group were in various spots, leaning against the bench top or sitting on it, while Jack and a couple of others were sitting on upside-down milk crates. Not a single one looked as though this was where they wanted to be.

"I knew she wouldn't stay away," Farron stated, shaking his head with a sly smile.

"Sometimes your powers of observation overwhelm even me, Farron," I quipped, my power practically licking its lips at the tension that was overflowing from every single person in the room.

Not to mention the special brand of agony that was Rowan.

"What's going on? Where is Rowan?" I demanded, putting my hands on my hips. "What's with telling me to stay away, Jack? Even if I didn't have the ability to pick up emotions, I would have been able to tell something was wrong. Is she okay? Where is she?"

"She's here," Jack answered, his eyes downcast. "But she's far from okay, love."

"Jack, I don't understand what you mean. She was unconscious but alive. And now, this?" I held my palms upward and shrugged.

"She's physically okay," Wren confirmed. "Dehydrated and exhausted, but okay, all things considered."

"I appreciate that, Wren, but you can understand that I need to see her for myself because you're all making me wonder."

Gabe shared a look with Jack, who gave him a small nod. "She's over here," he said, beckoning me over to the built-in room in the garage. As I approached, he opened the door, and I could see Rowan inside, her wolf form still curled up asleep from the tranquilliser, but this time she was locked inside a metal cage with just a bowl of water and some kibble.

"What in all of Hades is going on?" I hissed at him, rage boiling up under the surface of my skin as I made to step toward the doorway to her. "That's damn awful. She's a kid. Why is she locked up like that?"

"Ellie, please," he pleaded, placing his hand on my arm to stop me from going any further. "Let us explain."

"I don't have the patience to be mucked around any longer, Gabe. You wanted help to find Rowan, and I gave it, and now you've got her caged up like a feral animal. Not like the family you said she was. Not like the child she is. I never would have helped if I'd known you would do that to a traumatised kid," I said to him—to all of them—through gritted teeth.

"We didn't know this was going to happen," Jack said quietly from behind me, his tall but aged frame stooped with what my power told me was, without hesitation, shame.

"Sit." He gestured to one of the milk crates that were scattered around the garage.

"I'm not sitting down, Jack," I answered as I moved closer to where they were all gathered, keeping one eye trained on the room where Rowan was being kept. I bit the inside of my mouth to keep myself from saying something I might regret. "Please just explain what the Hades is going on here before I lose my mind."

"You know that Faoladh are vegetarians, right?" he said rhetorically.

I nodded anyway. "It's hard not to with the tonnes of tofu you all go through."

"It's not because we care about animals, at least not the way you think we do," he continued. "Thousands of years ago, when our kin were simple fae, we were blessed by the Morrigan with the ability to take the form of a wolf, at will, as a reward for our loyalty. That was the way it was for years until one of our kin went rogue and killed a human. No one knows why, but that doesn't matter squat now. The Morrigan was pissed at the abuse of her blessing, and she put a curse upon us." Jack stopped suddenly, a cough racking his body. "One of you louts pick it up for me, will ya?" he asked before another round got him.

Wren moved quickly to get Jack water from a fridge in another corner of the garage while Gabe took over. She tried to hand it to him, but he batted it away.

"Whiskey," he muttered. "It's not the day to be sober."

Gabe winced at Jack before continuing the story. "When the Morrigan discovered what had happened, she cursed the Faoladh to forever stay in wolf form if we were to taste the flesh of another human or animal again. Worse yet, the Faoladh who instigated the curse would be driven mad by their sin until it would destroy the entire clan it belonged to."

Silence, save for Jack's swig of whiskey, filled the room.

"So, you're saying that because Rowan bit me, she's cursed to stay a wolf forever?" I clarified. *Had I caused her to be damned to the pain she was in? No, it wasn't possible. She was in that state when I found her*, I rationalised.

"Don't forget the part where she'll go crazy and try to kill all of us," Farron added.

My instinct warred. *She couldn't be doomed because of one moment of fear.* But I knew better. Half of the Greek Pantheon was the embodiment of one bad decision ruining their lives. Yet, still, I couldn't wrap my mind around it.

I'd been around the world a few times in my thousands of years of life, and I knew that people and their beliefs weren't to be dismissed. Sometimes I wondered which came first, the belief or the basis for it, but that didn't matter in this situation. This wasn't some great philosophical argument atop Mount Olympus, where we could debate all night with bottles of wine and feasting and then recoup days of sleep afterward.

This was going to determine Rowan's life and, very possibly, her death. They had to be sure. The people I'd come to call family had to be sure. *I* had to be sure.

"I think I'll take that seat now," I said quietly as I sat down on the milk crate, adjusting a little to account for my sizable backside. They weren't designed for a plus-size woman to sit on. There was no doubt about that. "You're all sure of this?"

I looked around the room once I asked. Jack nodded, as did Emrys and Farron. Gabe, Wren, and Declan looked less certain, but none of them spoke in opposition to it.

"Has anyone considered that Ellie is a Goddess?" Clara spoke up from her position at the door to the garage. Declan leant on the door jamb behind her.

"She's not human," he added.

A murmur passed through the Faoladh in the room, but it was Wren who spoke. "We've been debating that. Some of us think it might not activate the curse, but as

Farron pointed out, Rowan's been surviving by eating wildlife. There was a half-eaten bin chicken right by where you found her. Blood on her mouth. It's a pretty logical conclusion."

Gabe crossed his arms and leaned back against the workshop bench behind him. The lack of physical interaction between Gabe and Farron made it clear that they were on different sides of this argument, even if Gabe seemed resigned to the group's consensus.

"First, you're going to have to explain to me what a bin chicken is. There weren't any chickens anywhere near where we found her, so how can you be so sure?" I asked. That drew a laugh from Wren.

"We call them bin chickens because they tend to scavenge in rubbish bins and dumpsters, but it's actually the Australian white ibis. It's like a tall, white bird," she explained.

Ah, that's what she'd been eating. "Okay, okay." I leant my elbows on my knees and clasped my hands together. I knew that curses and blessings existed, but I wasn't going to just blindly accept them if there was even a chance that we could save Rowan.

Especially since she hadn't actually done anything yet, aside from nipping at me. Well—biting me—but that was neither here nor there.

"Ellie," Jack said loudly. "We have no choice. This is the way our kin have lived for thousands of years. We cannot risk our survival on the chance that Rowan didn't activate the curse when we know full well that she's both bitten you and eaten meat. It's one life for the whole clan." He looked at the floor and shook his head, pain straining his voice thin. "This isn't the first time it's happened. My father was lost to the curse over fifty years ago. There was nothing we could do. I don't like it any more than any of you do, but I will protect this family."

The words he was saying lashed out, sending pain coursing through my heart. And it wasn't just my pain. No matter which side of the debate they were on, every one of them was hurting as they tried to process it all.

"None of you want to do this," I said as I lifted my head up and looked around at them all. "There's no point in lying. I can feel it. There's got to be something that you can do. Can't you call upon the Morrigan and ask for her help?"

"The Morrigan isn't someone you can speed-dial, El," Emrys answered. "Denny's always said that it's a last resort. She hasn't been called on for centuries."

"This is kind of a last resort situation, isn't it?" I questioned. "Rowan's life hangs in the balance. Does it get more dire than that?"

"My father lost himself to his wolf. Ma was there when he put himself down, love. She'd have done anything to stop that happening." Jack reached out for his whiskey and downed what was left. "I'm just glad she's not here for this."

"Dad, you're not going to leave her out of this," Wren chastised him. "That's the whole reason she should be involved. She's the only one that's seen this before."

"And suffered badly for it, Wren. You really want to put her through that all over again?" Jack argued.

"If it means that she can help us stop whatever this is, it's worth it. She might be old, but she's strong and she can handle this," Wren challenged him. "I'm calling her." She pulled her phone out of her pocket and walked back into the house.

"At least someone is trying," Clara quipped angrily.

"We never wanted this, Clara," Emrys replied. "None of us."

"Well, it's what we got." Wren interrupted as she reappeared. "I've given her the rundown. Gran, you're on speaker. Go."

"For starters, you lot did a good job finding Rowan. Know that I'm grateful for all that you've done, even though it's come to this." Denny coughed, her voice sounding hoarse and small. "Your father was the first in a long while, Jack. If you call upon the Morrigan, she will exact a price—nothing is without cost. We chose not to for your father. Our clan had to survive. There were young pups to think of, a new home, the future—" she started coughing again, the line filled with the hacking cough that made us all hold our breath as we waited for her next one.

"Gran, are you okay?" Wren asked.

"I'm not an invalid, child. Just asthmatic," Denny scolded her. Wren rolled her eyes in response. "This is a clan decision. They won't let me out of this godforsaken place until I can breathe without hacking up a lung. Just remember that this is more than just the future of Rowan you're dealing with. It's the future of our clan—and you'll need to decide soon. The curse manifests on the next full moon." Coughing echoed down the line until it cut off, the same silence as before filling the room.

"You and I are gonna have words later." Jack gestured at Wren, who remained defiant, her arms crossed, and lips pressed into a firm line. "How can we sacrifice our own kin for a child we've never met?" Jack asked.

"I'm sick of this," Clara said indignantly. "All that effort to find her and save her, yet you're willing to kill her now?" She looked around at everyone and sighed angrily. "You've got to be kidding me!"

This time, she looked directly at Emrys and Declan. "You two, you're just going to let her die because you're a little *scared* she might go off? Like, you couldn't just stop her even if you wanted to. You're all big bad wolves when you want to be, but a little girl has you running scared?"

They both hung their heads, although at least Declan tried to interject. Clara was having none of it. She turned back to the group.

"I've seen you all do the impossible, and yet you're just sitting here, taking this as a hit and not even trying to find another way. You're all cowards, the lot of you!" she yelled before storming out of the garage.

"Clara, stop, please," Declan shouted after her. He cast a quick look back at the group and then at her before cursing. "I'm going after her. She's not wrong, you know." Then he took off.

I watched him go and turned around to the rest of them. "I know you feel strongly about this. Especially you, Jack. But do you think you could give us some time to try some different options? She's not hurting anyone right now. Surely, we can take some time to make sure we've tried everything?"

I resisted the urge to use my power to force compassion into him, even though I knew it would get me the answer I wanted. This was one of those moments when using it would mean that I had taken their agency and choice away, and I didn't want to do that to the people who had become like family to me. I wanted them to make the right decision themselves, to be the people I knew them to be. It didn't mean I wouldn't use my power if I had to, but it meant that if I did, it would break more than just my heart.

"Darl, I want this least of all of you, but I won't lose the family it's taken me so many years and sacrifices to build." He put his head in his hands, a beat passing before he looked up at me again. "The next full moon is three nights away. I'll give you until that morning, but that's it. I'm gonna leave you young'uns to it. I don't have anything left in the tank after all this." Jack stood then, looking older than his years, if that was even possible, and made his way out of the garage and back into the house.

Thank the Gods.

I sensed a release of tension from most of the group when Jack was finally gone. It lightened the load on my own shoulders, a load I hadn't realised had been pressing down so hard on me because of the amount of people carrying it.

It was heavy and awful and terrifying, but they *needed* to feel the stress and the apprehension about the decision they were making if there was going to be even a chance to stop it. If I took it away, I took away her only chance.

"Do you all really feel that way, the way Jack does?" I asked, watching their faces closely and letting my power taste their emotions. "Do you believe the curse is real?"

"You know where I stand," Farron answered. "I get that she's a kid, but if she's a kid that's gonna kill us, what do you expect us to do?"

"Not that my opinion's worth much, but I expect that you'd do everything you could before just resigning yourself to it. There's got to be something you can try." I tried not to sound exasperated. I'd come to learn that he always saw things in black and white, missing all the grey in between. It frustrated me that he seemed so willing to just accept that Rowan needed to die.

"Farron, we've never seen it happen," Wren responded. "But we've heard about it our whole lives. It's just always been something we've accepted. Denny accepted it, and she lost her husband."

"And we've never been asked to kill a kid before," Emrys interjected. "How do we even know that it's real? If our grandfather sacrificed himself, it never actually happened. I mean, I've never even seen the Morrigan, and we're supposed to take this all as truth without a second thought."

"Calm down, Em. That's why we're talking about it." Gabe tried to reassure him.

I looked at Wren. "If she turns back to human form, that will prove that she's not cursed by the Morrigan, right?"

"Well, yeah. I mean, the whole point of the curse is that you *can't* shift back, so if she *can,* that should be a pretty clear indicator that she's safe from it," Wren agreed.

"So," I said, looking around, "what makes you shift?"

"It's a choice," Gabe answered. "The same way you access your power, I guess. We call on the magick in our veins and will it to shift, then, you know, we shift. Going back to human form is the same in reverse."

"Does that mean that in wolf form, you retain some of your human thinking?" I tried to disguise the surprise his revelation had thrust on me.

"It's part of why we don't operate in a 'typical' pack way," Wren answered for him. "We're never wholly wolf or wholly human. We are both, always. Otherwise, we'd have activated the curse thousands of years ago because the wolf doesn't care if it eats meat—only the human part of us does."

How incredible. They really weren't like the typical werewolf shifters who lost all sense of their humanity in their wolf form.

I could see the anxiety that my power tasted running through her as she twisted her rings around her fingers, again and again, before switching directions and starting over, twisting the other way.

"It's not just a choice though. Remember when you broke your leg and passed out?" Emrys directed the question at Farron. "You were in wolf form when you broke it, but when you lost consciousness, you shifted back to human automatically."

"That's a good point," Wren agreed, but the light in her eyes dimmed a little. "But we already know that won't work. The tranquilliser that sedated Rowan would have triggered her to change otherwise. So that's a no-go."

"Are you sure?" Gabe asked.

"You can ask Ever. You'll get the same answer." She looked at the pixie who'd done a very good job of making themselves somehow smaller and inconspicuous in the room. I hadn't even noticed them until now.

"No chance. It would have worked already if it was going to," they said.

"What about the Coven?" Gabe looked at Emrys. "Do you think you could call your mum and see if she could get them together?"

"If there's a spell that could help, she'll be the one to know it. I'll track down Declan, and we'll see what we can come up with," he confirmed.

"Got it," Emrys agreed.

I turned back to Gabe and the others. "I could see if I can try to absorb some more of the anguish that she's feeling again?" I offered.

"Again?" Gabe asked. "You've already tried?"

"Of course. Rowan's pain was so intense, I tried to approach her and take the edge off, but then ..." I gestured to my bloodied pant leg. "As soon as Kirra tranquillised her, I gave it another shot, but honestly, I've never encountered emotions so strong and overwhelming. It's kind of like she's still stuck in the raw, sharp pain of the moment of her loss."

"And you couldn't absorb it all?"

"No, I could barely absorb any of it, but that doesn't mean it's not worth another try. Maybe it was too much, too soon. Or it could be because I've never used my power on a Faoladh in wolf form before. Only the Gods know, but I'm not ready to give up yet," I explained, wriggling a little before sitting up straight again because the milk crate had started to imprint on my backside.

"That's good because I think we've established that neither are we," Gabe agreed. "At least this is a start. We've got things to try. Now we just have to make them happen."

Farron mumbled something under his breath.

"Just say it out loud, you pain in the ass," Emrys shot at him.

"I was just *saying* that it's easy to say that when Jack isn't around. The lot of you don't have two strings of courage to rub together when he's in front of you," Farron smirked.

"I don't know about you all, but I need a beer," Ever piped up, discharging the tension in the room.

"You're on the money there." Emrys grinned. "I do my best thinking with a beer in hand." He made a move toward the fridge near Gabe and Farron, pulling out a couple of cold ones before handing them out. "Ellie?"

"No, thanks. I'm going to head inside and see if I can find Clara and a hot cup of tea." Getting up off the milk crate, I was fairly certain I had a diagonal square pattern imprinted on my bottom. "I'm just glad we're on the same page. Hopefully, something will work."

I needed it to work.

Because if it didn't, I would have to risk everything I'd built with the Faoladh. I was not watching an innocent girl be killed because of an ancient curse that may or may not be in play.

CHAPTER SIXTEEN

I WATCHED THE SOFT rise and fall of Rowan's fur-covered chest as she slept the deep sleep of the sedated. It should have been reassuring, but each breath was like a tick of the clock toward the deadline Jack had set. Every minute seemed to be working against us, taunting us with our failures. We were almost six hours in, and nada, zip, nothing.

Ticking clock or not, once I'd found Clara and Declan, we'd collected Zane and Alora and headed home so that they could wind down. The whole time, I couldn't shake the feeling of being mentally kicked out that I'd encountered in Rowan, and it played on mind as we went through our usual evening routine.

Why hadn't my powers worked on her? The thought repeatedly wound through my mind, possibilities coming and going but finding no real answer. I debated summoning my mother, but I wasn't sure this was her area of expertise. Asclepius, however, might be more useful.

Unfortunately, Zane had noticed our lack of attention and taken it as a challenge. He'd worked out that if he dropped a poop pellet every few feet, Clara or I would chase him to try and stop him. It was only when we stopped running after him that he got bored with building up a pile in the hallway.

It had taken all my patience not to just drop to the floor and scream, but given Clara's barely contained frustration, I knew better than to start a release we couldn't stop. I'd offered to absorb some of her anger and replace it with some compassion, but she'd given me a stare that rivalled Medusa's.

Once the kids were asleep, I'd offered to take the first shift, but Clara had insisted on staying home with them so I could try to work on absorbing some of Rowan's pain. With the fire that still hadn't settled in her eyes and the waves of red pulsing through her hair, I was not about to argue.

Although, facing this failure firsthand was not my idea of a good time. With that thought, I closed my eyes and sent a call out to Asclepius.

Hopefully, he would answer. Quickly.

My wish was granted faster than I could make it out of the house and into the car.

"Good Gods, Asclepius!" I jumped as he appeared an inch or so in front of me.

"Apologies, my Goddess, I didn't mean to frighten you, simply to answer your call with haste." He bowed slightly before meeting my gaze.

"You don't have to do that," I told him, placing my hand on his shoulder. "I'm grateful you answered, especially earlier. You helped my friends immensely, thank you."

"It was my honour to assist the daughter of Nyx." He pressed his hands together. "The older lady did not take too kindly to my intervention, but the man, he was more accepting."

"I can't thank you enough. I don't mean to call on you again so quickly, but I'm having trouble helping a young wolf shifter. Every time I get inside her mind, she kicks me out again. I've never encountered it before," I explained. "I don't know what to do."

"This wolf, she's not of our Pantheon?" he asked, furrowing his thick, grey brow as he processed the information.

"Yeah, she's from the Celtic Pantheon. I've been able to help others of her kind before, but for some reason, I can't help *her*." I threw my hands up in frustration, accidentally dropping the car keys on the ground.

Asclepius leaned down and gently placed his hand on my elbow as I collected the keys and stood back up again. "Eleos, even Gods have limitations."

"Oh, that I know, trust me." I gave him a small smile. "But I can't let her down. Her life depends on it."

"It's possible that her wolf won't accept your presence or that the magick of the two Pantheons interacting is causing you to be repelled from her mind. Either way, your endeavours, while worthy, may be fruitless," he warned with kindness in his eyes but sorrow in his heart. Our commonality as healers made me feel heard, even if what I was being told wasn't what I wanted to hear.

"Thank you, Asclepius. Your counsel is appreciated."

"As you wish, Goddess." He pressed his hands together and disappeared into the ether again.

Gods, I missed being able to do that.

By the time I got back to Denny's, it was obvious that things hadn't improved in the time we'd been gone. Wren and Emrys had settled on different sides of the room, him with a beer and her with a strong, almost stinky coffee. I headed over to where Rowan lay, still in her wolf form, within the metal cage.

"While there's time, there's hope, Wren," I told her as I passed. "Why don't you go take a break, trade out with someone else for a little while?"

She nodded but avoided my gaze as she rose and left the room without another word. I could feel the shame and disappointment coming off her in waves, my power reaching for it, wanting to absorb it and replace it with something better, something kinder.

No, I admonished my powers. *We have work to do here with Rowan.* I could almost feel it curl back to me, reticent at the reprimand. As I entered the small room where she lay caged, I sat down cross-legged and placed my hands gingerly through the metal squares so I could touch her. Usually, I didn't even have to be near a person to impact them, but then, Rowan was a wolf.

I let my fingers nestle within the fur covering the side of her body, the feel soft and downy, her skin warm and breath even. My power was more optimistic than I was. Tendrils of it reached out, seeking her pain eagerly as though hungry to consume it. The first contact it made with her agony only excited it more, just as it had the last few times I'd tried. A pulse of her pain hit me, and I winced, the physicality of it surprising me. I bit down on the side of my lip, gritting my teeth against it, pushing my power further into her mind, a millimetre at a time, edging in slowly.

The sensation of siphoning her anger slowly started coming through, filtering through the magickal tracts within me as I released whatever compassion I could through those same paths and into Rowan. I'd managed to maintain it for five, maybe six minutes at the longest, and I was determined to last longer this time.

I *needed* to because I didn't know what else I could do if it didn't work—if Asclepius was right, and my power was useless against her wolf.

With each tendril that advanced into Rowan's mind, it was as though she responded with fire, burning the tips of them until they caught alight with her pain and trauma. I pushed further, the pain of it—of her mind—burning my power up from the inside the deeper I got, until I was no longer absorbing her pain but *experiencing* it alongside her. Every part of my power that was touching her mind started lighting up with flames of agony until I could no longer withstand it—until my power withdrew, and I couldn't tell where the burnt tendrils ended and Rowan's pain began.

"Oh Gods, oh Gods, oh Gods." The words slipped from my lips like a chant as I felt my power shoot back inside me with such ferocity it felt like my whole body was experiencing whiplash at once. "That ... that ... Oh, good Gods."

I took stock of myself. The natural recoil from Rowan's mind had sent me physically flying back against the wall of the small room, my back hitting the plasterboard hard before I slid to the floor. I braced my arms against the floor to keep myself upright. I looked up and checked on Rowan, her sleeping form unchanged as though nothing had happened at all.

"Whoa!" Gabe exclaimed, eyes wide with surprise, as both he and Emrys crowded the door to the small room. "What the hell was that?"

"That ..." I paused, catching my breath, "was Rowan kicking my power out of her mind." My head fell into my hands. "That ... was failure."

"Are you okay?" Emrys asked, worry clear on his face. "She's been kicked out every time so far," he updated Gabe, "but this was the most violent."

"And the quickest," I added, disappointment dripping from my words.

"But you're a Goddess," Gabe asked. "She's a kid wolf. How is it you can't overpower her?"

"I think Asclepius was right," I answered. They both looked at me questioningly, so I explained. "Rowan's in wolf form, and my powers are meant for humans. She's rejecting me, or her Celtic magick is. Either way, I can't get a foothold." I looked down at my hands as they continued to tremble beyond my control.

"I don't know what else to do," I confessed. I wiped my hands down my face and then clasped them together. "Have the rest of you been able to come up with anything?"

"Olive is working with her Coven on any spells they could try; Ever's talking with the pixies, but that's a long shot; and Jack, he's informed the family back home, but ..." Gabe trailed off.

"But what?" Emrys prompted him, his eyes narrowing as he caught his gaze.

Gabe sighed. "They're devastated, but their fear is greater. You don't know what it's like over there. They take the curse very seriously. Some of them are even vegan just to avoid any possible invocation of the curse. Rowan's grandmother, Siobhan, is terrified that waiting will anger the Morrigan."

My breath caught at the thought of Rowan's own grandmother pushing for her death.

"I know how horrible it seems, Ellie, but you have to understand that they're terrified that the curse will destroy their clan too. Her obligation is to keep the clan alive, even if it costs the life of her granddaughter."

"It makes no sense. How could I have more faith that Rowan is still in there—that she is still good—than her own kin?" I asked through gritted teeth. "There is no true good or evil in this world. It's never been as simple as that, and this is no exception. Rowan is not all bad, just because she did what was needed to survive, to protect herself. Just because things have always been one way doesn't mean that they should stay that way. There must be an answer, Gabe, a way to fix this without killing a young girl."

The silence that met my words was enough to invoke pure fear in me, sending me back to a time when I had no choice but to tend to the dying and the dead because of the wishes of the higher, mightier Gods and Goddesses. I might have been over three thousand years old, but at that moment, I felt as weak and as powerless as I had as a child. It was easy, comforting even, to believe that as a Goddess, I was stronger than all other things, but the truth was nastier and more complicated than that. You could only ever be as strong as the person who leads you, and at that moment, I didn't think Jack was strong enough to fight the pull of his history, his ancestors, and their ancient lore.

"I can't do this," I whispered, though it might as well have been a roar for the silence it was spoken into. "I can't try and fail, and try and fail, and try and fail again, all while Jack is planning Rowan's death on the other side of that door. What we're doing is not working." My voice cracked on the last couple of words.

Gabe crossed the room and knelt to look me in the eye. "None of this is easy, Ellie. Not one bit. If you need a break, take it because we need to know we gave it our all. If Rowan has to die, we need to know that we did everything we can. *That's* when we can give up. Until then, go and take a break. We'll stay and follow up with Ever and Olive."

I met his gaze, nodding slowly. "You're right. She doesn't need my emotions when hers are so overwhelming already. I'll take ten and go check in on Mason. I should be alright after that." Gabe stood up and held out his hand, which I took gratefully, using it for leverage as I got to my feet.

"I'll be back soon. Just ... just take care of her, okay?"

Emrys and Gabe both gave small nods, their focus shifting to their phones as I left the garage and headed down the hall. I prayed to any Gods or Goddesses who would listen that I wouldn't run into Jack. I couldn't contend with facing him right then. Fortunately, I didn't have to. The house was huge and long, but I made quick work of the hallways and found the guest bedrooms quickly. I'd gotten used to them when we'd stayed here while Halfling House was getting rebuilt, the whole time the Faoladh becoming more like family than friends.

And now, this.

The second door I opened revealed Mason, his trademark snore resurfacing every couple of breaths, as he lay on his side, one muscular leg thrown out of the covers. From the door, all I could see was the slight curl of his hair even where it was pressed against the pillow—only one because he was convinced two would crick his neck—which, by all rights, looked in good alignment as it led to the lean muscle of his back, the skin tanned and smooth, as it disappeared under the summer quilt Denny still had on the bed.

I closed the door and climbed into the bed, snuggling in next to him until almost every part of me was touching every part of him. Closing my eyes, I breathed in his scent and let my body relax as much as I could without forgetting the stakes.

"Mmm, miss me, huh?" he murmured as he rolled over so we were face to face, even though his eyes remained closed.

"Always," I answered, kissing him softly on his lips and settling into the crook of his arm. The warmth of the compassion that simmered inside him felt like a protective spell that pushed the rest of the world away for the smallest of moments, but nowhere near long enough.

"Do we have good news yet?" he asked, finally opening his eyes to look at me, his lazy half-grin gorgeous combined with his sleep-mussed hair.

"We found her," I told him.

He wrapped his arms around me tightly and drew me into a celebratory kiss. "Finally! That's great, El."

"No, Mason, it's not. It's really not." I placed my hand on his chest, creating some space between us. I could barely think when he looked at me like that. My voice hollow, I explained what had transpired after we found Rowan. "And now they want to sacrifice her," I finished, closing my eyes as I lay on Mason's arm and waited for him to absorb the whole sorry story.

The sound of his breathing hitched slightly, his emotions spiking enough that I knew he hadn't been expecting this news any more than I had. Cautiously, I opened my eyes and watched him pinch the ridge of his nose with his fingers.

"I just ... They're all on board with this?" The disbelief in his voice was almost tangible. My power could feel the complex web of emotions that were stirring within him.

"No, the others—Declan, Em, Gabe, Wren. Clara, of course—we're all trying to find a way to get Rowan to shift back into her human form so that we can prove that the curse isn't real. Jack's given us until the morning of the full moon, but that's disappearing so quickly."

"Any luck yet?"

"None. Every time I get inside her mind, she kicks me out again before I can even make a difference. Ever is talking with the pixies, and Olive is trying with the witches, but nothing yet." A tear forced its way out and trailed down my cheek. I went to wipe it away, but Mason beat me to it, his callused thumb wiping it away and then cupping my chin.

"El, sweetheart, you're trying, and that's the part that matters. With you on her side, Rowan has the best chance she could ask for. If anyone can do it, you can," he reassured me.

"That's the thing. I thought so too. I really, really did. I'm a *Goddess, for the Gods' sake!*" My frustration rushed out alongside my words. "I should be able to fix this, to fix her. To take away her pain and soothe her so she can come back to her human form and process her grief. All that's happening is that the more I try, the faster and harder she kicks me back out of her mind again. Asclepius thinks it's because her wolf is refusing me; our magicks are repelling each other."

Mason tucked one of my curls behind my ear, resting his hand in my hair before wiping those Gods-damned tears from my face. I *hated* crying. "You don't know what to do."

"I don't." I nodded, nuzzling my face into his hand. "I don't know how to help her."

The quiet encompassed us as I rested in his arms and tried to focus on my breathing instead of the overwhelming helplessness that was creeping into every nook and cranny inside of me. I felt Mason adjust himself, cradling me carefully so that he could sit up against the bedhead with my head in his lap. Minutes passed, and I closed my eyes, marking the passage of time by the strokes of his hand in my hair.

Mason was the first to speak, breaking the peace of the moments before. "Have you considered that maybe the anguish you're feeling from her isn't just emotion?" he asked curiously.

"What do you mean? Of course, it's emotion. I know what that feels like," I replied, tilting my head up so I could look at him. I felt slightly offended but tried to keep it in check because I knew he didn't mean it the way I was taking it.

"I get that, but it's like me. When you use your mojo on me, you calm my negative emotions and replace them with patience and compassion, but it doesn't wipe away the subconscious trauma of whatever caused the emotions. That's still there. Does that make sense?" he explained.

I stilled for a moment, time suddenly standing in place, as the pieces of the puzzle came together. "You're right ... Mason, you're a genius!" I sat straight up, his arms falling behind me and into my lap. "It's *subconscious*, not *conscious* emotion. I'm sorry, I've got to go." I jumped out of bed faster than I thought possible and shoved my shoes back on.

"Not that I'm done basking in the glory of being right, but where exactly are you going?" Mason asked as he propped himself up on his elbow, the sight enough to make my libido question my brain's choices.

"Home. Halfling House," I explained. "If I'm right, there's only one person who can help Rowan."

"Who?"

"Shade."

CHAPTER SEVENTEEN

I FELT SO STUPID that I hadn't thought of it before. I didn't want to get anyone's hopes up, so I asked Mason to keep it quiet until I could make sure I was right and then feigned needing to swap out with Clara. Declan's enthusiasm at the prospect was enough to keep the rest of them distracted by poking fun at him that I could slip out with no fanfare.

When I got back home to Halfling House, the chaos of the evening had passed. I hated leaving so much of the kids' care to Clara, but there wasn't much to be done about it. I gave her a quick update on the situation, and the look on her face screamed, 'I told you so' long before she actually said it.

I'd been trying to keep Shade away from this kind of thing, and yet here I was, about to drag him right into the middle of this disaster.

Shade had begged to be allowed to help last time, and I'd refused. All I'd wanted to do since the day I'd rescued his pale little self from that hospital in Canberra was protect him and give him the love he'd missed out on for most of his life. Part of that was keeping him away from all the crazy stuff that had been happening over the last few months, even if that had made him more pissed at me than grateful.

But that was parenthood, right? If your kids liked you, you were probably doing it wrong. It felt remarkably close to failure, but if the cost of keeping him out of all of this was Rowan's life, was it really worth it?

It didn't matter though. Not anymore. Whatever was going to happen would happen.

"I've got this, El," Clara reassured me as she checked the kids on the monitor. "Go eat your hat and get it over with."

I grimaced.

"You and I both know you should have let him come into his own on his own terms. Now, you don't have a choice."

"I know."

"You're the adult, El. If you can't admit when you're wrong, there's sure as Hades no chance that a teenager will learn to."

"I get it, I do. I just didn't want to bring him into all of this. I wanted to keep him out of it. For a while. Forever, ideally."

Clara chuckled quietly. "Forever was impossible. And a while was a long shot. He wants to help, don't stop him. He's ready."

"Is anyone really ready?" I asked, my mind filled with the memory of Clara and me, alone with the Animus that nearly killed me. She hadn't been ready for that. None of us had been.

"I was." Clara met my eyes, a knowing look in them. "You didn't think I was, I know. But the only thing worse than you deciding that for me would have been not giving me the chance to help anyway. Don't make that mistake with Shade."

She held my gaze unflinchingly, the clarity and truth in her words reflected in her eyes.

"Okay." I gave a small nod. "I won't."

It was time to talk to Shade.

I knocked on the basement door. Softly at first, then a little harder, after a couple of minutes passed with no answer. Eventually, it felt like I was thumping on the door so hard it would break it.

I'd paid enough to repair most of the place. I did not want to have to replace another door.

I knew he was down there; Shade was rarely anywhere else. The worst decision I'd made—in recent history anyway—had been to get him the set of noise-cancelling headphones he'd asked for. He couldn't hear a thing other than what was happening on the screen in front of him.

I hated just walking down into the basement and surprising him. He was a teenager. The Gods only knew what I could be walking in on, but I didn't have a lot of choice at this point. I opened the door and started down the stairs cautiously.

"Shade?" I called out every couple of steps, but it was no use. I could already hear whatever video game he was playing through his headphones. I'd warned him so many times that if he kept playing at full volume, he'd damage his hearing, but funnily enough, he managed not to hear that advice.

I crossed the basement floor and gently placed my hand on his shoulder, his body shooting up from his seat as he pulled his headphones off, shouting loudly.

"What the actual Hades?" he exclaimed, turning around to face me.

"Just me," I answered at a much lower decibel. "I tried knocking. Then shouting. And then, well, this ..." I trailed off.

"You could have called, El." Shade took in a ragged, deep breath and placed his headphones on their holder, before typing a goodbye into his computer setup and logging off the game.

"Called?" I asked.

"Called. On the phone. It comes through my headset, so I can answer it. Then I would have known you were coming down."

"Ah." I took in his explanation. "That makes sense. It just didn't occur to me to call you when we're in the same house."

"Yeah, well, you could always just scare the absolute crap outta me instead," he said in that deadpan, sarcastic way of his. "What do you want?"

"Sorry, I'll try to remember next time." I shrugged, ignoring the terseness of his tone. "Do you have a spot we can sit and talk?"

"Are you for real?"

I nodded. "I'm not 'for fake'."

He pulled his mouth into a deep frown and let out a deep sigh. "Whatever. Over there." Shade showed me to a spot in the corner of the room where he had a couple of bean bags set up. He walked over and dropped down on one of them, spreading out until he found a comfortable spot.

I followed and settled down on the other. It reminded me of the ancient *klinai* that I used to lounge on when I lived on Mount Olympus. Although they were decidedly more cloud-like as opposed to this, which felt like I was sitting atop a giant ball-pit in a bag.

"So ..." Shade said sullenly, looking at his hands, waiting for an answer. "Get to it. I have things to do."

"So," I copied, "do you think you could drop the angry teenager thing for a minute so we could have a real conversation?"

"Do you think you could stop being so high and mighty?" Shade glared at me. An awkward, tense silence sat between us for a few moments. When he realised I wasn't moving, he spoke again, but only after serving up a proper eye roll. "How can I be of service, your highness?"

"Nice." I stared back at him. "I need your help, but you won't be any good to me if you can't move past this anger you've had with me since the battle with the Animus."

The venom in his look wavered. "What?"

"I need your help."

"Seriously?" he asked, more disbelief in his voice than anger. "Real help? Not 'babysit the kids' help?"

"Real help," I confirmed. "But first, you need to understand that *I* wasn't trying to hurt you when I wouldn't let you help with the Animus. I made a promise to protect you, and I couldn't break that. I didn't think you were ready—"

"And it didn't matter what *I* thought. At least, not to you." Shade interrupted angrily, his temper flaring.

"It didn't," I admitted. "Not as much as it should have. What I understand now is that maybe it was more that I wasn't ready to have you in the line of fire yet."

"What's changed then?" This time, he sounded suspicious. "A couple of months?"

"No, Shade. Perspective. And necessity." I debated my next words carefully. "I need your help. And I know if I don't start asking for your help, you're going to start finding ways to insert yourself that might be more dangerous than the original threat."

Shade snorted and crossed his arms over his body. "No comment."

I laughed. "I appreciate the honesty."

"You didn't before."

"Shade, I've been a Goddess a long time—" I started to try and explain.

"You don't need to remind me every five minutes. I get it. Immortal, invincible, powerful Greek Goddess. It's impossible to forget."

"That's not what I was saying or what I was trying to say."

"Then say it," he demanded.

"I've been around a long time, but I've only been looking after you guys for the last twenty years. I don't always know what I'm doing, and sometimes, I make what I think is the right call, and it's not. And sometimes it's the other way around. I'm going to get things wrong—I clearly have with you—but I'm working on it. That's got to count for something, right?" I tried to meet his gaze, but he purposefully looked away. "I'm willing to try, and I mean really try, if you are. Please, Shade."

"You're just saying this because you need me all of a sudden," he said as he finally met my gaze. "You don't mean a word of it."

"Do you really believe that?" I asked, his black eyes holding mine.

Shade's shoulders drooped, and he broke eye contact, looking down at his hands as he rubbed his thumb into his palm. It was a calming technique I'd taught him not long after he'd come to live with me.

"No, I don't," he answered quietly. "This whole thing has just really sucked."

"For me too," I told him. We sat for a moment as the tension in the air slowly lightened enough that I could breathe properly again.

"This is about the missing wolf, right?" he asked, leaning forward. "You found her."

"How do you know that?" I asked. I hadn't kept him as in the loop as much I'd have liked to, so his knowledge surprised me.

"T's been around a lot while you've been gone. He reads the notes you leave."

"T?" I asked, thrown off a little. "Are you telling me you haven't been reading them?"

"Thanatos," he explained. "It's weird enough that he's a God, I'm not calling him *that* every time we talk. And yeah, I was pissed at you. I wasn't gonna read anything you left," he explained with a shrug.

Teenagers. "Oh, um, okay." Maybe that pairing had worked a little *too* well. I'd never known Thanatos to have a friend long enough to get a nickname, but there was a first for everything. The morning's events had proven that enough. I wasn't going to question it.

"The wolf?" he prompted.

"Rowan. Her name is Rowan," I told him. "When we found her, she was eating another animal, which is forbidden by the Faoladh. I'd thought they were just into animal rights or something, but not so much. Apparently, it's because of an ancient curse the Morrigan placed on them. The curse activates if they eat meat, trapping them in wolf form and sending them insane on the next full moon when they'll stop at nothing to destroy their clan."

"Heavy." Shade nodded. "Sounds like the stuff nightmares are made of."

Exactly, the thought flashed through my mind, *like the nightmares that come from deep sleep, from the unconscious.* I was feeling more and more certain that I was on the right track.

"Denny's still in hospital, so Jack's running the show. The Faoladh in Ireland are pushing to sacrifice her before the next full moon, but he's given us until the morning of the full moon to see if we can get her to shift back into human form. We're down to hours now. If we can't find a way to make that happen, they'll sacrifice her to save their clan," I explained, feeling the weight of it settling on his young shoulders.

"Nothing major then, just life and death stuff," Shade said sarcastically. "Why can't you calm her emotions? Wouldn't that help her shift back?"

"I've tried so many times, but her mind keeps rejecting me. I can barely siphon off the edge of her pain. I even asked Asclepius for help, but he thinks that it's the interaction of our different magicks because we belong to different Pantheons." I pushed a lock of hair behind my ear, glad that we were finally getting to the point. "I'm wondering if it might be a bit like Storm. Remember how she stayed in pup form whenever she was frightened? It took days to calm her enough for her to trust us with the vulnerability of her human form. I mean, I didn't have my powers then, but it makes sense, right?"

"Yeah, being in a different country, having a car accident, and watching your mother die all within twenty-four hours would be brutal. Way more traumatic than Storm, especially if she's old enough to get what's going on."

"Exactly. I've tried so many times to pull some of that terror from Rowan, but I think it's deeper, like buried in her subconscious. And I think that's more your territory."

"Aren't you afraid that she'll tear me to pieces or turn me into puppy chow or something?" he asked, his voice laced with sarcasm.

"Of course I am," I told him honestly. "But I'm also worried that by not asking you to help, Rowan might be stuck the way she is—terrified and alone—forever. Or worse."

Shade ran his hand through his hair and breathed out a big sigh. "And I'm your resident deep-sleep dude."

"Exactly. Do you think you could try?"

"Hell yeah." He answered more enthusiastically than I expected. "It's about time you took me off the bench and gave me a chance."

"Just promise me no stupid, half-formed, pre-frontal cortex crap, okay?" I said, hoping the seriousness of my tone was enough to pull him up. "I'll give you this chance, but you've got to prove to me that you can do this without putting yourself at risk unnecessarily."

"You won't regret this, Ellie. I'm ready. I'm more ready than I've ever been." He grabbed my hands and squeezed, a sly grin sneaking out. "Thanks for the chance. *Finally.*"

I squeezed him back.

And prayed to the Gods that I was making the right choice.

CHAPTER EIGHTEEN

THE DARKNESS OF THE night crawled across the mountains, spreading like a veil over the top of the trees and seeping down to the ground until only the stars glimmering in the sky separated the blackness of the sky from that of the forest that encircled most of Briarmoor. The rays of light from the moon taunting me with the fullness that was steadily creeping in.

I stood out on the verandah, waiting for Shade, watching as the world above me changed, hoping that the world around me would do the same.

"He's on his way out," Clara said from behind me. She wrapped the thick-knitted cream cardigan around her as though the weather had turned. "Olive just called to let me know that the spells haven't worked. They tried everything they could—transformation and restoration spells, healing tinctures, but no luck. It's only made Jack more certain that it's the Morrigan's curse blocking it." She came up beside me and nudged my shoulder before leaning against me. "Do you really think Shade can make this work when everything else has stuffed up?"

"Would I have swallowed my pride and literally begged him if I didn't?" I tried to infuse as much confidence into my answer as I could, twisting my ring around on my finger.

"Touché."

"I'm not going to lie though. I think this is going to be our last chance, Clara. If this doesn't work, I don't know what else I can try."

I felt the tendrils of dread taking root in my stomach, eating at the hope that had been there only a few hours before.

"All this work to keep Shade out of this—well, not this, but the hard side of this world—and here I am, putting the responsibility of Rowan's survival on his shoulders."

"You didn't say it like that, right?" Clara winced. "Shade's going to feel like it's his fault if he fails and Rowan doesn't make it. You'll need to get him out of there fast. Otherwise, he'll be dealing with a lot of extra trauma."

"Of course I didn't say it like that, but I didn't lie to him either," I replied indignantly, nudging her back. "I know the risks I'm exposing him to. It terrifies me, but you know that I'll do whatever I need to in order to keep him safe."

"Honesty, El. It'll get you into trouble and out of trouble, but you'll never know which until you try it." She gave me a small smile.

"Where'd you get all this wisdom from all of a sudden? Any chance you feel like taking over the parenting duties for a while? I could use a break from the mental load," I joked.

Clara nudged me, laughing. "Nope, not a chance. I'd do anything for these kids, but I'll stick with my current level of responsibility. I won't lie though. It's the best job I've ever had."

The edges of her mouth dipped down as I watched a thought flit across her face. She uncrossed her arms and locked eyes with me.

"Just promise me you won't be destroyed if this doesn't work. After this, you've done everything. There are no more stones to be turned over, spells or magick to be tried. Whatever happens after this, it's not because of you, it's in spite of you."

Tears pricked at the corners of my eyes at her words. I blinked them back and nodded, grasping her hand with my own and squeezing tight. "Thanks, Clara."

She leaned her head on the top of mine, her hair falling onto my shoulder. It was the deepest shade of red—so dark it was almost maroon—a colour very few people ever saw.

The colour reserved for the people she loved.

"Are you two done with all the soppy crap, yet?" Shade came sauntering out, his backpack slung over his shoulder as though we should be heading to school rather than to Denny's house to save Rowan. At the sound of his voice, we both turned around, unlinking our arms, which let me wipe away whatever tears had escaped before. For a pale, black-eyed, dream-eating, nightmare-wielding, bogeyman-style supernatural teenager, he seemed more excited than I was expecting.

"Soppy crap?" I arched my brow at him.

"Whatever." He rolled his eyes at me, but there was a smile behind them this time rather than the scowl I'd become accustomed to over the last few months. "Let's go." He headed over to the car, his impatience—or eagerness—clear to both of us.

"Okay. Clara, just give me a call if there are any problems. Thanks," I told her before heading over. "And just to be clear, I was the one waiting out here for you," I said pointedly at Shade. "You're the one who needed to get their things together. What could you even need other than your actual power?"

"That's for me to know and you to find out," he replied smugly as he got into the car.

"Good luck," Clara shouted from the verandah. "Keep me updated!"

I gave her a thumbs up and followed Shade's lead, turning my focus on what was to come next. As I drove out and onto the road, I called Mason, who answered on the first ring.

"El." It was only a single syllable, but somehow his greeting sounded ominous.

"Shade and I are on our way now," I told him, hoping that would be reassuring. For him or for me, I wasn't quite sure.

"Good, because something's going on here. I've been keeping to myself, but it seems like whatever deal you have going on isn't going to last for much longer," he warned.

I looked over at Shade, his black eyes darkening, if that was possible, as his eagerness was replaced with the sombre reality of what exactly the stakes were.

"What the Hades? Why would Jack go back on that? It's not like there's much time left anyway." About eight to ten hours if my math was right, and I was no Archimedes, the God of mathematics, that was for sure.

"I don't have the full picture, it's just what I could overhear, but Jack's a can or three in, and he seems to think it's all been a waste of time. He's scared they've placed the whole clan at risk by not dealing with Rowan straight away." Mason's gravelly voice sounded downright worried. "I've never seen him like this before. Jack's losing it with anyone who disagrees. They even got Denny on the phone, but she won't hear a word against him. She says it's his call. They've always been more set in the old ways than the younger ones, but this ... this is ..."

"Too much, way too much." I finished his sentence for him.

He barked out a bitter laugh. "Not exactly the words I was going to use, but close to it."

"Just do whatever you can to keep them from doing anything, um, permanent, if you can, Mason. We'll be there soon. They've got to at least let Shade try."

"I will, but I don't know that there's much I can do." Mason paused. "Or that I can do it for long enough. Just get here and get here quick." With that, the line went dead, and the dread that had started gathering in my stomach earlier grew stronger, taking solid root within me.

"Should you try the others?" Shade asked.

"We're close, but I don't think it would hurt. I should have called them as soon as I'd had the idea of asking you, but I didn't think that Jack would go back on his word. I think he's all messed up because the last Faoladh this happened to was his father." I shook my head. "He can't be thinking straight."

I sighed loudly as I tried to refocus. *I wasn't ready for this. Neither of us were. But that didn't matter anymore.*

"I'm calling Denny. She's been telling me how important it is to believe that there is good in all people, even the worst of them. She can't let him do this." The phone rang through to the hospital and then the ward, and finally, Denny answered with a cough for a greeting.

"Denny, you can't let him do this." I didn't waste time with pleasantries. "I have Shade with me, and I think he can help her. You need to stop Jack."

"He's summoning the Morrigan, love. He can't bear the weight of the decision any longer, so he's putting it to her. It's too much, and it's bringing back his memories of losing his pa. Our cousins are convinced that Rowan will bring ruin to their clan. And I'm stuck in this hospital like an invalid. Otherwise, I'd be there." She took in a sharp breath and battled through another cough. "I can try to get through to one of the kids, but I don't know if it will make a difference."

"Please try, Denny. Rowan's not out of options, not yet."

"I will, Ellie," Denny agreed, hanging up.

I didn't waste any time. Every minute we got closer, but the gnawing in my stomach told me I couldn't rely on that. I dialled Gabe and listened to the phone ring out.

Next, I tried Wren. Same thing, and I didn't have Farron or Declan and Emrys' numbers. I tried Mason again, but his phone rang out as well, mocking any hope I was holding out of someone answering.

Dread clenched tightly in my stomach. There was no good reason none of them would be answering.

"That's bad, right?" Shade commented, tightening his hand on the arm of his back-pack.

"It's not good," I acknowledged, my skin feeling tight on my face from the tension whirling within me. My power couldn't feed on my own apprehension or pain, but it was perched there, ready for the first passing emotion to be consumed. Shade and I were no different, really. Only I knew the consequences of what this type of power could bring.

And I was leading him into something that could be the worst of all I'd faced. Rowan would not—could not—open to me, but if she did to him, he could very well save her.

What she could do to him, however, I was not so sure. I could only hope that if he was able to consume her subconscious pain, it would feed him and not torment him.

Neither of us could take away the actual trauma that Rowan had experienced. There was no quick way to heal that. We, or more correctly, he, could only consume the symptoms of it, and hopefully, that would be enough to let her come back to her human self.

The lights of Denny's house came into view, and I turned down the driveway, parking to the side of the four cars parked out the front. It was a full house, and that didn't lift my mood, not one iota.

I turned to Shade, face to face, dropping the facade that everything would be okay. The mangled conglomeration of dire emotions I felt coming from the house and beyond were screaming at me that it would be anything but okay, and my power was eager to come out and play.

"Are you one hundred percent sure that you want to do this? I thought I had an idea of what I was asking you to get into, but that's changed. This ..." I motioned to outside the car, to the house and what lay past it. "I have no idea what this is that we're walking into, but I do know that if we don't—"

"If we don't, this girl, Rowan, will die. Someone just like me, that everyone had given up on, will die." Shade looked out the window as he spoke, his hands tightening around his bag until his knuckles whitened. "So, yes, Ellie. I'm ready."

"Shade, look at me," I demanded, waiting to speak again until his gaze was locked on mine. "This is not on you if it doesn't work. Rowan's life, or her death, is not your responsibility. It's the Faoladh's responsibility. I need you to know that. Not everyone gets a happy ending."

He let go of his bag for a moment and ran his hand through his hair before answering me. "I get that. Life sucks sometimes, but I'd feel worse if I didn't try to help. If you didn't let me try. So, I got this, either way."

The front door was unlocked when we got to it. That wasn't unusual. Denny's house was the main hub for all the Faoladh, and they weren't the best at remembering to lock doors. It was the emotions that hit me like a truck at full force. It hadn't even been this strong when I was here a couple of hours ago. Anxiety, bordering on sheer panic, raced through me, but not just my own. The place reeked of it. My power reached out of its own accord, finding it in every nook and cranny. There wasn't a place left untouched.

"Stay behind me, Shade," I instructed. He fell into line, not questioning me for what might be the first time in his life. He'd put his backpack on properly, as though he knew to be prepared for whatever we were about to find. It rustled with each movement, a sound that was oddly reminiscent of a box of Froot Loops being shaken up. *Surely he wouldn't bring a snack when he was about to have a meal.* The thought raced across my mind, but I had to let it go as I focused on finding the Faoladh.

As we made our way through, I could tell immediately that the energy inside was different. In the same way that the rooms usually vibrated with energy when everyone was present, the absence of that energy was starkly evident. I didn't waste any time searching in the bedrooms or guest rooms. Mason would have answered my call if he was still here. The only thing I needed to know was whether they still had Rowan locked away in the garage or if she was with them. My gut was already screaming the answer, but my mind needed the confirmation.

The hallway to the garage yielded nothing that the house before it had—just silence, the haunting emptiness of a house usually filled with loud, loving Faoladh. As I reached the door to the garage, I turned and held my finger to my closed lips, gesturing for Shade to stay quiet. I turned the knob and opened the door, the garage revealing itself to be as empty as everywhere else had been. Devoid of Faoladh, including Rowan. The only sign of any struggle was the drops of blood leading out of her cage to the back roller door, which had been left open to the outside. I knelt and touched the darkened blood, which was sticky and drying quickly.

Whatever had happened, whatever had been decided, the blood told me it hadn't been long since she'd been taken.

"Is it hers?" Shade questioned.

"I can't tell, but it hasn't been long since it was spilt. Small droplets get sticky and thick faster than larger pools of blood." I didn't let myself ponder the centuries of experience with the dying and dead that led me to gain that knowledge.

"Just give me a moment, and I'll see if my power can pick anything up," I explained. Closing my eyes, I let my power push outside of me, reaching further than my eyes or ears could. Searching out the unique taste of an overwhelming combination of anxiety, fear, and anger that could only come from a group of distressed people.

Found them.

As intense as the emotions were, a sliver of relief wove its way through me. Whatever they were doing—or planning to do—hadn't happened yet.

I knew the anguish of grief, and the only traces of it I could find were the familiar taste of Rowan's. I knew in my heart that the others, even Jack, would feel grief if they'd sacrificed Rowan.

Opening my eyes, I let them adjust to the darkness and stared at the open roller door and the dark bush beyond. "I don't think they've done anything yet, and that means there's still a chance."

"Good. Let's get moving then. I didn't wait forever for you to let me help just so some Faoladh could do something stupid and stop me," Shade said, readjusting his backpack and starting out the back roller door. "I'm guessing this is as good a place as any to start."

"You're right." I followed him outside the roller door and looked around at the different buildings of the compound. "That's the direction of the emotion I'm feeling," I said, pointing toward the bush at the edge of the buildings.

"If that's what we've got, let's roll with it," Shade agreed. "You leading, or me?"

"Me." I glared at him. "One step at a time, okay?"

Shade rolled his eyes at me but stopped in place until I was ahead of him. I walked quickly, trying to temper my desire to find them with the need to approach quietly. There were no instructions on how to sneak up on someone before they summoned the Morrigan for a sacrifice. Shade followed slowly behind me, a quick check over my shoulder every minute or so confirming it.

It was only minutes, but it felt like it was hours before we passed beyond the buildings and the firepit where Olive and the others had completed the protection spell. It was only a day later, but it might as well have been years for how much had changed.

As the grass turned to bush shrubs, I finally caught sight of a flicker of fire through the trees. The bush thinned the closer we got until I could see the outline of the people gathered in a clearing around the flames, the pacing form of Rowan captured between the fire and a border of what looked to be pink salt. The Faoladh couldn't cross salt—there was enough fae in them that while it didn't affect them as much as pure fae, it still held some power over them. From the looks of it, Jack had used the pink salt to trap Rowan so he could summon the Morrigan safely—for him anyway.

I motioned to Shade to stop as we got as close as we could without being seen, a few feet away from where the trees dropped away completely.

Jack stood closest to the circle around Rowan, in human form, with his hands held out, a book in one hand, the spine laid flat, the pages flicked open, and his walking stick in the other.

"You can't do this, Jack. You know it's wrong." Mason's voice caught my attention. I tried to search out where he was, but instead, I realised there was another circular barrier, keeping the other Faoladh and Mason at bay as well.

I wasn't sure exactly what it was, but this one wasn't salt. It looked to be like a filmy, white bubble that rippled when they fought to cross it on either side. Wren, Mason, Gabe, and even Farron were on our side of the barrier while Jack was trapped inside, persistently trying to pierce it with the end of his walking stick.

"The bubble ..." I whispered to Shade, who was next to me.

"It's that lady, the one with Dec and Emrys." Shade pointed just behind where Mason and the others were gathered.

"Olive." I said her name instinctively as I drew in a breath. She was chanting in a language I wasn't fluent in, with Declan and Emrys. Magick emanated from the trio toward the barrier. If I hadn't been seeing it, I wouldn't have believed it, but it looked like they were the ones holding the second barrier in place.

"Stay here," I ordered Shade. I started moving toward the back of the group, toward Olive, Declan, and Emrys. I needed to understand what was happening before I even thought of taking a step closer.

"Like hell," Shade hissed and followed. I didn't have time to waste on chastising him, so I just shot him an annoyed look and kept going, trying to keep each footfall in the dry underbrush as quiet as possible. Each crack of a twig or crunch of dry grass sounded louder than it should. It was only the sound of the chanting that gave us any cover.

It took a few minutes, but eventually, I'd managed to keep both of us hidden while approaching Olive, Declan, and Emrys from behind. My doubts about Olive still lay sleeping in the back of my mind, but I had faith that Declan wouldn't deceive me. Reaching out, I placed my hand on his shoulder, absorbing the spike of his fear at my touch while replacing it with a little mercy in the hopes we could avoid the 'freaking out' part of me showing up. It worked, sort of.

"Ellie," he breathed in between the words of the chant. "Thank God you're here. We need your help."

"How?" I asked, removing my hand from his shoulder but staying shadowed behind him.

"We're holding a barrier over Jack to stop the call to the Morrigan getting out. He's lost his mind. He wants the Morrigan to cast judgement on Rowan so that he doesn't have to. He's in pieces, El. I've never seen Dad so broken. We're trying to stop anything coming out, but it's stopping anyone getting through as well," he explained.

Olive and Emrys continued with the chant, but I could see beyond them, and without Declan's power, the barrier was wavering.

"Declan," Emrys uttered through gritted teeth.

Declan resumed the chanting, and I waited for the barrier to stop faltering before asking my next question.

"What do you think the Morrigan will do? If he gets the call out, she'll expect a price to be paid."

"If Rowan's guilty, she'll kill her. Cast her soul out into the Shadowland to suffer for the rest of eternity. And after that, I don't know. We haven't summoned her in generations, but the stories ..." Declan paused, uttering another line of the chant before starting again.

"The stories, they're not good, El. There's a reason why we haven't called on her, but I don't know if it's just nightmare fuel or if it's real. None of us do. That's why we're trying to stop this. But we can't hold it much longer."

The proof was right in front of me, the filmy, white barrier weakening in spots. Every couple of seconds, I could hear small snippets of Jack's summoning call seeping through.

We'd gotten here just in time, although I wasn't sure that time would be enough. I caught Declan's attention again, the furrow in his brow lined with sweat.

"If you can give us two more minutes, then I think Shade and I can deliver some nightmare fuel of our own, but we'll need the shield down," I explained.

Declan hesitated, his eyes flashing with uncertainty. He knew I was asking him to give me the only chance they'd have to save Rowan. And I could see the moment he decided to trust me.

"You've got it. Two, and then we drop it."

CHAPTER NINETEEN

THE TWO MINUTES WAS just enough time for Shade and me to get into position to the right of Jack and as close to the side of Olive, Emrys, and Declan's shield as possible while still being hidden. A surprise attack was our best shot. The emotions in the air were so heightened that they were nearly electric as I prepared to join the fray. My own heart ached as I tried to accept that someone I had trusted and come to see as family was now the enemy, but I couldn't dwell on it. The time for tears would come, but it wasn't this moment.

As soon as the white film of their shield faltered, I unleashed my gathered power and thrust every ounce of compassion and mercy I could muster at Jack. The wave of emotion stopped him immediately. His voice cut off, and he folded in half as though I'd thrown a punch instead.

Guilt rushed through me as I connected with his pain and anguish over what he was doing. I could almost read his thoughts, his emotions had such aching clarity—he couldn't face the responsibility of Rowan's life in his hands in the same way that he couldn't cope with the thought that his father's death could have been in vain if the curse wasn't real. Jack's fear spiked potently. He shifted to his wolf form, dropping the book into the brush as I threw barrage after barrage of power at him. Somewhere between the fourth or fifth wave, his wolf form shuddered, and he returned to human, his clothes worse for wear.

Jack wasn't a bad guy. I knew that in my heart, but he'd crossed a line with his weakness in leading the Faoladh and his willingness to pay whatever price summoning the Morrigan would demand just to shed the responsibility of Rowan's life.

The line between believing in good and assuming evil. The line we had to defend.

At the same time as I was stopping Jack from completing the summoning, Shade had leapt across the salt barrier and stood face to face with Rowan, who growled and bared her teeth at him, approaching him with the steady pace of an apex predator who'd decided on their prey.

Shade didn't even bother with pleasantries. He pulled open his backpack and whipped out an old box of doggie treats we had left over from Storm's days at Halfling House.

So, not Froot Loops. I smiled briefly before returning my focus to Jack, who remained cowed on the floor. Tears glistened on his face, proof of the overwhelming emotions he was battling. The ease with which I held him in place, crippled by compassion, surprised even me. I knew my powers returning was a process and that it would take time for me to be at full strength. With all the distraction of searching for Rowan, it was only at that moment that I realised I was stronger and more powerful than I thought I was.

My power was growing in presence and strength, and this was proof of that, even if it was the worst use of my magick, as a weapon and not for healing.

Healing. Fear for Shade pulled my attention back to him, where I watched as he reached out to Rowan with a doggie biscuit in his hand to see if he could succeed where I couldn't.

When the witches' shield disappeared, the other Faoladh had shifted into their wolf forms and created a crescent formation around Jack and me. Except for Wren, who had caught Olive as she collapsed from the drain of holding the shield for so long.

With my power subduing Jack, all I could do was watch as Shade continued to take small steps forward toward Rowan, one hand in front of him holding the biscuit, and the other reached outward, toward the rest of us, warding us off.

Warding Mason off.

That was when I realised where Mason had gone after the shield dropped—straight to Shade's side. *Thank the Gods.* It was hard to marry the relief I felt at knowing I could trust him to have my back with the fear of him getting hurt. His mortality was always stuck in the back of my mind. The fact that he knew I could handle Jack and that my heart was twisting, not being able to help Shade, made me fall a little more in love with him, even in the middle of this horrible mess.

Under Mason's eagle eye, Shade and Rowan faced off. His attempts to calm her with the biscuit drew growls and bared teeth, but it distracted her from his other hand, which he held in the air as he tried to pull at the subconscious nightmares that were consuming her. Through the corner of my eye, I could see the whispers of mist—of the subconscious nightmare consuming her—start to trickle out of her mind before vanishing into the thick, coastal air. Shade's frustration was clear on his face. Reddened cheeks, heavy breathing, and the lines of concentration forming across his forehead marred his youthful paleness.

It felt like an eternity passed as they squared off. Until, without any warning, Shade leapt forward and latched onto Rowan. Rowan let loose an otherworldly howl that made my blood freeze in my veins. If I wasn't an immortal Goddess, I'd have thought my heart had stopped.

"Shade! No!" Mason yelled, running forward across the salt barrier, breaking the circle of pink salt that was keeping Rowan contained.

The same words spilt from my mouth without thinking. "No, Shade, don't!"

It was a split-second, but it tore my focus from Jack, and I released my hold on him instinctively. The remaining Faoladh drew closer to him. I recognised Gabe's wolf form take the lead, keeping Jack in place but offering him comfort, a paw on his human hand. He was no risk to anyone now, between the compassion and mercy that still filled his mind and the close eye of the rest of the clan.

And so, I watched Shade, knowing that it was life or death now.

His and Rowan's.

Rowan's jaw snapped as she tried to get at Shade, his agile body missing each attempt by milliseconds as he manoeuvred himself onto her back and clutched his hands on either side of her head, just under her pointed silver ears.

Almost immediately, Rowan stilled, unnaturally so. The reason became clear as the telltale wisps of the torment inside Rowan's mind started flowing steadily from her mind to Shade's mouth, his every breath absorbing the anguish. I'd never really watched him do it before, not like this, and not with this much. Usually, it was the kids' nightmares, which were small and neat translucent white mist. Or my own, which had only happened when I was asleep and unable to witness it.

This time, I could see it all.

I could see the blackened veins that extended from Shade's eyes and from his mouth as he consumed Rowan's subconscious pain. Only this wasn't the thin, translucent wisps I was used to seeing him absorb from the kids. No, Rowan's anguish was like the smoke that comes from burning plastic, thick and black and intense, almost as dark as the obsidian of Shade's eyes. Eyes that were shining with power as an ethereal blackness enveloped his body and grew with every breath, with every bite, with every inhalation of Rowan's living nightmare, until he no longer resembled the teenage bogeyman I knew.

No, whatever it was that he had become, it was something I hadn't seen before. And it made my blood run cold even as my power burned inside me, reacting to the pain and torment it felt flowing from Rowan, as though it was calling to my power. It took all my strength to keep my power at bay, resisting the call Rowan's torment sent out to me so that Shade could continue his work.

Minutes passed, and slowly, so very very slowly, the stream of pain and anguish started thinning out, becoming gossamer-like, until it finally looked like the wisps of nightmares I was more familiar with.

As Shade consumed the last of her subconscious nightmare, I could see Rowan's wolf form release the last remnants of tension that were within her at the same time. It was such an enormous release of relief that I felt it emanate from Rowan through all of us, as though she were one large rock thrust into a river, the ripples vibrant and strong.

Shade let go of Rowan. The enormous ethereal shadow that he had become stood proud for a moment before unleashing an otherworldly scream that sent a shockwave of power through us all.

I looked around as I saw the momentum knock Mason to the floor, and then I felt it hit me, pushing me back a few steps. Fortunately, the other Faoladh were still tending to Jack while Olive and Wren were further back, having found the book Jack had tossed aside. By the time the wave hit them, it still caught them off guard, but no one else found themselves grounded unwillingly.

Fear overwhelmed me as I raced over toward Shade, Rowan, and Mason. *Gods, please let them be okay. Please.*

Mason was back on his feet before I even got to him. I grabbed his hand, and he pulled me toward him long enough for us to reassure each other we were both okay.

"I'll check Shade," Mason said. My maternal instincts pushed me to go straight to Shade, guilt shrouding my rational thought. *I brought him here. If he's hurt, it's my fault.* The thought gripped my heart like a vise. *What was I doing thinking he was ready for this? We still don't even know if he is mortal or immortal, or somewhere in between. And I've led him right into the wolf's den. Literally.*

I needed to know he was alright. That he was alive.

"No—"

Mason cut me off. "I've got this. The others need you more." With that, he squeezed my hand and gently pushed me toward Rowan. "Go. Now."

I wiped away the tears that had welled in my eyes. *He was right.* I hated it, but he was. I couldn't do much for Shade, but I could for Rowan.

We parted ways, and while my heart clenched at the thought of Shade being injured, I knew Mason would be more useful. He passed me as I knelt beside Rowan and placed my hand behind her ears reassuringly, her fur soft and silky. She looked up at me, her bright blue eyes empty of the wildfire of pain and anguish they had held before, replaced with deep sadness and grief. The kind I was far more familiar with from my years wandering this earth.

I wanted to go in there and take it away, my power itching to give her relief, but before I could even think of doing anything, I felt a glimmer of power flow over my hands, sending a shock of surprise through me.

A pulse of fae magick ran through her as I watched her silver and grey fur disappear into the ether as it was replaced with pale porcelain skin and wavy black hair. The whole time, her trusting gaze held mine as she transformed from the wolf they had feared into the young girl we'd fought to protect.

Rowan was human again.

"*Nach tubaiste bheag aoibhinn é seo?*"

Surprised at the unfamiliar voice, I looked away from Rowan and up at a woman who was simultaneously the most intensely beautiful and horrifically terrifying being I had encountered in the thousands of years I had been alive.

It was her.

The Morrigan.

"*Nach tubaiste bheag aoibhinn é seo?*" she repeated, her hands tightening on her hips as her patience waned quickly.

Words escaped me, and I stared up at her, my mouth ajar. I was a little rusty, but I recognised the Gaelic language. It was just that I'd thought Olive and the others had succeeded in blocking the summoning. Only Mason and Shade moved, closing the distance between us to stand behind me. Shade knelt down and pulled a jacket—and a doggie biscuit—out of his backpack. He placed the jacket over Rowan, who had clambered into my lap at the first words the Morrigan had spoken, although she still managed to snatch the biscuit from him too.

Relief wanted to edge out my fear as I realised Shade wasn't hurt, but the knowledge that one of the most powerful entities of the Celtic Pantheon was standing right in front of me overpowered everything else. I cast a quick glance at the Faoladh and the others, who'd formed a semi-circle opposite us, standing frozen in time as though the same shock ran through them too.

"Are you about to tell me that not one of you knows the language of your homeland?" she demanded in a thick Irish accent, disappointment dripping from every word of English that crossed her tongue.

Shame flushed across Jack's face as though that was his biggest mistake so far. Mason and I shared a look. I reached my hand out for Shade's, a rush of gratitude hitting me when he took it and held tight.

"It is a right shame," she bellowed at them. "To leave your kin and settle here is one thing, but for you to abandon your heritage is a whole other betrayal. And then, to have the gall to summon me to this delightful disaster ..." She glared down at Jack. "I have higher duties than coming when you call, like a commoner."

Jack stepped forward, his movements shaky. "The Great Queen, I ask your forgiveness, your mercy. We only sought you because we had lost one of our clan to the curse and wished for you to cast your judgement upon her before the end of our clan came," he explained, stuttering every few words as he gestured toward Rowan.

Gabe, Farron, Emrys, and Declan were still in their wolf forms and crept up behind Jack, staying a step behind him but close enough that they were there for whatever came next.

The Morrigan turned back to us, and her black eyes narrowed in on Rowan. "This young lass?" She moved closer, and I tightened my grip on Rowan, prepared to do whatever was needed to keep her safe, but the movement wasn't subtle, and it caught the Morrigan's attention. "My, what have we got here? The Greek Pantheon mixing about with my own."

"You'll find it's not that unusual here," I answered, focusing on keeping my words brief while sitting tall and proud. If there was one thing I knew, it was not to give a Goddess as powerful as the Morrigan a whiff of any weakness. I was no Goddess of war or strategy, but I'd cleaned up their messes long enough to be familiar with their take-no-prisoners approach.

A moment passed, those black eyes staring into the deep brown of my own as she took in what I'd said. "You're protecting her," she stated. "Why? She's not your kin." Curiosity made her eyes gleam.

"I make it my business to protect those who need it, not just those I call family," I told her. "And Rowan, she has good in her. She deserves a chance to show that." Rowan buried her head into my shoulder, deeper than before, if that was even possible.

"Agh, the lass took a bite of her kin, did she?" The Morrigan straightened up, turning to face Jack and the Faoladh again. "Who did she cross?"

The group exchanged looks amongst themselves, Jack appearing the most confused of all. Olive's curiosity had clearly gotten the better of her as she waited close by. Wren stood in front of Olive, a calming hand tucked into her forearm, holding her in place gently even as anger coloured her cheeks while she spoke.

"She's crossed no one, not a single one of us. Rowan was traumatised and stuck in her wolf form for days. Over a week. So, she did what any animal would do, she ate smaller prey to stay alive. That shouldn't be a reason for her to have to sacrifice her life!"

"Well, she did take a bite out of El too," Jack offered. "Whether she be human or Goddess, the lore is clear. No Faoladh shall eat the flesh of another creature, or they will be cursed to remain in their wolf form and to destroy their clan. That is why we called you, the Great Queen." He bowed his head to the Morrigan.

"And whose lore would that be?" the Morrigan drawled in her thick Irish tongue, one of her dark brows raised in question.

"Our ancient text, written by our ancestor, Conor McFayden, nearly four hundred years ago," Jack answered. "The book. Give me the book," he demanded.

Olive looked to the others, hesitating. I could almost see the wheels turning in her head as she considered whether handing the book to Jack was the best idea. Wren gave her a small nod, and she passed it over. At this point, I couldn't see a good reason to keep it from him anymore. He'd clearly managed to summon the Morrigan already. The wheels had been set in motion, and all we could do was wait.

And fight. The thought flitted across the forefront of my mind. I wasn't sure I'd be any match for the Morrigan, but we hadn't gotten this far just to lose Rowan anyway. I tenderly stroked her hair, my arms still wrapped around her as she kept herself crumpled up as small as possible in my lap.

"Here, my Great Queen, right here. It says it right here." Jack moved forward cautiously, his gait unbalanced as he held the book. He bent forward as low as he could and laid the book open at the Morrigan's feet, before creeping backward.

"McFayden ... Not the kin you should have had transcribing a thing, let alone your origin lore," she muttered before holding her hand out, the tips of her fingers wearing short silver claws. The book lifted from the ground, and it fell into her hand, the pages fluttering with the movement before being weighted down as she pressed the tip of one of her silver claws into the page, murmuring as she read the words written.

"Ach, I see, I see." With that, she snapped the book shut and snapped her fingers, the sound wiped out almost immediately by the sound of fire enveloping the book and reducing it to ash within seconds.

I watched as Jack's face became almost as grey as the remnants of the book. I swore I could hear the Faoladh's hearts stop at the sight of it destroyed.

"*Tá tú ar leathcheann.*" She shook her head and looked directly at the Faoladh. "Your kin, Conor, was a drunkard and a dunce. It is nothing more than the scratchings of your *leathcheann* fool kin." She gestured at the pile of ashes. "The curse was to keep you from in-fighting and harming each other, not from cooking up a feast. Shall you ever take the life of one of your kin, the curse will bring you and your kin's ruin, and I will delight in the destruction of the disloyal."

The timbre of her voice made the ground feel as though it were shaking beneath my feet. It took a moment for me to process the meaning of what she was saying. The Faoladh had the conditions of the curse wrong. They'd come so close to sacrificing Rowan and bringing the curse upon themselves unknowingly. They'd let Jack's father—Denny's husband—sacrifice himself for nothing.

I could feel the emotions of the group shift, a different kind of guilt and shame—and a fair share of 'I told you so' vibes—as they processed the fact that the lore they'd lived by their entire lives was not the truth.

"Rowan of the Faoladh." The Morrigan turned to face us, her expression neutral but intense. "You have committed no crime against your kin and will not be treated as so."

Relief flooded through me and through the rest of those gathered as the weight of Rowan's fate was lifted from our collective shoulders. Even Jack's.

"The rest of you ..." The Morrigan turned to face the Faoladh. "There is a price to pay for failing your Queen, but more so, for failing your own kin."

Silence fell, thick and fast.

The Morrigan stared down the Faoladh. It was as though we were invisible to her, as though anyone not of her Pantheon was irrelevant. She cast her eyes across the group, in human and wolf form alike, moving between each one in a slow and calculated manner.

"Our Queen," Jack called out, standing tall even though his body shook with the effort. Guilt crept in as I wondered if his frail condition was my fault, given he hadn't been all that well before tonight. Too much drink took its toll. "I offer my life in payment. I have lived a life of error, and it's only right that the ones with the future in front of them have the chance to fix our faults. Take me, please, my Queen."

"No, Dad!" Wren called out, struggling to get herself free from Olive's protective grasp on her. I thrust my power out at the Morrigan defensively, without a thought of the consequences, but it was too little, too late.

"Let it be done." The Morrigan flicked her wrist and pointed her fingers to the sky, summoning a flicker of black lightning that struck Jack, pushing him to his knees before leaving him as he collapsed to the ground.

A collective gasp filled the air as grief and sorrow filled the hearts of those who remained. *He was dead.*

"The price is paid," the Morrigan announced, filling the silence. She turned to me, her eyes filled with fire. "This is not your domain, Goddess. You'd do well to keep out of it."

Returning her focus to the Faoladh, the Morrigan stood tall and addressed them, her voice carrying across the clearing. "I've left you without guidance, and it's time to fix it. Our Pantheon's strong, but others are nigh on war." She cast a look at me so brief that I thought I imagined it, until she continued. "You must be strong, ready to fight for what is ours. One of you will be coming with me to scribe your true heritage. The rest of you will do as you've done until our return."

With that, the Morrigan disappeared into the ether, leaving all of us staring in silence until Gabe asked a question that sent ice running down my spine.

"Where's Wren?"

CHAPTER TWENTY

THE MINUTES THAT FOLLOWED the disappearance of the Morrigan were chaotic. Emrys and Declan set out to try to scent where Wren had gone, but it was useless. She had been taken by the Morrigan, somewhere far beyond the stretches of Briarmoor's bush, perhaps even out of this realm. It took a fair amount of convincing from Olive, but eventually, Emrys and Declan shifted back to their human form and worked with Gabe and Farron to carry Jack's body back to the house.

Back home.

Despite the warm evening air, Rowan wouldn't stop shivering. Shade and I had done what we could to siphon off the distress that had trapped her in her wolf form. The trauma of the last week or so of her life would take much longer to heal.

Mason helped us to our feet, Rowan's hands clinging around my neck as though to let go was unthinkable. Shade followed closely, never more than half a foot away at any time, which was a good thing considering Rowan started to whine if she looked up and couldn't see him. Whatever had passed between the two of them, it was something I had never seen before, and I suspected, may have linked them in a way I didn't quite understand. Not yet anyway.

The walk back to the house was long, the darkness no longer threatening, instead a blackness that was only disturbed by the hazy orange fire that continued to burn in the distance. Silence accompanied us, save for Rowan's occasional whimper. I could feel the grief that had struck down the Faoladh, amplified by the grief that was winding its way through my own body until words felt pointless.

We had saved Rowan, but two of their own—my friends—had been taken in exchange. It was a cost that we'd only just begun to feel the consequences of.

The house was quiet as we walked in, even though the lounge was far from empty. Jack's still form lay on one of the couches, his head resting on Denny's lap, where she wept silently as she stroked the side of his ashen face. The others—Gabe, Farron, Declan, and

Emrys—sat in vigil around them, sorrow painted across their faces as they watched her mourn. The only unfamiliar face was Ever's, their usually glistening, joyful demeanour gone as they put their finger to their lips, the universal sign for quiet, and came over to me.

"How did she get here?" I asked.

"Wren wasn't answering my calls, so I was on my way over, but then I got a call from Denny at the hospital. She'd discharged herself and gave me an earful until I agreed to come get her. We made it just in time to see them bringing Jack inside ..."

My heart contracted at the thought of Denny's pain at that moment. I felt worse still, knowing that it wasn't the end of the grief she'd feel.

"Does she know about Wren?"

Ever's eye's widened, surprise registering. "I thought she was with you—"

"You don't have to whisper. I can hear you both perfectly well. I'm grieving, not deaf." Denny's voice cut through our conversation as she turned to look at us.

Rowan let out a whine as she shimmied herself behind me, Shade stepping closer so that he was right beside her.

"Is that Rowan?" Denny's voice softened. I nodded cautiously. Denny was my friend, but she'd also just lost her son, and possibly, her granddaughter. Grief twisted people in so many unknown ways.

"The boys told me what the Morrigan said, what she did. How wrong we got it all, for so long." The corners of her mouth dropped, almost unwillingly, as she fought off a sob that transformed into a cough, although this one was only short, thankfully. "The only good to come of this night is your precious life, lass." Denny gestured for Rowan to come to her. It was a gentle movement, well intentioned, but it set Rowan off, eliciting a screech from her before she bolted back out the door and into the night. There wasn't a second for me to react before Shade spoke.

"I've got her." Then he took off after Rowan.

Instinct made me want to run after them both, but sense kept me in place. No matter how much Denny wanted Rowan to stay here with the Faoladh, it was clear that she wasn't ready for that just yet. I could tell Denny needed to cling to something good coming out of this mess. It was just that Rowan wasn't ready to be that silver lining right now.

"Denny, I'm sorry, but—" I started, moving closer to her.

"She's scared of us," she said sadly. "And rightly so."

"It won't be forever. Denny, but it's been a lot. For all of you, for her, for us," I replied softly as I knelt next to her. "Let me help you the way you helped us with Storm. I can give her a place to heal until she's ready to come back to you."

"Ellie." Gabe interrupted cautiously. "She belongs here, with her kin."

"The kin that almost got her killed." Farron grabbed Gabe's hand tightly, making Gabe turn to him. "She had to watch her mother die, and then when she came here for help, she was tranquilised, locked up, and then subjected to the Morrigan's judgement. This isn't a safe place for her right now."

Gabe paused and looked down for a moment before meeting my gaze. "It's Denny's call."

Denny looked around at the group and came back to me, her hand still absentmindedly stroking Jack's hair. "We'll accept your offer of a home for Rowan—temporarily." She reached out with her other hand to squeeze mine as I stood. "Thank you for what you've done for us and for what you will do, love. You too, Mason."

I nodded and squeezed her hand back before tucking a rogue lock of hair behind my ear. "You were there for us when we needed you, so we're here for you. All of you," I replied as I looked around the room at my friends.

"As for the rest of us, it's our time to grieve. We have a life to honour, no matter how its end came. Jack's heart was true, and his life well-lived, even if he made mistakes."

"It's rude to call Declan a mistake, Gran," Emrys interjected with a sad smile. Declan elbowed his brother, who feigned pain by clutching his side and falling to the side.

"You two, now's not the time for this. Respect your grandmother," Olive admonished them in a hushed voice.

Denny's bark of laughter cut through the telling-off Olive was giving, brightening the room for a moment. "No, they're right, Olive, love. Jack was never one for quiet and crying. If it was anyone else, he'd already have the whiskey out and be three sheets to the wind."

"So, whiskey then, Gran?" Declan asked tentatively, as though he thought she might change her mind.

"Whiskey it is, Declan. One for all of us. Jack too."

"Consider it done," he replied, disappearing into the kitchen.

"Mason, do you think you can get us a permit for a bonfire?" Denny asked.

"Not a chance, Den. Bushfires, remember?" He scratched at the five o'clock shadow that was growing later by the minute. "I can probably get them to look the other way if you keep it in the clearing and do it late at night or early morning," he offered.

"Thank you." Denny gave him a small smile. "Now, I'm not trying to be rude, but if you two wouldn't mind taking Rowan and Shade home. There are people we need to gather. I think it's time to say goodbye in our own way and on our own terms, loves."

"Of course, we'll leave you be."

Mason and I said our goodbyes and retreated outside, the darkness of the late hours of the night making it hard to see Shade and Rowan perched on the edge of the outdoor area, sitting in companionable silence.

"Time to go, Shade, Rowan."

Neither questioned why Rowan was coming home with us, and I was grateful not to need to explain it just now. Taking my hand, Mason and I led the way back to the car, and we were on our way back to Halfling House within minutes.

The next few days passed quickly. The sun rose and set, the temperature dropping as the edges of the Australian autumn gave way to the true chill of the season, as though even summer had given up trying to hold the inevitable back. The turn of the weather gave the firefighters the chance to gain the upper hand and steadily beat back the flickers and flames that had consumed so much of the land. As they disappeared, the leaves fell, and the animals returned, finding homes in the blackened stretches of bushland and peeling crevices of the eucalyptus trees.

The Faoladh farewelled Jack with a traditional pyre funeral. The wake lasted a few days, and the case of whiskey I had delivered barely lasted one of them. Mason was able to hand off most of his duties to Mac, whose recovery courtesy of Asclepius was near miraculous. That was how I found myself waking up to the most delightful sight in the world, even if the sound wasn't all that enjoyable. I waited until his most recent snore petered out before giving in to the urge to gently run my fingers down the side of his face, stopping only when I reached the coarse, unshaven tip of his chin.

I was falling in love with a human. A mortal. The thought pierced my heart as I allowed myself to finally admit it. To love him, I would lose him. He would grow old and frail, and time would do away with him, while I stayed the same, watching and waiting until it stole our love, and I was alone again.

And still, there was no denying it. I was falling in love with Mason, and I couldn't stop myself. I didn't want to.

"Y'know, some people would say it's dangerous to wake a sleeping man," he murmured, wrapping his arm around me and pulling me close so I could nestle into him again.

"Those people haven't met you." I grinned into his chest. "The most dangerous thing about you is that snoring."

He chuckled, opening his eyes to look at me. "Says the Goddess with the power to kill a man with an expired cappuccino mix."

This time, I laughed out loud. "Shh ... It's bad manners to wake kids up."

He raised his eyebrows a good inch. "I'm noticing some definite double standards here."

I shrugged, shooting him a flirty smile. "Forgive me for wanting a moment alone with you before I have to share you with everyone else."

Mason laughed, the kind that I could feel start deep in his stomach. With that, he cupped my chin and drew me into a kiss that shortened each breath and made my whole body want to become one with his, lust sizzling between us at the same time as my power reacted viscerally to the love that was growing unchecked, unencumbered, and unwary between us.

The challenges, the disasters, and the near misses of the world disappeared.

It was just us. Until it wasn't.

"Ellie, Mason, you've got incoming!" Clara shouted up the stairs, her voice breaking into our moment of bliss only a second before Zane and Alora came rushing into the room, bouncing up and down with a level of energy that should have been criminal, if it wasn't so adorable.

I slid off Mason's lap. *Thank the Gods we didn't sleep naked.* I cast a quick glance at Mason, which seemed to mirror the same thought, as we both moved to my side of the bed, sitting on the edge.

"Mama E! Mama E!" Zane yelled, his wings fluttering inconsistently so that he was bobbing up and down until he slammed his little body into mine. I wrapped my arms around him and looked down at the luminescent, bluish-teal scales that edged his round face and big eyes.

"What's so exciting?" I asked, pretending I hadn't a clue.

"A wolf, there is. A wolf, Mason, mister," Alora explained as she flashed briefly from the doorway to Mason's lap. At least after living at the Faoladh compound for a while, neither Zane nor Alora found wolves particularly scary anymore, but it was still an exciting development.

"Rowan did it?" Mason said, surprise in his voice.

"It sounds like she did," I agreed, not ashamed of the pride that had snuck through. "I wasn't sure she would be ready for a while, but I'm happy to be wrong. Come on, Zane, Alora, let's go down and have some breakfast."

"Race?" Alora looked up at Mason's face, excitement brightening her small, perfect features.

"Race. Race. Race!" Zane exclaimed, bouncing on my lap.

"Okay, okay, okay," I told them. "You know the rules. You have to sit on our shoulders and hold our hands. First one in their seat at the table wins."

The two of them got into position. Mason and I exchanged grins, and we were off. I let Mason take the lead at the stairs because Zane had won yesterday, so it was Alora's turn. They ended up beating us by all of a couple of seconds, a loss that Zane was slowly learning to take in his stride, even though he spent a few minutes sulking in his chair until the breakfast hit the table.

Mason sat down with the kids while I joined Clara at the bench, her masterful pancakes filling the kitchen with the type of smell that would mean even Shade would have to venture up for breakfast.

"You should go into the lounge," she told me, nodding her head in its direction. "I think you'll like what you see."

"You sure you don't need a hand?"

"I've got it covered. Go. Before it gets less cute and more teenager-y again."

Making my way to the lounge, I heard Shade's voice. Ever since we'd come back from the Faoladh compound that night, Rowan had stuck to Shade like glue. Whatever he'd done to help her with her trauma had bonded them in a way I still didn't quite understand. Either way, she felt safest with him here, and that had been something I'd made clear to Denny wouldn't change until Rowan was ready for it.

"You're safe here, Rowan. You could be a wolf forever, and you'd still be safe here. Ellie might be a pain in the ass—a lot—but once she promises to keep you safe, she means it."

"That's what my clan's job was." Rowan's voice was small, sad.

"You don't have to be afraid of what you are." Shade paused. "What you are isn't what matters. It's *who* you are that does. And you're good, Rowan, even if you had to do things they didn't understand. You're good."

To hide my eavesdropping, I made sure my footsteps were louder than usual as I walked into the lounge room, where I saw Shade on the couch and Rowan sitting cross-legged on the carpet, her hair almost touching the floor when it hung loose like this morning.

"Nice pyjamas," Shade snickered. I looked down. They were my sushi-themed flannelette set.

"You're lucky I was able to match the shirt and the pants, so don't complain," I teased, although I wasn't entirely lying. My socks were odd, mostly just because I couldn't bother to pair them up anymore.

I sat down on the floor next to Rowan. "How's the morning been?"

"Good." She smiled shyly, her gaze flicking to Shade. "I could shift into my wolf form and back again without anything going wrong."

"That's great news," I told her enthusiastically, but I could see some disappointment dim her pride.

"I-I-I just," she stuttered. "I'm not ready to go back—to them, to the house. The cage." Tears welled up, obscuring the bright blue of her eyes. "Please don't make me go back, please."

"Rowan," I said, sterner than I intended, but maybe that was what she needed. "You're not going anywhere, I promise. Not unless it's what you want, and even then, it'll only be when you want and how you want it."

I scooted over so I was closer to her, and she automatically leaned over and laid her head in my lap so I could stroke her hair.

"That's what I told her, El. We don't get rid of anyone." Shade reinforced my point.

"He's right, Rowan. I don't even kick out surly teenage boys who ignore me for months at a time, so why would I kick you out?" I reassured her, throwing a bit of shade at Shade, who had the wits about him to just blush rather than argue. "I've already spoken to Denny, and the others just want you to get to know them at the pace you're happy with. Denny will probably overload us with food until you give in to a cup of tea with her, but we can handle that."

"You mean it?" Rowan asked, her bottom lip still wobbly but her well of tears lower.

"I do, on my honour as a Goddess," I vowed. "You'll always have a place here."

"And chores," Shade piped up.

I shot an annoyed look at him. "We'll worry about chores tomorrow. For now, let's go get some of Clara's amazing pancakes before the kids—or Mason—eat them all. How's that sound?"

"Good," they both said in unison, and we headed back into the kitchen just in time for the last tray. As I watched them all battle over the maple syrup, butter, and ice cream, I couldn't help but be grateful for this little slice of happiness in the world.

Sometimes, the good won out.

Dear Reader,

Thank you for reading my book and choosing to spend time with the delightful characters of Halfling House. I hope you enjoyed reading it as much as I loved writing it. If that's the case, I would be so grateful if you could leave a review or a rating so that other readers can fall in love with The Briarmoor Chronicles too.

Much love,

Victoria.

Want more of Briarmoor and the adventures of Halfling House?

The next instalment of The Briarmoor Chronicles,

"Sanctuary at Halfling House" by Victoria Vassallo

is out now!

Find it here:

https://mybook.to/SanctuaryHalflingHouse

NEWSLETTER

WOULD YOU LIKE A FREE EBOOK?

Join Victoria's newsletter and you will receive your very own copy of **Halfling House Origins** for **FREE!**

Plus, you'll be the first to get updates on Victoria's newest books, her writing process, sneak peeks, and book reviews.

http://www.victoriavassalloauthor.com

Don't want to miss a thing? You can also follow Victoria on socials:

Facebook | Instagram | Goodreads | TikTok | Amazon| Bookbub

AVAILABLE TITLES

The Briarmoor Chronicles

Prequel

Halfling House – Origins

Series

Welcome to Halfling House – Book One

Merry Magickal Mischief – A Halfling Christmas Adventure

Rescued by Halfling House – Book Two

Sanctuary at Halfling House – Book Three

Alliance with Halfling House – Book Four – *Pre-order Now*

Alternatively, scan this QR Code for more:

PRONUNCIATION GUIDE

Are you finding some of the words a little tricky? Never worry again with this quick pronunciation guide to The Briarmoor Chronicles universe!

Alora – Ah-lawr-ah
Eleos – Ell-ee-oh-ss
Faoladh – Fey-lah
Farron – Fah-ron
Wren – Ren
Themis – Them-is
Asclepius – As-klee-pi-us
Thanatos – Than-ah-tos

ABOUT THE AUTHOR

VICTORIA VASSALLO CAN BE described in many ways, however, the most accurate would be a tea-loving storyteller obsessed with creating worlds inspired by ancient myths and legends.

More importantly, perhaps, Victoria is an Australian solo mother-of-two who spends her days working in the Administration field while her tertiary degrees sit gathering dust and disdain with each year that passes.

Fortunately, the magic she finds in her writing holds the real world at bay and keeps the mystical and magnificent possibilities endless as long as there is a breath to draw and a page to write.

ACKNOWLEDGEMENTS

There are many people I would like to thank for helping to bring this story to life:

T & L, the curiosity and joy with which you see the world inspires me to keep finding the happiness and sharing the love of a good story. Without you, this book would never be possible.

Mum and Dad, thank you for being there for every step of the journey, and for always being the first to sing my praises.

I and C, thank you for listening to me at my best and my worst, and loving me at both.

H, thank you for letting me add 'Best Friend of a World Champion' to my achievements list. Also, congratulations!

I'd also like to thank the incredible communities of 20Booksto50K©, Successful Indie Author, Fans of Indie Urban Fantasy, Fans of Urban Fantasy, and Books and Btches. The incredible indie authors within these communities continue to inspire me.

Another big thank you goes to the amazing authors behind UFAC who have taken me under their wings and helped me as I navigate these indie author waters. The kindness, support and memes have been integral to getting this book out in the world.

Lastly, but perhaps most of all, thank you to the amazing ARC Team for The Briarmoor Chronicles and the readers who choose to fall in love with the characters and the world of Briarmoor. It's a gift that I will treasure every single day.

www.ingramcontent.com/pod-product-compliance
Lightning Source LLC
LaVergne TN
LVHW090945080826
845145LV00003B/899

* 9 7 8 1 7 6 3 5 3 9 1 5 0 *